The Rebel and the Thief

ALSO BY JAN-PHILIPP SENDKER

The Art of Hearing Heartbeats

A Well-Tempered Heart

The Heart Remembers

The Long Path to Wisdom: Tales from Burma

The Rebel and the Thief

JAN-PHILIPP SENDKER

Translated from the German by Imogen Taylor

Other Press

NEW YORK

Originally published in German as *Die Rebellin und der Dieb*
in 2021 by Karl Blessing Verlag, a division of Penguin Random House
Verlagsgruppe GmbH, Munich, Germany

Translation copyright © 2022 by Other Press

Production editor: Yvonne E. Cárdenas
Text Designer: Jennifer Daddio
This book was set in Marcia and Zapfino by
Alpha Design & Composition of Pittsfield, NH.

1 3 5 7 9 10 8 6 4 2

Library of Congress Cataloging-in-Publication Data
Names: Sendker, Jan-Philipp, author. | Taylor, Imogen, translator.
Title: The rebel and the thief / Jan-Philipp Sendker ; translated from the
German by Imogen Taylor.
Other titles: Rebellin und der Dieb. English
Description: New York : Other Press, [2022] | "Originally published in German
as Die Rebellin und der Dieb in 2021 by Karl Blessing Verlag, München"
Identifiers: LCCN 2022010799 (print) | LCCN 2022010800 (ebook) |
ISBN 9781635423044 (paperback) | ISBN 9781635423051 (ebook)
Subjects: LCGFT: Romance fiction. | Novels.
Classification: LCC PT2721.E54 R4313 2022 (print) | LCC PT2721.E54 (ebook) |
DDC 833/.92—dc23/eng/20220311
LC record available at https://lccn.loc.gov/2022010799
LC ebook record available at https://lccn.loc.gov/2022010800

Publisher's Note
This is a work of fiction. Names, characters, places, and
incidents either are the product of the author's imagination
or are used fictitiously, and any resemblance to actual persons,
living or dead, events, or locales is entirely coincidental.

TO

Anna, Florentine, Theresa, and Jonathan

AND IN MEMORY OF

Kyal Sin

(2002–2021)

ONE

I don't have much time to tell my story. It's only a matter of hours till they find us—maybe a day if we're lucky.

How did this happen? How did someone as quiet and obedient as me end up being a thief on the run? How do any of us end up where we do?

The truth is, I don't know. I crossed a line to help my sister—a line I hadn't thought I'd ever even get close to.

I was helpless and decided to do something about it. Then one thing led to another. Not because I had any particular plan, but because life never stands still; it's not a film you can pause or rewind.

It was never a dream of mine to be a hero. A lot of people see me that way because of what I've done, but that was a question of circumstances, and those circumstances were out of my control.

Did I have a choice? Looking back, maybe I did. But at the time I was making the decisions, it didn't feel like it.

I was in trouble, and I took the liberty of not dwelling on the consequences of my acts. I never believed I could save the world. The most I had hoped for was to save a few people from sickness, hunger, and death.

It all started with my little sister crying in her sleep.

It wasn't even proper crying—more like a faint whimper broken by the occasional cough. Despite the heat, she had slid close to me and flung an arm over my belly; I could feel her warm breath on my skin. A sob wracked her body. I didn't know what to do.

But maybe that wasn't the beginning. Maybe it all started much earlier, when someone bought a bat or a pangolin at an animal market in China and was infected with a virus—or when negligence in a laboratory led to the escape of a deadly disease that traveled around the world, killing millions in its wake, including, probably, my auntie Bora.

It may even have started earlier still, when my parents decided to leave their country to seek their fortune—or at least escape their misfortune.

Who can tell when and where a story begins and ends? Life, my father says, is a circle. We're born, we die, we're born again... There's no point looking for beginnings and ends.

My sister was trembling, as if she were cold. I was sweating.

It had been over a hundred degrees that day, and the heat built up in our shack like water at a dam. The nights brought little relief. Hungry mosquitoes whined around our heads; a spider crawled up my leg. I didn't even try to shake it off—I was afraid of waking my sister. We were lying on our raffia mats, and it must have been after midnight because the evening voices had died down. The old drunk next door had settled in for the night. The cantankerous couple opposite us seemed to have dropped asleep in exhaustion. Even the shanty belonging to the widow with six children and as many lovers was quiet at last.

Our parents were asleep beside us; I could tell from my father's snoring and my mother's heavy breathing, broken by bouts of coughing. She was sick too. Maybe she'd caught what her sister had. Whatever it was, she had a cough and a temperature and was getting weaker by the day. It might be malaria, pneumonia, TB. Or it might be the new virus. We'd never find out, just as we'd never know for certain what Auntie Bora died of.

Yesterday, with my help, my mother had made it to the bathroom. Today she hadn't got up at all. Every breath she took sounded painful and labored.

I'm not especially sensitive to sounds. The gnawing of rats at my ear, the buzz of insects, the shouts of people arguing in the shack next door, the low moans of lovers and indigents—I heard them and at the same time I didn't. They went right through me without leaving a trace. My sister's sobbing was different. It gave me an almost physical pain. It reminded me too much of my other little sister, Mayari, who had died three years before. She had whimpered like that too, in the nights before she fell asleep and never woke up.

"Thida," I whispered, "what's wrong?" It was a stupid question. I knew quite well she was hungry.

I wondered whether there was anything left to eat. I'd had a little packet of cookies hidden between the boards, but she'd had them the day before. The bananas were long gone. There were no leftovers from dinner, because there hadn't been any dinner. Or lunch for that matter. The only meal of the day had been a bowl of rice and a mango that we'd split between the three of us. It was a mystery to me where my father had found that mango. Chewing gum sometimes helped the hunger, but I'd swapped my last piece for half a cup of rice a couple of days back.

I stroked Thida's sweaty hair out of her face, and she looked at me with half-open eyes. Her lips moved, but there was no need for words. My belly was empty too. A hole in my gut. If you've never been hungry, you don't know what it feels like. I'd had cramps all day. But I'm eighteen, I can take it. Thida is five.

A rat scuttled across the room, stopping halfway to stand on its hind legs and sniff the air. I threw a flip-flop at it. Not even a rat would find anything to eat in here, and I was afraid it might get it into its head to bite Thida.

Not long since, we hadn't known what hunger was. My father had worked as Mr. Benz's security guard for fifteen years, and we'd been pretty well-off. Mr. Benz wasn't his real name, but when we first knew him—before he started building shopping malls and converting paddy fields into housing plots—he had had a Benz dealership, and I can't remember ever calling him anything else.

My father had started out as an assistant gardener and quickly worked his way up to security guard. Most of his days were spent on a stool in a little hut next to the gate, dressed in his gray-blue uniform and meticulously polished black boots. Every morning when Mr. Benz left the house with his chauffeur, he would jump to his feet, slide the heavy, black-barred gate open, and then stand to attention and watch the car drive away, not moving until it had disappeared into the traffic. This scene was repeated every evening when Mr. Benz returned home, or when Mrs. Benz or the children went out. Other than this, my father's job as a security guard demanded little of him. The grounds were surrounded by a high wall topped with shards of broken glass and three rows of barbed wire. For a time, there were also surveillance cameras connected to a monitor in my father's hut. He used to spend hours switching from one camera to the next and staring at the identical black-and-white images. I sometimes kept him company when I was a kid, but nothing ever happened, and I would soon tire of it. Not so my father—or at least he never let it show if he did. Then the cameras stopped working and no one bothered to replace them.

My mother cooked for the family, and Auntie Bora did the shopping and helped out in the kitchen. In our last year there, I was put in charge of the big gardens and the tennis court after the previous gardener was fired for taking secret photos of the grounds on his phone.

I was also responsible for looking after the spirit house. There was a big old banyan tree in the garden, inhabited by a spirit who watched over the villa and its grounds. Long ago, a small house had been built for this spirit, and every day I would leave offerings in it on behalf of the Benz family: a vase of fresh flowers, a small glass of water—things like that. The Benzes were Christian, but Mrs. Benz was very superstitious and went to the spirit house several times a week to make sure it was clean and the flowers fresh. I often saw her lay large pomelos or mangos in front of the altar, and ask the spirit for a favor or protection. In the months after her daughter's accident, she was there every day.

My parents, aunt, sister, and I lived together in a bungalow next to the gate. "Bungalow" is perhaps too grand a word for our little house, but my parents called it that, and from what they said, it was by far the biggest and nicest they had ever lived in. It had two rooms. In one of them, we unrolled our five sleeping mats every night; in the other was a table, a television, our altar, and two shelves. At the back of the house was a bathroom with a shower and toilet. The walls and floors were concrete; the roof was corrugated iron. During the monsoon, the pelting rain made such a racket that we couldn't hear ourselves think. Our greatest luxury was the air-conditioning—even on the hottest, most humid nights we never had to sweat.

We ate in the main house, in a little servants' room off the kitchen. We wanted for nothing. We had it good. So good, that hardly a day went by when my mother didn't give a deep sigh and ask what we'd done to deserve such good fortune.

All that changed overnight.

First, Auntie Bora came down with a temperature. She had a cough, a sore throat, and a headache. We supposed she had caught a cold at the market, and thought nothing of it. Colds, even bad ones, came and went.

But the fever continued to climb.

And then came the virus. Or rather, the news of a virus. Or perhaps only the fear of a virus—back then, it was hard to know.

The government appealed to all citizens on Facebook, asking them to wash their hands regularly with soap, cough into their elbows, wear masks, stay at home if they had a temperature, and keep their distance from each other. All borders to neighboring countries were closed.

Mrs. Benz had asthma, and the family was worried for her. My mother was the only one of us still permitted to enter the house. As well as a mask, she had to wear disposable gloves, a protective gown, and plastic overshoes. She was only allowed to leave the grounds to go shopping, and the rest of us weren't allowed out at all. The Benzes asked if we were all healthy; unsuspectingly, we told them about Auntie Bora's fever and cough. That was perhaps a mistake, but something tells me they'd have found out sooner or later.

Mr. Benz gave us half an hour. My mother cried; my sister cried. Auntie Bora didn't cry. I expect she was too weak by then.

My father and I began to get ready. It didn't take long; our few belongings could be packed in a matter of minutes. My T-shirts, underwear, two pairs of pants, two longyis—it all fitted easily into one of the plastic bags that Mrs. Benz had kindly asked the chauffeur to leave on our doorstep. Precisely twenty-nine minutes later—my father is a stickler for punctuality—we were outside the gate, leaving behind us the only home my sister and I had ever known. No one came to say goodbye—but then we hadn't expected them to.

I took charge of the bags with our belongings. My mother carried our altar in one hand; with the other she kept a firm hold on Thida, who had her stuffed elephant tucked under her arm. My father pushed the moped, with the small television and our raffia mats strapped to its luggage rack. Auntie Bora was so feverish she could barely keep on her feet and had to cling to my father for support.

Our biggest problem was that we had no idea where we were going. We had no relatives in town. We were all the family there was.

My parents came to this country twenty years ago looking for work, and my sisters and I were born here. My father started out taking whatever employment he could get. He worked as a builder, a dishwasher, and a gardener; he polished cars at a car wash, swept streets, collected garbage, and worked as a night watchman at a parking lot. Meanwhile my mother minded other people's kids, massaged other people's feet, and washed other people's laundry. They never made much money, but it was enough to keep us from starving and give us a roof over our heads. They were proud of that. Then someone recommended them to the Benzes and they started working there.

What we didn't have were official papers. No work permits, no visas, no ID, no passports—not even birth certificates. Nothing. We were "illegals." We didn't officially exist. This meant that I couldn't attend a normal public school when I was a kid, but had to be taught by monks in a nearby monastery, together with other "illegal" kids. It meant that we couldn't take my sister to a hospital when she fell sick. It meant that my father didn't go to the police when his first moped was stolen, and that my mother didn't press charges when a man did things to her that she only just managed to confess to her husband.

Going back to my parents' country wasn't an option. The borders were closed, and in any case, our family belonged to the Koo minority. Even in their own country, the Koos were only tolerated; they'd had no rights for centuries. It was complicated.

We made our way down the road; Thida kept asking where we were going.

We spent the first night under a bridge, the second in a subway entrance, and the third at a disused building site. Auntie Bora coughed a lot, wheezing and gasping as though she might choke to death at any moment. My father and I took turns carrying her on our backs, and it made me sad to feel how sick and exhausted she was. She'd grown so thin she felt like a bag of bones.

There were some workmen living on the building site. Their job was to make sure that no one stole any tools or building material, though things went missing all the same—sacks of concrete, boxes of nails, spools of cable. At first, these men tried to send us on our way, but my father's entreaties—and Auntie Bora's cellphone—changed their minds. When Auntie Bora died two days later, they helped us dig her a grave at the edge of the site.

My father spent the days looking for a job. He set off soon after sunrise, confident that with his credentials as security guard, gardener, car washer, and street sweeper, he would soon find something. Every evening he returned disappointed. No one had work for him; everyone was afraid. Despite the long years of working for the Benzes, we had no savings. My father was a Buddhist; he wasn't interested in personal property. At the end of every month he had taken what was left of our wages and delivered it in person to the local monastery. Their need was greater than ours, he always said.

The day after Auntie Bora died, the workmen told us that the police were starting to patrol the disused building sites and arrest any illegals they found. We decided it was too risky to hang around any longer—we might get separated or thrown into jail. And so we packed our things and moved on.

The news on Facebook was depressing. The president had declared war on the virus and the government had announced a state of emergency, but still the disease continued to spread. There was a ban on public gatherings. Schools and universities were forced to close; most stores were shut down too. Train and bus services were limited and irregular. People were advised to stay at home. But what about those of us who didn't have a home?

On a plot of wasteland surrounded by a construction fence, we found a settlement of shacks, huts, and shanties put up by other illegals. Billboards on the fence told us that one day a building development called Beautiful Tuscany would stand on this site. After long, tough negotiations, my father managed to swap his moped and our television for a small shack, complete with dishes, three pots, and a pan.

Our new residence consisted of a single room with a dirt floor, just big enough for our four sleeping mats and a firepit. Thida could poke her fingers through the holes in the plank walls, and the roof leaked even in a light shower. The only toilet in the settlement—a makeshift pit surrounded by plastic sheeting—was only a few feet away, and the stench of shit and garbage filled the air night and day. When we wanted water, we had to lug it in cans and buckets from a canal two blocks down the road.

Still, we were relieved to have a home again.

All day long, Thida and I wandered around between the shanties with nothing to do. We were used to spending time together. Sometimes, at the Benzes, she'd helped me with the gardening; I'd taught her how to cut the grass with shears, weed the beds, climb a palm tree—and how to clean the spirit house and change the flowers and water without disturbing the resident spirit. Now we sat for hours in the shade of the "Beautiful Tuscany" billboard, playing with marbles someone had swapped her for her barrettes.

At first we'd amused ourselves by watching videos, but then I was forced to sell my phone. I had trouble letting go of that phone. I'd saved up for it for six months. Not being able to make calls wasn't so bad; there was no one I wanted to speak to anyway. But it was more than just a phone. It was my window to the world, my refuge. With those little white buds in my ears, I could withdraw, and for the first time in my life I was free to choose what I listened to.

Thida and I soon discovered that life in a settlement of poor people and illegals (I prefer to avoid the words *slum* and *shantytown*) was not only boring, but full of unpleasant surprises. We'd been there only two days when someone came in the night and stole one of our cooking pots. Three nights later, my mother's phone disappeared. The

general atmosphere was one of suspicion and distrust. There was a fat man called Bagura who was
something like the boss of the settlement. Bagura
had a white beard, long hair, and red teeth; he sat
outside his shanty all day, sweating and chewing
betel nuts, and occasionally scratching himself between his legs and belching loudly. He always had
a big handkerchief in his hand, and with this he
alternately mopped his brow and blew his perma-
nently blocked nose. People came to him when they
were hard up, bringing their last possessions to sell
to raise money for food—cellphones, gold earrings,
nose rings.

Bagura had a wife who was even fatter than he
was. He also had two sons, Yuri and Taro, who did
his haggling for him. They were universally feared
because of their reputation for forcing down even
the lowest prices.

Bagura settled any disputes that arose; for
some reason I couldn't fathom, no one dared question his decisions. I didn't like him or his sons and
gave them a wide berth. People said they had spies
everywhere and that nothing in the settlement
was hidden from them for long. Many believed that
Bagura had connections to the police—this, apparently, was why the authorities left us in peace,
and I had heard that, to thank Bagura for protect-
ing them, every family in the settlement made him

a weekly gift of a few coins, half a cup of rice, or a couple of cigarettes. I never asked my father if this was true—or, indeed, if he himself made such payments.

The settlement grew fuller by the week. There were soon two, or even three families living in some shacks, and new shanties went up at the edges of the site —flimsy constructions of wood, corrugated iron, and plastic sheeting. The government announced that the war on the virus had entered the next phase. They ordered people to stay at home except to go shopping or in an emergency, and to keep at least six feet apart when they did.

It wasn't easy for us to follow the new rules. Our shanties stood cheek by jowl, with rarely more than a yard between them and only just room inside to sleep. How were we supposed to get through a day without going out, let alone weeks? Luckily, the fence around Beautiful Tuscany was high, so we didn't worry too much about the authorities to begin with. We thought that as long as we kept to ourselves, no one would care whether we followed the rules.

By this time, all building sites, restaurants, hotels, guesthouses, factories, and stores had been shut down—only grocery stores and drugstores were kept open. There were no more dirty dishes for the illegals to wash, no more cheap T-shirts to be sewn, no hotel rooms to clean, no laundry to iron. Rich people laid off their nannies, cooks, chauffeurs, and gardeners. Anyone without relatives to go to fled to one of the settlements that were springing up in parks, under bridges, on riverbanks, and on the outskirts of the airport.

My father was convinced that our impoverished circumstances were the result of our karma. He thought we must have grossly violated the Buddha's rules in our former lives to be punished with such a fate. The monks at the monastery school had taught us the same, but I found it hard to understand what my little sister's karma had to do with her hunger. For me, Thida was just Thida—a sweet, generous, gentle girl, who always shared everything and wouldn't harm a spider (even if they did creep her out). She didn't deserve such misery.

That night, then, I lay beside her, listening to her whimpering and trying to work out where I could find her something to eat. Sometimes in the past few weeks, trucks had stopped near the settlement—from churches, the Red Cross, the UN, or some international aid organization whose name meant nothing to me. Men and women had stood on the truck beds, throwing bottles of water and packets of rice, noodles, flour, and instant soup into the crowd. Word spread through the shanties like wildfire, and anyone fit enough ran there as fast as they could.

People thronged around the trucks, stretching out their hands in supplication or anger, pushing, jostling, cursing. I arrived too late every time. Either the food had already been distributed, or the volunteers didn't throw far enough, or people snatched the packets from in front of my face. I would return home empty-handed, wondering what I was doing wrong. Was I too polite? Or just not hungry enough? But if I wasn't, my sister certainly was, and I felt shame at my inability to help her. The food trucks clearly weren't a solution, and in any case, I wasn't sure when the next truck would come—or if there'd ever be another. It had been days since the last.

Where else could I lay hands on food for Thida? I thought of the cellar in the Benzes' house, where the storeroom was bigger than our shack. I'd been down there a few times to fetch things up to the kitchen for my mother—rice, noodles, oil, cans.

I was going to have to steal. To become a thief. Did I have it in me? Once, when I was a little boy, I'd pocketed a piece of sugarcane candy from the nice old Indian at the market, who often slipped us kids treats. He didn't notice and even gave a friendly wave when we went on our way. I felt so guilty that I returned to his stall the next day and left the money for the candy on the counter when he wasn't looking. Not the most auspicious start to a career as a thief.

This was different, though. I wouldn't be stealing for myself, but for Thida. The Benzes had more than enough, and when the crisis was over and my father and I had work again, I could return what I'd taken. I would only be "borrowing" the food.

I was pretty sure that the Benzes wouldn't have hired a new security guard. That didn't mean, of course, that I could sneak in at the gate or climb over the barbed wire, but I had another idea. I knew a place behind the bushes at the foot of the garden wall where the Benzes' dogs used to dig like wild things. Something drew them to the spot; they'd churn up the earth and burrow right under the foundations of the wall. I was always having to fill in the holes. That part of the garden abutted an undeveloped and overgrown plot of land that I could get into without being seen—if I dug in the right place, it wouldn't be long till I was under the wall and out on the other side. There was a barred door to the cellar at the back of the villa, and I knew where Joe, the Benzes' son, kept a key for when he came home late at night and didn't want to wake anyone. The dogs would recognize me; I wouldn't have to worry about them.

I had made up my mind. I got up, grabbed my flip-flops, stepped over my sleeping parents, and crept out of the shack. If all went to plan, I'd be back by dawn.

TWO

I knew I was taking a big risk. Anyone caught on the street after curfew without special permission faced a hefty fine, and if you couldn't pay, you went to jail. The better-heeled neighborhoods were even said to be patrolled by soldiers who shot suspects on sight.

It was about an hour to the Benzes' house from our settlement if you walked straight there. But I had to avoid the broad, brightly lit boulevards and thoroughfares; only the dark backstreets and alleyways offered relative safety. The cloudless, moonlit night didn't make things any easier.

I took a piece of rusty corrugated iron to dig with, climbed through a gap in the fence, and slipped out onto the street. The silence was creepy.

At first I met no one but stray cats and dogs, and they kept out of my way. After walking for a few minutes, I found myself at the corner of Patriots Avenue, an eight-lane thoroughfare with so many lights and streetlamps that you could see every cockroach on the road. In the past, I'd seen traffic jams here even at midnight, but now the place was deserted, as if everyone had fled the city. I needed to cross the avenue and walk a good quarter of a mile under the streetlamps before I could turn off into the next alleyway.

Head down, I hurried past a hotel and a row of shuttered stores, and was about to dash across the road when I heard sirens and roaring engines in the distance. I looked around nervously. There were no parked cars or cookshops to hide behind. The noise came closer. I wriggled under a bench at a bus stop and lay flat on the ground, clutching a metal bench leg in both hands, as if it could protect me. When I thought of the grief it would cause my mother if I got picked up by soldiers, I felt physically sick. Two police cars streaked past with blue lights flashing, followed by three, four, five military trucks. Even when they were well out of sight and earshot, I didn't move. My body was rigid with fear. I contemplated turning back, but the thought of Thida's hunger drove me on.

I didn't start to feel safe until I reached the Benzes' neighborhood. I knew my way around here; the streets were relatively narrow and only dimly lit, and they were lined with parked cars that would provide cover if necessary. Through the black-barred gate at the Benzes, I saw the banyan tree and the spirit house in the pale moonlight, and I thought with regret how good we'd had it here. I crept on to the vacant lot next door. Two palms and a bougainvillea spilling over the wall marked the spot I was looking for. The soil was soft and damp; the rainy season had begun with a heavy downpour the day before. The corrugated iron made a good spade; I could use it to cut through roots and shovel earth out of the steadily growing hole. The bottom of the wall was a good arm's length down, and it took me half an hour's sweaty work to break through to the other side. Another half hour and I'd made the hole big enough to crawl through.

Garden lamps buzzing with insects lit up the villa, a white, two-storied house with a roof terrace overlooking the city as far as the river. A broad driveway led to the pillared portico of the main entrance. I'd heard that an American businessman had built the place at the turn of the century as a miniature version of the White House.

I crept past the sprawling hibiscus and bamboo, hurried over the neglected-looking lawn, and dived down the stairs that led to the cellar door. The key was behind a loose brick in the wall. I turned it soundlessly in the lock and slipped inside. My heart was pounding in my throat. Keeping my fingers on the wall to get my bearings, I groped my way through the darkness. If I remembered right, the first two doors led to lumber rooms and the third to the laundry; beyond that was the storeroom.

I worked my way forward, one door at a time, and when I came to the fourth door, I pushed it open a crack, squeezed through, and pulled it shut behind me. I took a few deep breaths, then felt around for the light switch. What I saw when the light flickered on was like something in a dream: the room was stacked from floor to ceiling with bags of rice, boxes of noodles, flour, sugar, salt, bottles of various kinds of oil, fish sauce, soy sauce, spices, eggs, vegetables. I spotted pasta and mineral water from Italy, jams from England, beer from Germany, crates of wine from France and Australia. The Benzes had laid in enough to last them for years.

I heard the abbot's voice in my head: "You must not steal. The Buddha forbids it." He had been a patient teacher, sympathetic and understanding, but absolutely intolerant of pupils who disobeyed the

Buddha's teachings. I saw him before me, his shaven head, his wise eyes, his round, wrinkled face with its gentle smile. For ten years he had taught me at the monastery school, and all that time I had been an eager and biddable pupil. He would not approve of what I was about to do.

In my mind I began to argue with him: My little sister is crying with hunger. My mother is sick. We don't have the money for a small bag of rice or even a cupful, let alone medicine. My father and I can't get work, no matter how dirty or badly paid. I would trim the lawns of the rich with nail scissors till I had blisters on my fingers. I would clean their toilets with my bare hands if they'd let me. But they won't. Employment has become as scarce as gold.

Gingerly I hefted a twenty-pound bag of rice off the shelf. A bottle of oil. Two cartons of eggs. Noodles. Then it occurred to me that I had no idea how I was going to carry all this stuff. And suddenly I heard noises. A door creaked. Someone was tiptoeing down the stairs. I didn't dare move, but held my breath and looked around for somewhere to hide. The footsteps came closer. It was too late to run away—or even to turn off the light.

I was trapped.

Out in the passage, someone pushed down the handle and opened the door.

It was Mary.

She cocked her head to one side, just as she had as a child. "Niri. What are you doing here?" She sounded curious rather than surprised.

Mary. My heart began to race the way it used to. It was like going back in time. Mary and I hadn't spoken for four years. If I'd heard her voice at all during that time, then it had been only once, at a distance. I'd never dreamed we would one day stand face-to-face again.

"I saw you from my window. How did you get over the wall?" She hobbled into the room, closing the door behind her. She was wearing a red dressing gown embroidered with flowers and tied at her waist in a double knot. Her long black hair was piled up in a bun on top of her head.

"I didn't come over it, I came under it."

She looked at my filthy arms and hands, and raised her eyebrows in respect. "Not bad. But you should have cleaned yourself up a bit. You're leaving quite a trail." She pointed at the dirt on the ladder and on the shelves I'd touched.

I was so ashamed, I said nothing. I was embarrassed, too, by my appearance. The grime on my body and clothes wasn't all from my tunneling effort. It was weeks since I'd last had a proper wash or shower, or even cleaned my teeth. I probably stank.

"How did you open the door?"

"I know where Joe hides the key."

"You were lucky. My father's about to have a burglar alarm installed. Another few days and the sirens would have woken the entire neighborhood."

"What were you doing at your window in the middle of the night?"

"What do you think? I was bored. Couldn't sleep. Weren't you scared of getting shot? I thought there was a curfew."

"I don't think they'd really shoot you just for being out at night."

"Oh yes, they do. There's been quite a spate of burglaries around here recently—didn't you read about it on Facebook? A lot of houses are empty, because people have fled the virus and gone to their second homes by the sea. Yesterday the police shot a taxi driver who was walking along Patriots Avenue in the middle of the night. They thought he was a looter. You were lucky. What's it like out?"

"Creepy."

She looked at me. "You're pretty brave."

The admiration in her voice made me feel better. But maybe I was imagining things.

Mary and I were almost exactly the same age. She'd turned eighteen a few weeks ago; I'd been eighteen for a few months. As kids we'd spent a lot of time together. Even when we started school and she was chauffeured back and forth to a private school while I was taught by the local monks, we had continued to see a lot of each other. Every afternoon I would wait patiently by the gate, and as soon as she saw me, Mary would jump out of the car and run to meet me. Unlike her brother, she came to the bungalow almost every day. I helped her with her math homework; she helped me with reading and writing.

Like brother and sister, my parents once said wistfully.

All that would change. Mary suddenly had little time to spare for me; she spoke to me less with every passing week. Her mother asked me to start calling her Mary rather than Narong, because that's what she was called at school. I continued to wait for her at the gate every day, but instead of jumping out of the car to meet me, she only waved furtively from the back seat. It hurt terribly. I felt so abandoned. There was no one to explain what had happened, and I was left wondering what I could have done to deserve such punishment. No one, I told myself, loses his best friend for no reason.

Every afternoon, I would prowl around the villa, hoping that when she'd finished her homework or piano lesson or whatever she got up to in there, she'd come out and play with me—or at least glance out the window. I would stand at a distance watching her play tennis with her brother, who was now called Joe rather than Yakumo, and I was always happy when he called out to me and asked me to fetch the balls out of the bushes for them. That way, at least, I was close to her. I wanted to ask what I'd done wrong, but I never got the chance to speak with her alone.

One day, my mother gave me a letter from Mary. I remember retreating with it to a remote corner of the garden and opening it with trembling fingers. It was a long letter—four closely written pages decorated with flowers.

Mary asked me what I was up to, how I was doing. She described the dreary afternoons alone in her room and told me how much she missed me. She asked me in long, convoluted sentences if I felt the same, and apologized for all the times she'd ignored me. It hadn't been by choice. When she'd started school, her parents had told her to play with me less; later they had forbidden it altogether. They said it was time she made new friends. We would soon be twelve; we weren't little kids anymore. The time for playing was over.

She ended by suggesting that we meet in secret. We'd had a hiding place when we were little, a den we'd built ourselves out of twigs, sticks, branches, and dried palm leaves. It was over by the wall in the far corner of the garden, where even the dogs rarely strayed.

I waited there half the afternoon and then, just as I was about to leave, I heard a rustling in the bushes. As soon as we saw each other, we knew it wouldn't be our last secret tryst.

That first meeting was followed by a second and a third, and soon I was waiting for Mary every day again. She didn't always come, but that didn't matter; it only made it all the lovelier when I did get to see her. I had nothing else to do, and it was enough for me if I saw her two or three times a week. Her afternoons were filled with piano practice, riding classes, tennis lessons, and homework—with visits from grandparents, aunts, and cousins. It wasn't easy for her to sneak out unnoticed.

She always brought something to eat and drink, and we would lie in our hiding place talking. Mary told me about her school, the teachers, the other girls. She complained about her parents, who insisted on silence at table once grace had been said, about her brother, who alternately provoked and ignored her, and about the excruciatingly boring services every Sunday.

When her mother was out, we had more time, and Mary would bring books to the hiding place for me and a sketch pad and pencils for herself. She loved drawing and could conjure a flower, palm tree, or bug with only a few pencil strokes. Sometimes she drew from imagination; at other times, I would bring her a flower, a sprig of blossom, or a dead butterfly from the garden. She would sit there, pencil in hand, so absorbed that she forgot everything around her.

At such moments I envied her.

We could go for hours barely talking. We lay side by side, drawing and reading, or simply staring at the sky through a hole in the roof. As long as we were together, all was right with the world. We had no need for more.

A week before Mary's fourteenth birthday, her parents discovered our hiding place. Her brother had seen her sneaking a picnic hamper out of the house and followed her. Mary begged him not to give her away, but that evening at dinner, Joe told their parents everything. The next morning, Mr. Benz summoned my father to his office and instructed him to see to it that all contact between Mary and me was immediately broken off. Much as it would pain the family after so many years, any attempt to breach this ban would leave them no choice but to look for new staff.

I had never heard my father so serious. He made me promise solemnly that I would keep out of Mary's way in future. The fate of our family was in my hands.

Eight days later, I saw Mary for what would turn out to be the last time for many months. She had been given a horse for her birthday and was in the car on the way to the stables with her mother—I knew her timetable by heart. They were both on their phones. Mary looked sad. When she noticed me, she waved and made some secret sign I didn't understand. Two hours later she fell off her horse, breaking both legs, a hip, and several vertebrae. She was an excellent horsewoman; no one understood how it could have happened.

Almost a year would pass before she returned to the villa—a year in which I spent many afternoons alone in our hiding place, hoping for a message from her, though a little hazy as to how such a message would reach me.

My father told me that Mary's parents had flown in a specialist from America who had performed several operations—but despite this costly treatment, she was left with a crooked hip and one leg shorter than the other.

When at last she came home, my mother said she was like a different person. The once-lively girl had become quiet and withdrawn. The cheerful girl was now subdued. The strong girl had grown weak. (How wrong my mother was on that last point.)

My father lectured me on keeping my promise. I mustn't even think of visiting Mary or writing to her.

But I did write, of course—and not just one or two letters, but half a dozen. I wrote them in secret, knowing that I would almost certainly never be able to get them to her. Sneaking into her room was too dangerous, and sending the letters by mail or leaving them in the mailbox was hardly better. I kept them hidden away in a book of Buddhist wisdom given to me by the abbot. When my father chanced upon them, he was almost as angry as I'd ever seen him. He told me I was ungrateful and irresponsible—had I forgotten the possible consequences of my actions? Had I forgotten Mr. Benz's threat to the family? He confiscated the letters; I don't know what he did with them. After that, I resolved not to think of Mary anymore. At first it was impossible, but as time went by I was surprised to find that it became gradually easier.

Almost three years passed. Then, shortly before the virus broke out, I began to glimpse Mary again from time to time. I would see her sitting at her window, and I had the feeling she was watching me. Watching me climb the tall palms to saw away the withered leaves. Watching me crawl across the lawn, trimming the grass by hand because the noise of the lawn mower gave Mrs. Benz headaches.

I concentrated on my work. On the few occasions when our eyes did meet, we both turned away, shaken.

Mary stood in the storeroom and looked around her. "Wow. Crazy. My parents must have a starvation phobia. There's enough here to last a century. Take whatever you need. That's what you came for, isn't it?"

I nodded. "We've nothing left. Thida's hungry."

"Pack up as much as you can carry. I was afraid I'd never see you again. Do your parents still have their phones? I tried to call you, I wanted to know how you were getting on. You all just vanished."

"My mom's phone was stolen, Dad and I had to sell ours."

She nodded, as if to say, shit happens.

"Where are you living now?"

"In a settlement on a disused building site, not far from the Good Life Mall."

My answer seemed to satisfy her. "How are you going to carry all that food? You can't walk around at night with a bag of rice over your shoulder. You need a backpack. Wait here."

Before I could reply, Mary had opened the door and disappeared down the passage. A few moments later she returned with a gray hiker's pack that her brother sometimes used.

"It's Joe's. He won't miss it."

"But he uses it," I objected.

She shrugged. "He'll think he's lost it, and my parents will buy him a new one faster than he can ask for one."

I took a twenty-pound bag of rice and threw her a questioning look.

"Take two. Take some noodles too. And a bottle of oil. Sauce. Eggs. As much as you can carry. Believe me, no one will notice."

I crammed the backpack with food. The straps cut into my hands when I picked it up. "Thank you."

"Don't thank me. As you can see, we have more than enough." She turned away and hobbled down the passage. I would have liked to stay, but if I wanted to be back in the settlement by dawn, I mustn't waste time. We slipped out of the cellar together, and Mary followed me across the garden to inspect my tunnel.

She stared at it for a long time, as if trying to work out whether she'd fit through herself. Then she said: "Cover it with branches on the other side. I'll take care of this side with some palm leaves. I don't think my brother ever comes to this part of the garden, but it's better to be sure."

"Why?"

"So you won't need to dig a new hole next time."

Was it an invitation? I wasn't sure. But her voice suddenly sounded like little Narong's, so achingly familiar that I felt a sharp pain somewhere inside me.

I gave a hint of a nod.

"Now get out of here. I need to go and eliminate your trail."

THREE

It was getting light when I reached the settlement. I desperately hoped that my father was either asleep or absorbed in his morning meditation, because I had no idea how to explain to him my sudden possession of rice, noodles, flour, vegetables, oil, and soy sauce. I decided to hide everything (though I didn't know where) and to get it out a little at a time—only as much as we needed for the day's meals. If I kept the quantities small, I could always say they were alms from a monastery, or donations from a Red Cross truck.

The place was still deserted, apart from a few dogs roaming the narrow alleyways and the odd rat scuttling between shanties. I heard children's voices coming from some of the shacks and the murmurs of waking people. Our front door stood ajar. I pulled it open cautiously.

"Where have you been?"

Startled, I turned around. My father looked me sternly up and down. "Dad. What are you—"

He cut me short. "That's what I'm asking you. Where have you been? What were you doing wandering the streets at night? Don't you know how dangerous it is? You could have got yourself arrested—or shot."

I stared at the ground and said nothing. It was unusual for my father to be so upset. I tried to work out what was uppermost in his voice—anger or concern.

"What's that backpack?"

"It's got food in it for Thida. She needs to eat," I said, vaguely hoping this would be explanation enough. A moment later I regretted my choice of words. I'd made it sound as if Thida had sent me.

Our one-armed neighbor across the way was peering at us through her open door. My father signaled to me to go inside, and followed me into our hut. My sister lay snuggled up to my mother; they were both still asleep. We crouched down beside them, and my father unpacked the backpack, setting the food out on the floor. His eyes widened when he saw the mountain of rice, noodles, vegetables, sauces, but he said nothing. I wondered what he was thinking. It was enough food for at least a fortnight.

"You stole this."

"Thida's hungry."

"Do you think I don't know that?" he hissed. "There are hungry children in every shanty in the settlement. Does that mean their brothers and fathers go out thieving?"

I didn't reply and kept my eyes fixed on the sandy floor. I thought of Mary. "You're pretty brave," she'd said. Maybe the others weren't so brave.

"The Buddha says you mustn't steal. He doesn't say only those with full bellies mustn't steal; everyone else can take as much as they need. He doesn't say we can do bad things as long as we mean well. Do you think there was no hunger in the Buddha's day? Do you think he didn't know what he was asking of people?"

My father looked piercingly at me; I felt an almost physical pain. I wanted to apologize, but didn't know how—or what for.

"You're creating bad karma," he said. "And not just for yourself—for all of us. We can't eat this food; it doesn't belong to us. Take it back where it comes from. I'll soon have work again. We're not going to starve."

How can you be so sure, I wanted to ask. Where do you think the next bowl of rice will come from?

We won't get full bellies from meditating. I didn't dare argue with him, but I had no intention of sneaking back to the Benzes' cellar and returning the food to the shelves.

"We can share it," I suggested. "We'll just take as much as we need for today and tomorrow, and give the rest to our neighbors. That way we'll feed a dozen families, probably more, and turn our bad karma into good. What do you think?"

"What about the other families who are just a bit farther away?"

I had no answer to that.

"Is it just tough cookies for them? Do you think that's fair?" My father thought for a long time. "Or will you go on another looting spree tonight so that their kids get fed too?"

I said nothing.

"And what about all the other children in the city? Once you've started stealing, where do you stop?"

My father closed his eyes. It was rare for him to talk so much. I looked at him out of the corner of my eye. He was barely forty, but already he had gray stubble on his chin, and he had grown more gaunt in the past weeks; the dark skin stretched taut over his ribs. His chest rose and fell steadily. Beads of sweat were forming on his forehead.

"All right," he said at length. "I accept your suggestion. Just this once. But you must promise me you won't steal again."

I nodded. I knew it was pointless to pursue the subject. And I meant to keep my promise. The thought of disappointing my father was at least as bad as the fact of my sister's hunger. Also, he wouldn't be so quick to forgive a second time.

"I can't hear you," he said.

"I promise," I said softly.

"Good. Then take what we need for two days and share the rest among the neighbours. Don't tell anyone where you got it."

As I made to stand up, he grabbed my arm. "Another thing, Niri. I'd like you to start meditating with me every day at dawn. An hour a day, starting tomorrow."

My sister woke looking tired and drained, worn-out by the hot night. She stared at us in silence. I had the impression that her eyes had grown larger over the past weeks, but maybe it was just that her face had got thinner.

Our mother was awake too. We helped her sit up, and she coughed and struggled for breath. Her body was burning hot. I wished I could at least wash her face with a cool, damp cloth. Auntie Bora had been through exactly the same thing in the days before she died. The last hours were grim. She wheezed and gasped until she couldn't breathe anymore.

My father looked worried. He was frightened for Mother, though he did his best to hide it. I could tell by the twitch in the corner of his mouth, the pinched look in his eyes. He couldn't fool me.

I handed her the can of Coke that Mary had given me for Thida. She drank a few sips and nodded gratefully. She didn't ask where I'd got it.

Thida helped me with the cooking. She was good at lighting fires and usually puffed away spiritedly at the embers, not stopping until she'd got a blaze going. Today, though, she only flapped her hand at them a bit. I put water on to boil and we squatted by the fire and stared impatiently at the simmering rice. The smell of the rice water and the memory of our mother's vegetable curry made our bellies ache. I could have reached into the pot with my bare hands. The last minutes were the hardest. By the time the rice was steaming on our plates, Thida and I couldn't wait. We both burned our tongues.

Our mother ate only a few spoonfuls; my father and I took it in turns to feed her. She looked so tired—dark rings under her eyes, wrinkles around her mouth that I'd never noticed before. Who would have thought that eating and breathing could be such hard work? Her eyes were drooping. We helped her back onto her mat, and she murmured a faint thank you.

Moments later, she was asleep again. My father slipped out without a word.

Thida had been sitting by herself in the corner, watching us.

"Is Mom dying?"

"How should I know?" She had only said out loud what I had been thinking, but still—or maybe because of that—her question angered me. "I'm not a doctor."

Thida's face filled with silent horror. I was shocked at my own thoughtlessness. "Sorry," I said. "No, she's not dying, not now."

"Tomorrow?"

"No, Thida, not tomorrow either."

"Will she get better?"

"Yes, she will, definitely. Don't you worry about her."

"Auntie Bora didn't get better."

"No, but she was older," I lied.

"No, she wasn't."

"Well, she looked older." It didn't matter what I said now; the damage was done.

"Would you like some more to eat?"

Thida ignored my question.

"Shall we play a game?"

She got up, lay down next to our sleeping mother, and turned her back on me.

FOUR

Distributing the food among our neighbors proved harder than expected. I had thought I would simply go from shack to shack, handing out portions of rice or noodles until I ran out, but it wasn't quite like that. I started off with the widow with six children. She stared at me, first surprised, then suspicious. If I thought this meant my father and I could go touching her up, she said, I had another think coming. Eventually, though, her hunger got the better of her, and she brought me a tin dish, which I filled with rice.

The woman with twins, who lived next door to the widow, was no friendlier. What was I expecting in return? When I told her I wasn't expecting anything, her skepticism only grew, and even her children stared at me as if I were evil incarnate.

Reluctantly, she handed me a dented saucepan and I decanted another measure of rice.

By the time I came to the old drunk's shanty, I was surrounded by a dozen children. They stared at me, wide-eyed and curious; most of them stretched out their hands to me in silence, their arms as thin as Thida's.

The drunk was asleep on the floor, on some old newspapers. I pulled out a sheet from under him, rolled it into a cone, filled it with rice, and left it at his side. By the time he came around, I thought, the rats would probably have eaten most of it.

When I emerged from the shanty, the alleyway was heaving with women and children. How was I to decide who got food and who didn't? They crowded in, pushing and shoving. I called out to them, telling them they'd all get some. But they must have known it wasn't true. I had only enough to feed a handful of them. They began to snatch at the bag of rice and packets of noodles. I pushed them away and shouted at them. Directly in front of me, a child started to cry. Another called out anxiously for his mother; the others ignored him. They pulled and tugged at my longyi and at the food in my arms. The bag of rice split open and the contents spilled out onto the ground. The kids pounced on it, egged on by their mothers, scrabbling to gather up as much as they could.

In a last attempt to establish order, I let out a yell of fury. But it was no use. The children continued to scuffle in the dirt over the rice. Suddenly desperate to get away, I dropped the noodles too, and elbowed a path through the crowd back to our shack. The noise of the fight and the cries of disappointment followed me all the way.

That evening we were visited by Bagura and his sons. With his big belly and broad shoulders, Bagura almost filled the door. Strands of sweaty hair hung in his face. He huffed and blew, angry and making no attempt to hide it. A pretty mess I'd made in the settlement with my charity efforts, sowing discord among people. Now, as well as being hungry, they were envious and resentful of one another. The rumors were oozing out of the woodwork like foul-smelling, poisonous fumes, fogging people's senses. Women suspected one another of providing "services" for us; respectable men had been planning to raid our shack, thinking we had a whole stockpile of rice. It hadn't been easy, Bagura said, to stop them. If ever I got it into my head to hand out alms again, it was absolutely crucial that I go through him and his family. I just had to leave the food with them and they'd see to it that it was fairly distributed.

When this tirade was over, my father was silent for so long that Bagura and his sons began to fidget.

"It won't happen again," I said at length.

Looking at the faces of Bagura's sons, I could tell they'd been hoping for a different answer.

Although we rationed the rice and noodles carefully, and although my mother ate practically nothing, and my father and I only enough to ease the worst hunger pangs, the food was gone in three days. After five days, Thida was as weak and hungry as ever.

My father turned increasingly to meditation. The hour I spent sitting beside him every morning was torture. I tried to focus on my breathing and ignore my hunger and my thoughts of Mary, but it was no use. I could think of nothing else. The hole in my stomach grew with every breath I took—and my longing to see Mary grew with it.

At night I lay awake, thinking of the promise I had made to my father.

I didn't want to disappoint him.

I thought of the kids who came to our door every day now, hoping for another handful of rice or noodles. I thought of their mothers.

I heard my sister whimpering.

Just once more.

FIVE

The hole looked just the way I'd left it. I cleared away the leaves, twigs, and branches, and was about to climb in when I noticed a small yellow bag embroidered with red elephants hanging on the wall. It felt as if it were filled with gravel or coarse sand. Curious, I opened it. Inside there really was a handful of gravel. There was also a note from Mary:

> *Hi Niri,*
>
> *Our alarm is now up and running, so don't come too close to the house. If you throw gravel at my window and wait three minutes, that will give me time to disarm the system. If the alarm goes off anyway, do not make a run for it—they'll shoot you dead on the spot. The key's*

*in a new hiding place: under the stone next to
the stairs.*

> *Good luck!*
> *Mary*

I slipped into the tunnel and slithered under the
wall. On the other side, I carefully pushed aside the
dry palm fronds and poked out my head. Something
rustled in the leaves beside me—probably a snake.
Not far off, a dog barked. Otherwise, all was quiet. I
crawled through the bushes on all fours until I was
level with Mary's window. I was just about to throw
a first smattering of gravel, when a light went on
briefly in her room, and I saw her wave to me.

Slowly I counted to three hundred, and then to
fifty. Better safe than sorry. Even so, I was scared
to venture onto the lawn. I scuttled bug-like across
the grass toward the cellar, expecting at any moment to hear screeching sirens.

Mary was waiting for me in the passage. I followed her into the storeroom, and she closed the
door and switched on the light.

"Hello," she said.

She smiled awkwardly, but I had the feeling she
was pleased to see me. She was wearing a white
nightdress embroidered at the collar, and a dressing gown with two big pockets. She didn't look tired
at all.

"Hello," I replied. "Thanks for the warning."

"I didn't want you waking my parents," she said, smiling again. "They wouldn't appreciate the disturbance."

"Do you sit at the window every night?"

"Most nights. I have trouble sleeping."

"Why?"

"I have pain in my back and hips since the riding accident. Especially at night."

"Every night?"

"Most nights," she said again.

I would have liked to say something comforting, but I didn't know what. "Can't the doctors do anything?"

"My father sent for specialists from Singapore and America, and they operated four times, but nothing's made a difference. They say the pain will go away eventually, my body needs time, but I know that's not true. I'll stay a cripple."

"You're not a—"

"Stop it," she said curtly, and I did.

"I hadn't expected you back so soon," she said, after a pause.

"The food's all gone. I gave most of it to our neighbors."

"Your neighbors? Are you some kind of Robin Hood?"

"Who's that?"

"You don't know Robin Hood?"

"No."

"He's an English folk hero. Said to have lived in the thirteenth century. He's famous for robbing the rich to give to the poor."

"I only did as my father told me. He was mad at me and didn't want us to keep the stuff."

"He was mad at you because you got food for your sister?"

"Because I stole."

"From people who have more than enough . . ."

"Theft is theft."

"Says who?"

"My father. And the Buddha."

"Jesus, too, but that doesn't make it true. What you're doing is different. You're stealing because you have to. Take as much as you can carry."

Once again, I crammed the backpack with rice and noodles, flour and oil and sauces.

Mary watched me. "What will your father say this time?"

"He mustn't find out. He'd make me bring everything back. I'll have to hide it somewhere."

Just then, we heard noises overhead. Mary switched off the light and we listened.

"Where are you?" she whispered.

"Here."

"Come to me."

I reached out for her and stepped gingerly in her direction, one arm outstretched. My fingers touched her shoulders, her hair. I couldn't see a thing, it was so dark—as if someone were holding my eyes shut.

"Here."

We stood very close; I could feel her breath on my skin. She was breathing fast, like when we used to run races in the garden. Our arms touched. Then our fingers. Very timidly, we took each other's hands. I'd never touched a girl before. Not like this.

There was a magic to the darkness. In the black of the cellar, I could forget the shameful contrast between my grubby longyi and Mary's clean, white nightdress. With the lights off, we were just Mary and Niri. Like when we were little. Why couldn't it stay dark forever? At least for the rest of the night.

"You believe in reincarnation, don't you?" she said, her voice low.

"Yes. Don't you?"

"I shouldn't, I'm a Christian. We believe that when you die, you go to heaven or hell. Somehow, though, I have the feeling that you and I must have met in a previous life. It's as if we've always known each other."

"Haven't we?"

"Not like that."

"What do you mean?"

"Not the way little kids know each other."

"Then how?"

She let go of my hand. Her fingers brushed my cheeks, mouth, lips. I was so excited I had to turn aside.

Overhead, the footsteps moved away.

We were silent. The darkness was suddenly too much for me, and I switched the light back on. Mary looked as if she'd been crying.

When we were little, I had sometimes cheered her up by making faces, or made her laugh by walking on my hands. I used to be good at it.

Those days were over.

"Is there anything else you need?"

"I could do with some old newspapers."

"Newspapers?" She looked perplexed, as if trying to remember what the word meant. "No one here reads newspapers."

"I just need some paper, for wrapping."

Mary thought for a moment. "My mother reads *Vogue* and *Marie Claire*, stuff like that. There might be some old issues in one of the lumber rooms."

We found a shelf with several stacks of magazines, and I put some in my backpack.

Back in the settlement, I spent the rest of the night rolling glossy ads for cars, perfume, and watches into cones, filling them with rice, and leaving the packets on people's doorsteps. There wasn't enough for everyone, but I hoped there would be a little less fighting than last time. At least this time I could claim I had nothing to do with it.

My father saw through my ruse immediately. As soon as he heard that some mystery person had distributed packets of rice, he demanded to speak to me. This is it, I thought. He's going to ask me to explain myself. We were sitting in our shack. He had sent Thida out to play with her friends; my mother was asleep. I felt hot and kept my head bowed, waiting for him to rant at me for breaking my promise, to tell me how disappointed he was in me—that he had trusted me and I had abused his trust. I waited for him to remind me sternly of the Buddha's teachings.

I would ask him to forgive me, I thought—but again, I wouldn't feel that I'd done wrong. I would assure him it would be the last time, while stubbornly thinking: here's another promise I'm going to break. The Buddha's teachings, I told myself, cannot fill the bellies of hungry children.

But none of that happened.

My father didn't rant at me. He sat there in silence and closed his eyes. This was something he often did, and it drove my mother crazy. She said it was disrespectful. He said it helped him to concentrate—to escape the distraction of all the images, colors, and movements he saw when his eyes were open.

Geckos scuttled across the wall behind him. Flies crawled over his forehead, nose, and mouth. He didn't stir. The longer he said nothing, the louder the silence between us grew, and the worse I felt. My sense of righteousness melted away like ice in the sun. What right did I have to defy him? After all my father had done for me, how could I be presumptuous enough to think I could follow my own rules? I was ungrateful. You didn't have to believe in karma to know that no good could come of my actions.

Minutes passed before he finally broke the silence. "Did I ever tell you the story of the little novice Dada?" he asked. His eyes were still closed. "I fear I didn't," he went on, answering his own question.

"No, I don't think you did," I said, glad that he was speaking to me again.

"Dada was an orphan who lived in a monastery in the mountains around Lake Minle. His parents had died when he was very young, and the village monks had taken him in. He was a shy boy who spent a lot of time alone, spoke little, and was quick to learn. The monks were impressed by his intelligence, modesty, and helpfulness, and for his devoted obedience to the Buddha's teachings. Dada was particularly close to animals. He took great care to make sure that no one in the monastery did harm to any living creature. Even the pesky mosquitoes mustn't be killed, but only driven away with vile-smelling substances.

"One day he heard that the villagers had caught a tiger and were keeping it shut up in a bamboo cage. Since none of them dared kill the creature, they had decided to wait until it died of hunger and thirst. Dada went to see the poor tiger for himself.

"'Let me out,' it called to Dada, 'or I'll starve or die of thirst.' Dada wanted to help, but he knew, of course, what a dangerous beast the tiger is. 'I can't,' he said, 'you're wild and bloodthirsty.' 'Don't be afraid,' the tiger said. 'If you set me free, I'll run off into the jungle and you'll never see me again.'

"Could he believe the tiger?

"Dada didn't know what to do, so he went to the abbot of the monastery to seek his advice.

"The old monk didn't hesitate for a moment. The tiger, he said, was a wild and bloodthirsty beast. It had already eaten several of the farmers' cows, and the people had a right to protect themselves and their livestock. They were acting in self-defense.

"Dada wasn't convinced. The tiger may have eaten a cow or two, but the villagers weren't starving, the rice harvests were abundant; people were well-off; they had more than enough.

"He thought of the Buddha's teachings. The first was: *You must not kill a living being.* And that was precisely what the villagers were doing. Dada was a good Buddhist; he couldn't just stand by and let them get on with it.

"So the next day Dada went to the cage. He reminded the tiger of its promise not to harm anyone, but to disappear into the jungle forever. Then he opened the cage door. The tiger leapt out. Almost crazed with hunger, it pounced on Dada and swallowed him whole. On its way across the fields, it gobbled up another couple of children who were out playing. Then it disappeared into the jungle and was never seen again."

My father opened his eyes, but he didn't look at me; he stared straight ahead at the plank wall. After a few seconds he turned to me. "I'm worried about you, Niri."

I was about to say that he had no need to be, but thought better of it. It wasn't up to me to tell him what to worry about and what not. Instead I asked, "Why?"

"Because what you're doing is misguided. You're deluding yourself."

SIX

Life in the settlement grew tougher every day.

A young man, barely older than me, tried to hang himself. The roof beam wouldn't take his weight, and he ended up bringing down not only the shack where he lived, but also the building next door. People said he'd been driven by shame. He had lost his job and was no longer able to send money home to his family.

More and more shanties were wracked by the familiar sounds of coughing and wheezing. Most people recovered—some didn't. On Bagura's initiative, a makeshift cemetery was created on another disused site next to the settlement.

One morning after our daily meditation session, my father asked me to fetch him a bucket of clean water from the canal. He washed more thoroughly than usual and shaved himself.

"I've been thinking," he said as he scrubbed stains from his longyi. "I'm afraid I'm unlikely to find work in the current situation." There was a meaningful pause before he went on. "So I've decided to borrow some money."

I asked myself who would lend my father money, but nobody came to mind.

"I'm going to ask Mr. Benz for a loan," he said firmly. "I'm sure he'll give me one."

I doubted that was a good idea. "Why Mr. Benz? He threw us out. It's his fault that we're in this situation in the first place."

"They were scared. Auntie Bora was sick. Mrs. Benz is asthmatic. Everyone's scared these days."

"And why do you think he'll help us now?"

"We worked for him for almost eighteen years and I wasn't sick once in all that time—nor was your mother. We were always hardworking, and the Benzes were always good to us. Mr. Benz knows he can rely on me. He knows I'll pay him back every cent. When I tell him how tough things are right now, he won't hesitate—he can't."

"Do you want me to come with you?"

He shook his head.

I walked to the fence with him. He seemed cheerful, but I felt uneasy and didn't like him going alone.

"Are you sure you don't want me to come?" I asked, though I didn't know what possible use I could be to him.

"Quite sure."

I watched him go with a spring in his step. He grew smaller and smaller, until eventually he disappeared altogether.

Impatiently I waited for him to return. When I saw him shuffling home with bowed head that afternoon, I guessed what had happened.

He sat down in front of our altar without a word and meditated until nightfall.

Thida and I made a watery tomato curry with rice. Our father barely touched his food and we ate in silence—Thida kept throwing me questioning glances. Later, when she had fallen asleep beside me, Father whispered through the darkness. "Niri," he said, his voice shaky, "He wouldn't even see me."

I reached out to take his hand, like when I was a kid and he walked me to the monastery. But my groping fingers found nothing but dust and dirt. We were too far apart.

———

At first it was only a rumor, spreading rapidly through the settlement, jumping from one person to the next like a virus. The widow told the woman with one arm; she told the twins, and from them it was passed to the market woman, the car washer, the garbage collector, the blind couple, and back to the widow.

Then, one evening, Bagura and his sons appeared in our door again, and demanded to talk to my father and me. At that point, the rumor became a threat. Bagura looked concerned. He'd had a visit from the police that morning, he told us. Things didn't look good. Not good at all. Not only was the virus spreading all over the world, not only were more and more people falling sick and dying, and more and more stores and factories closing. Now, on top of all that, a newspaper in New York—an influential newspaper that was read all over the world—had found nothing better to do than report on the fate of illegals here in our country during the pandemic. Some of the residents of our settlement had been quoted in the feature; there had even been photos of our wretched shanties. The mayor and the minister of tourism were not pleased, to put it mildly. They said we were a disgrace to the town and called for the settlement to be cleared. The police gave us three days to get out.

Bagura paused, and his eyes flicked from my father to me and back again. Of course, he went on, as so often in life, there was a way out. In return for a token of gratitude and respect, the police were willing to temper justice with mercy, and drop demands for immediate clearance; after that, the furor would presumably die down anyway. The mayor had other problems to deal with.

There had originally been talk of a hundred thousand leik, but Bagura had negotiated relentlessly and managed to reduce the sum by half. As a small concession, the police had also offered to accept gold in any form—chains, bracelets, anklets, earrings, nose rings. Bagura had been obliged to explain that no one in our settlement any longer possessed anything of value.

"I'm not sure what you want from us," my father said, after due pause. "We have no money."

"I know." Bagura waved this aside. "But your son," he said, giving me a long, hard stare, "seems to know a source flowing with rice, flour, noodles, and various other things. Maybe also money."

All eyes turned on me.

I was already hot and felt myself growing hotter. Fat beads of sweat formed on my forehead. Stealing fifty thousand leik was a different thing altogether from pilfering a few bags of rice. No one could ask that of me. And I didn't want to have to ask Mary. Even if the Benzes had that kind of money in the house, she would never steal that much from them. This wasn't petty theft anymore. My father certainly wouldn't condone it. Never. I looked at him, expecting, maybe even hoping, for a firm no. I waited for him to say "You mustn't dream of it." But he said nothing. His eyes were vacant. I searched his face for some clue as to what I should say, some small hint. Nothing. He sat there before me, silent, unmoving; he didn't even close his eyes. He seemed to be looking right through me.

"Dad?"

Not a word. Not a wink, not a frown, not the slightest shake of his head.

"Dad?" I needed him to tell me what to do. I couldn't decide on my own.

Silence. Only his quick breathing told me that he wasn't as calm as he looked.

Never in my life had I felt so alone.

Bagura cleared his throat. He was waiting for an answer.

I was already on the other side of Patriots Avenue, with the most dangerous part of the walk behind me, when I got the feeling someone was following me. I kept my head down and walked on, then ducked into an alleyway and hid in the first doorway I came to. A few moments later, Yuri and Taro sidled past. They spotted me immediately.

"What are you doing here?" I called.

"Keep it down," Yuri whispered—he was the older of the two. "You'll wake the whole neighborhood." He grabbed my arm and twisted it behind my back.

"Ow, that hurts. Let go."

He twisted harder. "We want to know where your source hangs out," he said.

"I'm not telling you."

"You're taking us there right now."

"No way."

Yuri gave my arm another twist; the pain brought tears to my eyes, and I was afraid he was going to break it. Taro punched me in the stomach; my knees buckled and I crumpled to the ground. Yuri let go of my arm and I fell over like a sack of rice. He knelt on my back; I couldn't get my breath.

"I can't breathe," I gasped.

"Where do you go? Who helps you?"

"I—can't—breathe."

"Where's your source?"

I would have liked to be brave. I would have liked to tell them to fuck off, to make clear that they wouldn't get anything out of me, even if they broke my arm or beat me half to death. But I wasn't much of a hero. I wasn't any kind of hero. My back ached and I was afraid of choking to death. "I'll show you," I mumbled.

Yuri raised his knee slightly. Air rushed into my lungs and I felt immense relief.

"What did you say?"

"I'll show you." What harm can it do, I thought. Let them see where the Benzes' villa is. It's not as if they can get in.

Yuri stood up and they waited for me to get to my feet. My belly hurt, my face was smarting. I had cracked my lips and chin when I fell.

The brothers walked on either side of me and we went on our way, keeping close to the walls. We still had a few blocks to go, and my doubts grew with every step. It was a mistake to lead them to the villa. What would happen if they got in? What would they do to Mary?

I could, of course, pretend I was lost, but they'd never believe me. I could lead them around in circles, but eventually they'd notice—and Yuri wouldn't take his knee off my back so quickly a second time. My only chance was to run away. Yuri and Taro were a few years older than me, a good head taller, and considerably stronger. But like their father, they were also fat. They had power but no stamina, and they weren't fast runners. I just had to make sure I got a head start, and they'd never catch up with me.

Two blocks farther, I risked it. We were crouching behind a Toyota pickup, watching the street. All was calm. Yuri was next to me, so I bided my time, knowing that he'd try to hold me back if I leapt to my feet. Then he put a hand on the ground to push himself up and jerked his head as a signal to move on. I slammed my heel down on his fingers. There was a crack of broken bones and a yelp of pain. I was up and running before Taro had even figured out what had happened.

My flip-flops went flying through the air. I ran barefoot on the warm asphalt, jumped over a ditch, turned a few corners to be on the safe side, and took a sharp left into a small, dingy alleyway. Yuri and Taro puffed and cursed behind me; the distance between us grew with every step I took. After two or three hundred yards, they were only a dim sound in the distance; soon after that, the sound died away altogether. I ran on in a zigzag, and didn't approach the villa until I was sure I'd shaken them.

Mary was sitting at the window. Maybe, I thought, she'd been waiting for me all evening and half the night. And last night. And the night before. She signaled to me; I counted to three hundred. Moments later, we met in the storeroom.

She looked at me in alarm. "What happened to you?"

"I fell over."

Mary went into the laundry, dampened a cloth, and handed it to me. "Here, wipe the blood off. No, wait, I'll do it, it'll be quicker." She carefully cleaned my wounds.

I had to tell her why I'd come, but I didn't know where to begin. Was it even acceptable to ask for so much money? Where was she supposed to get hold of it? And yet it was our only chance. If I returned empty-handed, bulldozers would lay waste to the settlement in a matter of days.

Mary rinsed the cloth and then looked at me searchingly. "Who was it?"

I pretended not to understand.

"You didn't fall. Someone hit you. Come on, tell me who it was. And why they did it."

Reluctantly, I told her the whole story.

She listened intently. When I came to the end, she said nothing but looked thoughtful.

I waited.

"Fifty thousand leik?" she said. "Now?"

She was silent again.

With every second of silence, my fear grew. At the same time, something inside me hoped she would say no. I didn't want to get Mary into trouble. I had no right to confront her with such decisions.

"My father keeps cash in the house," she said at length. "There's a safe in his office. I know where the key is."

"Fifty thousand leik?" I couldn't believe anyone kept that kind of money at home.

"More."

"We'll never be able to pay it back."

"I know."

"But you'll help us anyway?"

"Yes."

"You don't have to."

"Of course I don't. I'd like to see someone try and make me."

An image of Yuri and Taro flickered into my mind. I thought of the brutality people were capable of, and knew that Mary had no idea. But I said nothing.

"Maybe I want to help you. Ever thought of that? Wait here a moment. I have to fetch the key from its hiding place, take the picture down, open the safe, and then put everything back again. I'll be gone a while. If you hear voices or noises upstairs, it means my parents or Joe have woken up, and you must get out of here as fast as you can and come back tomorrow." Without waiting for a reply, she turned and hobbled out. I closed the door and switched off the light. Her scent lingered in the air.

The minutes alone felt like an eternity. I listened out nervously for voices, footsteps, creaking doors—but the house remained quiet. There was nothing I could do but wait.

When at last the door opened again, I had lost all sense of time. Someone slipped in soundlessly and closed it behind them.

"Sorry to take so long."

Even with the light off, Mary found me immediately. She took my arm and pressed a thick envelope into my hand.

"Fifty thousand in thousand-leik bills. All very new and crisp-looking, and there are plenty more in the safe. Gold coins too. My father clearly doesn't trust the banks anymore. But don't worry, I can't imagine he counts his money every day."

I wanted to say thank you, but it didn't seem quite adequate for what she'd done for me. Since I couldn't think of a more appropriate response, I said nothing.

When I left, she slipped me a second envelope containing something hard. It felt like money and a cellphone.

"In here are two gold coins in case of an emergency and my old iPhone. I've charged it and put in a SIM card. I couldn't find the charger, but I'm sure you'll find one somewhere in the settlement."

"Thank you," I said. I was too embarrassed to explain that we didn't even have electricity.

SEVEN

On the way back, I took even more care on the streets than before, hiding in doorways and behind bushes, fighting surges of panic. What would the police or army do if they caught me with fifty thousand leik and two gold coins? Arrest me for theft? They were more likely to confiscate everything and send me on my way, then shoot me from behind for being a "looter on the run."

Just before I reached Patriots Avenue, my strength failed me. Earlier that night, fear had put speed into my legs; now it made them so heavy I could barely move.

I found a pickup at the side of the road with a tarp over the truck bed and climbed in underneath. By day I would be more visible, but a lot less suspicious. There was a curfew from ten until six.

I stretched out under the tarp and thought of Mary. I hadn't realized how bad her pain was, and hoped she was in bed by now and managing to get some sleep at last. I had the impression I was only just beginning to understand how much I'd missed her these past years—how lonely I'd been without her. I had buried my longing for her somewhere between the palms and the hibiscus bushes, but it had sprouted stronger than ever, and each time we met, it grew a little more. Our secret meetings in the storeroom reminded me of the forbidden afternoons in our den. Back then, her brother had betrayed us. I wondered how it would end this time, and was still pondering the question when I fell asleep.

I was woken by a downpour. Fat raindrops drummed on the tarpaulin, and for a moment I didn't know where I was. Alarmed, I felt for the envelopes. They were still in my longyi.

The rain stopped and I peered out from under the tarp. There were more cars on the road than I had expected, and a few passersby too. They were all wearing masks. I hadn't thought of that. Without a mask, I would be stopped by the police. I clambered out of the pickup, and set off for the settlement, head down. I felt no easier than at night. Whenever I passed someone, I was afraid they would know, just by looking, how much money I was carrying.

Halfway down Patriots Avenue I saw six policemen coming toward me. My first impulse was to turn and cross the road or run away, but I soon thought better of it, realizing that I'd only draw attention to myself.

Between the police and me, a few people were waiting at a bus stop. My bare feet and grubby longyi and T-shirt showed clearly that I wasn't one of them, but I joined them anyway. A young woman saw the police approaching and gestured toward my maskless face, a questioning look in her eyes. I shrugged helplessly. There was a trash can beside her that hadn't been emptied for a long time, and I was about to stuff the envelopes into the overflowing garbage when the woman thrust a mask at me. It was used and reeked of sweat, but I quickly put it on and assumed a bored expression, as if I were waiting for the bus. The policemen passed us. One of them noticed my bare feet and filthy clothes. He threw me a suspicious glance, and for a moment I thought he was going to stop, but he seemed to think better of it and trotted on after his colleagues.

My father was waiting for me at the fence in the blazing sun. He'd been worried, but when he saw me, he was relieved rather than angry and didn't ask any questions.

We went straight to Bagura, who was sitting in the shade of his shack chewing betel nuts with gathering impatience. His sons sat beside him. Yuri's hand was tied with a thick bandage. He glared at me, but said nothing. Bagura stood up and asked us inside. Under the corrugated iron roof, it was just as hot and stuffy as in our shack, but the air tasted of sickly-sweet rose perfume, fried garlic, and chilies rather than cesspit. It must have been the biggest shanty in the settlement. There was even a second room, where someone was clattering pots and pans. The walls were hung with posters of a many-armed elephant and other Indian gods, and there was a proper bed with a proper mattress, an old table, several wooden stools, and a shelf filled with books and magazines. On the bedside table I spotted a black-and-white photo of a little girl staring solemnly and wide-eyed at the camera.

Bagura sat down on one of the stools. "Have you got the money?"

My father handed him the fat envelope—I had kept the phone and gold coins a secret. Bagura opened the envelope and counted the bills. Once. Twice. Eventually he nodded approvingly. "Fifty thousand leik!" He turned to me. "Respect. Good job. We're all in your debt." Then he threw a stern look at his sons. "Taro and Yuri too, right?" he added sharply.

They nodded reluctantly.

"I heard they caused you a bit of trouble last night. I'm sorry about that. It won't happen again, I assure you."

If my father was proud of me, he didn't let it show.

I don't know what Bagura told people in the settlement, but our family's standing changed overnight. Suddenly everyone greeted us—me in particular. Really, everyone. Some were respectful. Others were friendly, inquisitive, obsequious, distrustful, grateful, or admiring. People stepped aside for me in the narrow alleyways. They offered me stools in their huts. They let me go first when I was queuing for the toilet. Those who still had a phone took photos of me—me and their children, me and their husbands or wives, me and their sisters and brothers-in-law. At first I was embarrassed and a little weirded out by so much attention, but I'd be lying if I didn't admit that I came to enjoy it. The admiring glances, the awed whispers, the sudden show of respect.

Neighbors congratulated my father on having such a fine son, or asked how my mother was getting on. Complete strangers dropped by with herbs that supposedly cured coughs and fevers, or offered to bring us water from the canal.

Men of all ages asked my father's advice on just about everything.

Thida had new friends, who hung around our shack all day.

People made me the strangest offers. One man tried to sell me his dead wife's gold nose ring. Her sewing things. An incomplete pack of cards. Dented saucepans.

A woman pulled me into her shanty, grabbed my hand, and pressed it to the huge bosom that was spilling out of her T-shirt. A man offered me his fourteen-year-old daughter.

After the offers came the requests. Men took me aside and told me in hushed tones about their sick wives who were going to die soon, leaving their children motherless if they didn't get medicine quickly. One mother pressed her screaming infant into my arms and told me that her breasts were empty and the child would starve if I wasn't quick.

The hardship was great and growing greater by the day. I wanted to help these people, but how could I when there were so many of them?

It wasn't long before I came up with a solution. One part was hidden under my raffia mat; the other was sitting outside his hut as usual, sweating and chewing betel nuts.

I was in luck; Yuri and Taro were nowhere to be seen. Awkwardly, I dug out the gold coins. Bagura's eyes widened. He examined them thoroughly and was wise enough not to ask where I'd got them.

"Two ounces of Australian gold. If I had the money, I'd buy them off you," he said, handing them back. "But if I had that kind of money, I wouldn't be sitting here."

That was the answer I had feared. "Could you help me find someone who might be interested?"

He ran a hand through his white beard, scratching himself between his legs with the other. "I'd put each coin at about eighteen or twenty thousand leik. Very hard, though, to find someone who'll pay you that much in the current climate. If I were you, I'd wait."

"But I need the money now."

He frowned. "That's your business. If I'm lucky, I can probably get twelve grand for each coin—thirteen, max. I'd take fifteen percent. That suit you?"

I nodded.

"Come back in the early evening. With a bit of luck, I'll have the money for you by then."

Was it a good idea to give Bagura the coins, just like that? Did I have a choice?

That evening, he sent Yuri and Taro out of the hut and asked me in. He set a dish of sunflower seeds on the table and helped himself, then dropped onto a stool with a groan and gestured toward another. "Sit down."

He pulled a fat, sweat-soaked envelope from his longyi and handed it to me. "As I feared. I couldn't get more than twelve thousand for each coin. Minus fifteen percent makes ten thousand two hundred. Count it."

Uneasily I opened the damp envelope and pulled out a wad of worn ten-, twenty-, fifty-, and hundred-leik bills.

"I got you mainly smaller bills," he said, leaning forward and fixing me with an equivocal look. "They're easier to pay with than the thousand-leik bills, and it isn't such a disaster if you get the odd forgery."

Awkwardly I counted the money, miscounted, started over. Bagura watched patiently, occasionally spitting a sunflower-seed husk onto the ground. He seemed in no hurry.

When at last I was finished, I stuffed the bills back into the envelope. Bagura pushed the dish of seeds toward me. "Help yourself."

"Thanks."

"Listen here, kid," he said, without taking his eyes off me. "It's no business of mine what you want all this money for, but if you're planning to do what I think you are, I would advise you to be careful."

"What do you mean?" I asked suspiciously.

"Don't tell anyone that you have this much money in your possession. People in need can be dangerous."

I nodded.

"Don't raise false hopes."

I pretended I didn't know what he was talking about.

"'Don't tempt people to follow you into the hell of good intentions.' Know who said that?"

I shook my head.

"I did," he said, smiling. "And believe me, hells are my specialty. You've already seen what can go wrong."

"How many people live in the settlement?" I asked.

"What is this settlement you keep talking about? Do you mean this wretched slum?" He didn't wait for a reply, but went on: "There are about a hundred shanties, but new ones go up almost every day, and a lot of them are home to more than one family." He calculated. "I'd say at least one thousand three hundred residents."

Now it was my turn to do the sums. Twenty thousand four hundred divided by one thousand three hundred: about fifteen leik per head. It wasn't much.

"Better than nothing," Bagura said, as if he'd read my thoughts. "A family of five gets seventy-five leik. That's enough for a week."

"For food, yes, but not for medicine."

"You can't solve all the problems at once." He mopped his brow with his handkerchief, and looked at me, his heavy body leaning over the table, his head propped on his hand. I couldn't interpret his look—it was skeptical, curious, but maybe also approving.

I took the envelope, tucked it into my longyi, and stood up.

"How are you going to distribute the money?"

"No idea."

"If you go from door to door, you won't get far. After the second, you'll be lying half-beaten to death in the dirt, and the envelope will be gone."

I didn't want to believe him, but it wasn't impossible. I sat down again. "What do you suggest?"

"Yuri, Taro, and I will accompany you. As long as we're there, no one will hurt you. We'll do it for another five percent."

I shook my head.

"Three," he said.

"One," I said. "Two hundred leik and not a cent more."

Bagura laughed. "You're not just brave, my boy, you're smart too. Agreed."

The four of us went from door to door. I handed out the money without making a big thing of it and made sure we kept moving. Soon a small crowd was following us, but as Bagura had predicted, they kept a respectful distance and left me in peace.

When I walked through the settlement again late that evening, I stopped in amazement and took several deep breaths through my nose. At first I thought I must be mistaken. But I wasn't. The vile stench of shit and piss had vanished. For the first time since we'd moved here, the alleyways were filled with the smell of freshly cooked food.

The next morning I went to Bagura, to thank him once again for his help. He was sitting outside his shack as usual, dripping with sweat. Yuri and Taro had gone into town. I was about to sit down too, when we heard loud shouts and shrill, excited voices. A boy came running up and said Bagura must come right away, or something terrible would happen. Reluctantly, Bagura heaved himself up, and we followed the boy to the only decent-sized open space in Beautiful Tuscany, not far from the latrine. A crowd of people had gathered there. Bagura elbowed his way through and I followed close behind. Sitting in the middle of the crowd was a woman I knew. She had moved to the settlement not long after our arrival and lived a few shacks away from us with her husband and daughter and another family. She and her husband argued a lot; we would hear their crude, abusive squabbling all the way from our shack, and sometimes, too, the unmistakable sound of hands slapping flesh, followed by shouts of fury from the husband. He had left her the week before and moved in with his mistress, who lived just down the alley.

A few days before, I had bumped into the deserted wife on my way to fetch water from the canal, and we'd got talking. Until the outbreak of the virus, she told me, she had worked as a nanny for a rich family. They had taken her everywhere with them, giving her the chance to see New York, Sydney, Dubai. There was no mistaking the pride in her voice. There was no mistaking, either, her outrage at being reduced to living in such a shithole. She complained vociferously about the stingy widow she lived with, her unfaithful husband, the rich family who had fired her without warning—in fact, about pretty much everything and everyone. I felt sorry for her, but I was glad when she chose to vent her anger on someone else on the way back.

Now she was sitting on the ground, her daughter crying on her lap. I knew the girl too; she was Thida's age and the two of them often played together. The woman was clasping her tightly with one hand; in the other, she held a lighter and a plastic bottle filled with a see-through liquid. She was threatening to set fire to herself and her daughter if her husband didn't come back to her.

People stood around, staring; they made no move to do anything. Life in the settlement didn't offer much in the way of entertainment.

Bagura approached her slowly, motioning to me to follow.

"Don't come closer!" the woman screamed, her eyes bulging. Her daughter cowered on her lap like a small, frightened dog; I could see her trembling.

Bagura waited. He told her to calm down—they'd find a solution. He'd speak to her husband and sort things out. There was conflict in every marriage, and conditions here weren't conducive to peace and harmony. Everyone was struggling.

Then he took another step forward. The woman poured the liquid over her head. A reek of gasoline filled the air.

People shrieked and backed off.

The woman held the lighter in the air and struck it.

Bagura kept very calm. He kneeled down on the ground and began to talk to her quietly. I couldn't make out what he was saying; I heard only the sing-song of his voice. It sounded the way I imagined a snake charmer's might sound.

The flame went out.

Bagura talked and talked, and after a while his words seemed to have a soothing effect on the woman. She lowered her hand. Tears were running down her cheeks. There was still a strong smell of gasoline.

Bagura turned his head to me. "When I give you a sign, I want you to walk up to them very slowly, take the girl in your arms, and carry her to safety."

He went on talking to the woman until she nodded and released her grasp on her daughter. Bagura threw me a quick glance. I took a few steps, squatted down on the ground, and held out my arms. But the little girl wouldn't come to me.

"Give me the lighter," Bagura said.

The woman shook her head, but so hesitantly that I could see he had almost persuaded her. Something had broken her resistance.

"Give me the lighter," he repeated.

She threw it at his feet and fell to the ground on her side, crying bitterly. A murmur went through the crowd.

"You saved their lives," I said, when we were back outside his shack. Bagura clutched his wadded handkerchief in both hands and looked utterly exhausted. He only nodded.

"What did you say to her?"

"That I understand that she resents living in this shithole. We all do, and nobody knows how long we're going to have to stick it out. That things may get worse, much worse. That her husband's a bastard, but God knows she isn't the only woman to have been cheated on and lied to. That she has no right to destroy her daughter's life. That plenty of people would give the world to have such a beautiful child. That she should fucking well pull herself together and stop taking herself so seriously."

I stared at him in disbelief. "Really?"

"Yes." He mopped his neck with the handkerchief. "It could have gone very wrong."

EIGHT

My mother's health was worsening. I heard it in her feeble cough and her struggle for breath; I saw it in my father's worried face. He hardly left her side, and every evening he put a small dish of our precious rice on the altar and prayed. Come morning, all the rice was gone. Thida thought the Buddha had taken it and would heal our mother in return. I knew my father was only feeding the rats.

When I saw Mom lying on her mat, her face drawn and her body so thin you could see every bone, I hardly recognized her.

My big, strong, beautiful mother. The woman who had given birth to me. The woman who had carried me around on her back when I was a baby. She was nothing but a bundle now. Too worn-out to sit up. Too feeble even to raise a spoon to her mouth.

Desperate, I went to Bagura and told him how things were. He offered to go to a doctor with us.

"But we're illegals."

He waved this aside in a gesture typical of him.

"I know a doctor who treats illegals. At a price, of course."

"Would he come to the settlement? My mother's too weak to go into town."

"Of course not." Bagura shook his head at my ignorance. "He works at Saint Joseph's Hospital. I could arrange a taxi for us." He did the sums in his head. "It would cost you one thousand two hundred leik altogether, plus expenses for medicine, if the doctor thought it worth prescribing anything."

"We only have twenty leik, max."

"No more gold coins?"

"No."

Bagura sighed, as if he already regretted making the offer. "I could lend it to you. You're the most creditworthy person I know." He laughed in a way I couldn't interpret and continued his sums. "Ten percent interest a day. Nonnegotiable."

I thought of Mary and felt sure that, given the circumstances, she would help us again.

My father agreed to let Bagura take my mother and me to see a doctor. I thought it best not to mention the costs, and he didn't ask.

I carried Mother to the taxi on my back. Bagura sat in the front, next to the driver. He had doused himself in a sickly-smelling deodorant and put on a freshly laundered white shirt and a clean longyi; a worn, light-brown shoulder bag dangled in front of his belly.

With the driver's help we lifted Mother carefully onto the back seat. I got in beside her and held her tightly in my arms all the way. It was hot and humid; sweat poured down my body despite the headwind. An oppressive feeling crept over me: Was this our last journey together? Would she even make it to the hospital? She tried to say something, but spoke so softly that I couldn't hear her. I bent down and put my ear close to her mouth. "Take care of Thida," she said. "She needs you."

The hospital was on a side street not far from the cathedral. It was a modern, white, three-story building with a long flight of broad steps leading up to the entrance. Bagura asked the driver to stop under a nearby tree and wait for us. Then he disappeared for a few minutes. When he returned, he led us to a back entrance, where a nurse was waiting for us. She gave me two face masks and unfolded a wheelchair. I lifted my mother out of the taxi and into the chair. The nurse hustled us along a corridor so crowded we could hardly get through. Some people were lying on gurneys; most were sitting on the floor. They weren't all as emaciated as my mother. Some looked well-fed, but still leaned apathetically against the wall, their eyes vacant. Bagura led the way, pushing them aside with his feet. Some were crying. A man begged a doctor to do something for his heavily pregnant wife, but the doctor ignored him and hurried on his way.

The nurse opened a door; I wheeled my mother in and was glad when the door closed behind us.

We were in a small, windowless room, empty apart from a few chairs. A noisy AC unit blew slightly cooled air through a hole in the ceiling, but it was still stiflingly hot.

After a while, a man in a white coat came in. He was small-built, bespectacled and bemasked, and spoke in a low voice. He said he was pressed for time—how could he help? Bagura gestured toward my mother. The doctor turned to her, peered into her eyes and mouth, felt her pulse, and examined her chest with his stethoscope. He asked her to breathe deeply in and out. I could see her struggling. "Deeper," he said kindly, and listened. Once, twice. His eyes darkened. He walked around her and applied his stethoscope to various places on her back, tapping with his fingertips.

"We're going to have to x-ray," he said, and stopped to think for a moment. "We can do it right now—it'll be an extra thousand leik."

Bagura turned to me. "Do you want to? I'd lend you the money. Under the same conditions. A thousand leik. Ten percent interest a day."

I considered.

The doctor sighed impatiently. "Yes or no?"

Bagura looked piercingly at me with his dark, almost-black eyes, as if he could read the answer to the doctor's question in my face.

"Yes."

He pulled ten crisp hundred-leik bills from his bag.

The nurse opened the door and wheeled my mother out into the corridor. The doctor followed. "Wait here. We'll be an hour, max."

Now it was just the two of us, but we weren't alone. The groans of the ill and dying drifted in from the corridor. I don't know whether it was the heat or the noise or my anxiety about my mother, or maybe everything together, but I was finding it increasingly difficult to breathe. I felt dizzy and had to lie down on the floor.

"What's the matter with you?"

"I don't know. I don't feel well."

"You must have something to drink." Bagura disappeared and came back with two bottles of water. I sat up and sipped it and was soon feeling better.

We heard the plaintive cries of a woman. I couldn't make out a word of what she was saying, but I knew anyway.

"Are they all illegals out there?" I asked softly.

"Illegals! Never! They wouldn't be here if they were—you know that. All this lying around in corridors is new. The hospitals are overcrowded. Everyone's scared of this mysterious virus."

"Aren't you?"

He made his dismissive gesture. "You?"

"No."

"We'll starve before it gets us. I've survived malaria, dengue fever, and two bouts of pneumonia. I'll survive this virus too. And anyway, there's supposed to be a vaccine at some point." Bagura laughed scornfully.

"Don't you believe it?"

"I don't know, I'm not a medic. But I do know that we'll be the last to get it."

Until now I hadn't given much thought to the virus or the distribution of the vaccine, should there ever be one.

"I'm a Dalit, I know what I'm talking about."

"What's a Dalit?"

Judging from the look Bagura gave me, I should have known. I shrugged apologetically.

"Dalits are the 'untouchables' in India," he said. "The lowest of the low. The filth that everyone tramples underfoot."

I'd heard about them.

Bagura took a handkerchief from his bag and mopped his brow. "I left India when I was about your age," he said.

"Why?"

"Why?" He seemed to consider my question. "I was born in a village near Mumbai. At school, none of the children wanted to sit next to me. When my mother cooked school dinner, only the Dalits' children ate her food; the others wouldn't touch it. They'd rather have died of thirst than have drunk out of my water bottle. My father cleaned latrines because it was the only work he could find. It would have been the same for me. If I'd been lucky, I might have got a job in a slaughterhouse, or as a street sweeper or an undertaker. The worst fucking jobs were only just good enough for us. But I wanted to be a teacher. No idea how I came up with that. I might as well have decided to fly to the moon. Everyone laughed at me. The other kids, the teachers, our neighbors, my brothers and sisters. Everyone except my parents. They were furious. Whenever I mentioned it, my mother shouted at me and my father beat me. They meant well, of course."

"I don't get it."

"They were worried for me. The way they saw it, teaching was a totally unrealistic goal, and I was a lunatic who was wasting his life with reckless fantasies. They wanted to protect me from that."

"Did you listen to them?"

Bagura rocked his head back and forth, as if weighing the question. "I didn't try to become a teacher. But as you can see, I'm not cleaning up other people's shit in my parents' village either. When I was eighteen, I stuffed my few possessions into a plastic bag, climbed onto the roof of a bus, and rode to Mumbai. When I got there, I worked in cookshops and lived on the street. I began to get interested in politics. I wanted to understand why things are the way they are; I even joined the CP."

"The what?"

"The Communist Party."

He could see I didn't have a clue what he was talking about.

"Marx? Lenin? Mao?"

I shrugged.

Bagura groaned. "Forget it, kid, it's a long time ago. At any rate, I signed on to a ship a year later."

"You were a sailor?"

"No, I was cook's boy on a container ship. Sailed all over the world for seven years. I'd got myself fake papers in Mumbai and wanted to leave my old life behind. To get away from my caste, my country, my family. But shall I tell you something, kid?"

Bagura looked at me.

"You can't get away. Wherever you come from, whoever you are, whatever you've done in life, you take it with you. No matter where you go and how long you stay away. Even if you sail to the end of the world."

He took a big gulp from his water bottle.

"Once I'd figured that out, I signed off and went ashore. The ship was docked right here in this country. I did all kinds of odd jobs. I worked as a cook and married a woman who was an even better cook than me. We had a cookshop of our own and could hardly move for customers. Someone spread the rumor that our yellow curry with ginger and potatoes increased your potency, and we had men queuing up around the block. That made our neighbors envious, and one morning I came to work and our kitchen was nothing but a charred mess. I built us a new one from our savings—my wife was against it, said it would only happen again, but I didn't listen to her. She was right of course. The new kitchen went up in flames too, along with all the tables and chairs. After that I gave up."

His voice had gone quiet. He turned to me. "Why am I telling you all this? You have enough troubles of your own. You should rest."

I must have fallen asleep, because I was woken by the doctor's voice. "The X-rays show that your mother has pneumonia. I don't know if it's viral or bacterial—we'd have to do more tests for that and right now the hospital's too full, so I'll give you a prescription for antibiotics. She needs to take one pill three times a day, morning, noon, and night. Before meals, with a big glass of water, not with tea or coffee. You understand?"

I wondered how she was supposed to take the pills "before meals" when there were no meals, but I said nothing.

"If it's bacterial," he went on, "it'll soon clear up and she should be quite well again in six to eight weeks."

And if not?

He scrawled something illegible on a form, took a rubber stamp from the pocket of his coat, stamped and signed the paper, and gave it to me with a smile.

Bagura thanked him, bowed several times, and handed over a brown envelope that immediately vanished inside the white coat. The doctor gave us a last friendly nod and left the room without another word.

We stopped off at a pharmacy. Bagura bought the antibiotics for another hundred and twenty leik. We also bought two big bottles of clean water and two packets of cookies in a 7-Eleven. For a sick person, Bagura said, a cookie was a meal in itself.

Back in our shack, I broke two cookies into little pieces and gave them to my mother, together with the first pill. She had the second that evening, under the skeptical eyes of my father and Thida.

And then a miracle happened.

Only the next day, my mother's eyes began to follow our movements again.

On the second day, she asked for something to drink. Quietly but clearly.

On the third day, she sat up without help and ate some rice.

On the fourth, there was a smile on her face.

Until then, Thida had followed developments suspiciously. She had kept aloof and waited, as if afraid of a relapse. But something in Mother's smile must have convinced her that the changes might be permanent. Her fears vanished.

After that, she didn't leave Mother's side. She insisted on sleeping next to her, leaving me to sleep next to Father. By day, she followed her wherever she went, even queuing up outside the toilet with her, and in the evenings, she watched over her until she fell asleep. She seemed to feel that her presence alone was enough to prevent a relapse.

Every day, we got back a little more of our mother. Her voice, her smile—even the stern look she gave when she was cross.

"Now," Thida said one evening, "everything's the way it used to be. Almost everything." She was convinced that the Buddha had helped Mother because we'd given him so much rice. The Buddha and her big brother.

I couldn't believe what power there was in those little white pills. No bigger than my little fingernail. Lighter than a betel nut.

Three times a day, morning, noon, and night.

Such tiny things, and they had it in them to decide between life and death, fortune and misfortune.

Pneumonia surely wasn't the only disease where a few pills determined whether or not someone survived. Could it really be so hard to provide them for everyone who needed them?

NINE

Our mother's continuing recovery made a difference to our father too. He began to smile again.

His breathing steadied.

He grew more talkative.

Instead of meditating for hours on end, he sat with us, got the fire going, cooked rice. Even his posture changed. He stood taller, strode out, held his head high.

"You saved your mother's life," he said one morning.

"Bagura helped me," I replied. "We'd never have found a doctor without him."

"You know what I mean. Mom and Thida and I are grateful to you." There was a long pause and he looked at me. "Very grateful. But it has to stop."

"What?"

"You know what I'm talking about."

I averted my eyes and said nothing.

"Where does all this money come from?"

An immense weight seemed to bear down me. I had been fearing this question for a long time and still had no answer to it. There was no way I could tell him the truth. "Someone's helping me..." I stammered.

"Who?"

My stomach cramped; I fought for breath. The weight bore heavier with every question. What could I say?

"Niri?"

"Dad, please."

"Who's helping you?"

"Why do you have to know?" I asked defiantly. Just be glad I'm taking care of things. Be glad I get us money for food and doctors and medicine—it's not as if you do. Why should I justify myself?

My lack of respect outraged him. I could see him struggle to check his anger.

I had no choice but to keep quiet.

When he realized that I wasn't going to say any more, he got up and left the shack. He returned a few minutes later, his voice softer and more patient. "Mom and I are worried about you. We've already lost one child. We don't want to lose another. Would you want Thida to grow up without a brother?"

"No," I said quietly.

"If you don't stop, we'll have to leave town and go and live in the country or by the sea."

What would we do there with no land to cultivate, I wanted to ask. With no relatives to put us up. No fishing boat.

The truth was, we couldn't go anywhere. We were trapped in the city. Trapped in Beautiful Tuscany.

My father knew that as well as I did. He must have been at his wit's end to act as if we had a choice.

Just then my sister came running into the hut.

"Nai Nai is sick. Can you help her?"

"I don't think so."

"Why not?"

"Because I'm not a doctor."

"But you helped Mom."

"That was different."

"Why?"

"Because she's our mom."

"Nai Nai's my friend."

"I know. But I can't help her."

"You're mean."

"No, I'm not."

"Yes, you are." Disappointed, she turned away.

"Thida," our father said sternly. "Stop this nonsense. Niri can't help Nai Nai."

My sister clenched her fists, the way she always did when she was angry. "But she looks all silvery. He *has* to help."

"Silvery?" I asked, surprised.

"Yes, come and see."

It was hard to resist Thida's imploring gaze. I got up and she pulled me out the door by my hand, not letting go until we reached Nai Nai's shanty.

Nai Nai was lying on the floor, whimpering, surrounded by her parents and several children. My sister hadn't been fibbing; her body was as shiny and silvery as a metal can without a label. Her father told me she'd been begging with a group of children from the settlement. Somewhere they'd found a bit of silver paint left in a can and sprayed Nai Nai with it, thinking the disguise would encourage people to give them a few more leik. Now she was vomiting, her skin itched and stung like hell, and nobody knew how to remove the paint. They'd tried water, but without success. I had no better suggestion.

I crouched down next to Thida. "I'm sorry," I whispered, "I really can't help her." Disappointed, she followed me back to our shack.

Not long afterward, Taro appeared in the door. His father wanted to see me.

———

Bagura was lying on his bed, coughing. He looked worn-out. Yuri was sitting beside him, fanning the air with a piece of cardboard.

Had I seen that he had visitors that morning?

I had. Three police SUVs had parked at the fence, and half a dozen men in clean, freshly pressed uniforms had got out and made a beeline for Bagura's hut.

"They want more money," he groaned. "They say the mayor is rather unhappy, not to say furious, that this disgraceful slum is still standing. Apparently there are only two ways of placating him. Either they send in the bulldozers, or we give the mayor a little token of our gratitude and respect too."

"How much?"

"Fifty thousand for the mayor. Fifty thousand for the police."

I gave a loud groan.

"I know. There's no limit to their greed. The more you give, the more they want. And another thing—not far from here, just behind the General Hospital, is a similar slum that's set to be demolished next week. It's an even bigger shithole than this, I can tell you. But it's full of women and children, and where would they all go? They've heard that you saved us and now they're asking . . . Well, you can guess . . ."

"Yet more money?"

"The site's smaller. The police are asking for twenty thousand."

"And the mayor?"

"You're quick to learn, my boy. But he doesn't seem to know about this particular slum, so I guess he'll go empty-handed this time." Bagura coughed again, making a face.

"Are you all right?"

"I don't know. Maybe I caught something in the hospital. I'll get over it." Bagura smiled wearily. "One last thing. I don't know where your money comes from, but the police mentioned a robbery in the Noro Hill villas. They think it's the work of a gang. The army started patrolling the streets there today. Be careful."

"I will, I promise."

TEN

The settlement lay silent, as if sunk in a deep sleep. Only the occasional whisper came from the shacks. The streetlamps on the other side of the fence shone brightly, bathing the tumbledown shanties in a yellow glow.

As I left our shack, I noticed someone else making his way toward the fence—a tall, thin figure moving nimbly along the narrow alleyways. I knew at once it was Santosh. His height gave him away. He was the only one in the settlement who could see over the top of the fence—so tall and skinny that everyone called him Lanky. He was a good two heads taller than me.

Santosh had a wife and four children. Thida sometimes played with the kids. He wore crooked glasses with grimy lenses, spoke in a gentle voice, and was said to have worked as a kind of private tutor before the crisis. With Bagura's help he was trying to set up a school for settlement kids. He had spent days scouring the site and surrounding streets for waste wood to make little stools, even somehow managing to get hold of paper and pencils. Anyone who wanted to learn to read or write was welcome. From what I heard, there were few takers, but that didn't stop Santosh, who blithely added math and geography to the curriculum. The general lack of interest persisted, of course. The children couldn't be bothered, and their parents had other things to worry about.

Two days before, I had stood behind Santosh in the queue for the toilets. He was holding one of his sons in his arms. In his usual good-natured way, he had asked after my mother and pressed on me how important it was that Thida learn how to read and write. I had nodded dutifully, secretly doubting that he would find anyone to teach in these times.

Where could he be going at this late hour? I followed him at a distance, and saw him peer over the fence and squeeze between two boards.

His longyi was dark, but he was wearing a white undershirt. Why had he made no effort at camouflage? Was it the only shirt he possessed, or didn't he care? The curfew was now only from midnight until six, but it was as strict as ever. Walking the streets without a special permit could mean death. What was he planning to do? I couldn't picture him as a looter. Then again, if someone had told me a few months back that I'd be climbing into people's houses at night and stealing gold coins and wads of cash, I would have called them crazy.

Who knows how far a person will go in times of need?

How many of us know our own limits?

Until a few weeks ago, I had thought I knew mine, but maybe such a belief is the privilege of the full-bellied and the content—the illusion of those who have a roof over their head and wake up in the morning knowing what they'll have for supper.

I also pushed my way between the boards. I saw Santosh, head down, scurrying along Loi Sam in the direction of Independence Boulevard. We seemed to be going the same way.

On the corner of the boulevard was a supermarket with an empty, brightly lit parking lot, and at the far end of this were garbage containers and stacks of crates and boxes. I'd heard that the whole place was under video surveillance, but this didn't stop dumpster divers from the settlement coming to try their luck.

Santosh crossed the asphalt with his head held low. He had no cover and barely stopped to look around him. A living target. Any patrol would have spotted him a mile off in that white shirt. His need, his hunger, his children's hunger—something must have been gnawing at him horribly to make him act so rashly. Santosh, of all people, I thought—careful, sensible Santosh. Even when he reached the containers, he didn't take shelter in the shade of the building, but walked straight to the boxes and started to open them.

I was about to move on when a military patrol appeared on the boulevard. Two jeeps turned out of a side street and rolled slowly toward the supermarket, three soldiers on the back of each. The soldiers looked about them in all directions, their rifles at the ready, as if they were expecting attack at any moment. Santosh was too busy with the boxes to notice them; it was only a matter of seconds before they discovered him. I had taken cover behind a bush and wanted to warn him, but didn't know how.

"Santosh," I called, but he was too far away.

"Santosh. Sa-a-antosh." Too quiet, much too quiet.

I would have had to yell at the top of my voice— but then the patrol would have discovered me too.

The jeeps were less than two hundred yards off. The soldiers were wearing night-vision goggles; one of them spotted Santosh and leaned forward to the driver. The truck slowed to a halt.

Sa-a-antosh. You idiot. You madman. You lunatic. Duck. Take cover. Make a dash for it. Run—run for your life.

The seconds that followed are tattooed on my mind. I see them repeat themselves over and over, as if on a loop.

Santosh is standing with his back to the parking lot, slightly bent over.

He is rummaging around in a box.

The soldier calmly raises his rifle.

Sa-a-antosh.

Takes aim.

"Sa-a-antosh." I abandon all caution and yell as loud as I can. My shout is lost in the bang of a shot.

The lanky body jerks and slumps to the ground. Lies motionless on the asphalt. The jeeps move in. One of the soldiers peers in my direction, as if he's heard me yell, despite the shot. I press myself flat on the ground and close my eyes, clawing the soft earth with my fingers. I am trembling all over. I smell warm, damp soil. A solitary mosquito whines at my ear.

I don't know how long I lay there.

By the time I'd mustered the courage to raise my head, the jeeps had vanished, taking Santosh's body with them.

Murderers, I thought. Cowardly, base, underhanded murderers. Shooting an unarmed man in the back—a man who was searching the garbage for food for his starving children. Anger and disgust rose in me. I felt sick and stood up to vomit, but I hadn't eaten for days and retched up nothing but bile. It made my throat burn. Part of me wanted to creep back to the settlement and hide away with my parents and Thida until someone came to tell me it was all over.

That the virus was gone.

That we could leave the settlement.

That we were needed again

The other part of me felt such fury that it wanted to destroy something. I would have liked to take a rock and throw it through the supermarket window. But that wouldn't have brought Santosh back to life.

I had a job to do.

We had debts with Bagura.

The settlement needed money.

I swallowed my anger. It tasted as bitter as stewed tea.

I only vaguely remember the walk to Noro Hill and the Benzes' villa. It seemed to go on forever, and I moved through the streets in a daze, not even feeling fear. Eventually I found myself at the foot of the wall and crawled underneath to the other side.

The light was on in Mary's room. She wasn't sitting at the window, but she signaled the go-ahead as soon as I threw the gravel.

She got a shock when she saw me. "My God, what happened?"

We sat down on boxes of French wine and I told her, haltingly, what I had witnessed. I would have liked to weep in her arms, but I couldn't; there was an awful, crippling void in me.

"I could have saved him," I kept saying.

"You couldn't."

"I should have warned him earlier."

"They'd only have shot you both."

"You don't know that. We might have managed to flee together."

"Almost every morning I hear of injured or dead people on the streets. Curfew violators, supposed looters. You wouldn't have had a chance."

"I looked on and watched them kill him."

"No. You make it sound as if *you* shot him. It isn't your fault. The city's crawling with uniformed murderers, and he didn't take care. Those people are sadists, killers. Do you hear? It. Isn't. Your. Fault."

Maybe she was right. Maybe she wasn't. Santosh had been careless. What idiot wears a white T-shirt to go dumpster diving? Who stands with his back to the street in a situation like that?

And yet.

I buried my face in my hands and felt Mary stroking my hair. Her fingers smelled of turpentine. Her hands were smeared blue, yellow, red, and black.

Instead of a nightdress, she was wearing an artist's smock spattered with paint. She saw the surprise on my face. "I've been working," she said. "I've done a lot of painting since you were last here. Would you like to see?"

I nodded. "In your room?"

"Yes."

"Aren't your parents and brother at home?"

"Yes, but they're asleep. If we take care, it'll be fine. Are you scared?"

"No," I lied.

"Come on then." She opened the door and hobbled out quickly, as if afraid I might change my mind. In the passage, she handed me a flashlight from the pocket of her smock, and I lit the way as she struggled up the stairs. With every step, my doubts grew. Was this a good idea? If we were caught, Mary wouldn't be able to protect me. Nothing she could say would stop her parents from calling the police.

At the top of the cellar stairs, I paused. Mary noticed and turned around. "What's wrong?" she whispered.

The flashlight lit up her face. It was so full of joy that I couldn't bring myself to disappoint her. "I'm coming."

The two dogs, Kato and Mo, came to meet us. They sniffed at my legs, wagging their tails, clearly pleased to see me.

Mary opened the door to the big entrance hall, then waited and listened. When she didn't hear anything, she hobbled across the hall to the curved staircase. I followed breathlessly. Apart from the fireplace, there was nowhere for me to hide if someone turned on the light upstairs. Mary heaved herself up the first step. It gave a loud creak. I held my breath.

Silence.

The next step creaked too. I wanted to go back to the cellar. Straight back. That second.

For a moment Mary didn't move. Then, signaling to me to carry on, she put a foot on the third step. This one creaked only very softly, almost imperceptibly. In this slow and nerve-wracking manner, we made our way to the top of the house.

All the bedrooms were on the second floor. We slipped into Mary's room and closed the door behind us. It was even bigger than I'd imagined. The broad bed, covered in a mosquito net, took up an entire corner. There was a window seat with a red cushion, a desk with a computer, and a whole wall lined with closets and bookshelves and a big television. Unlike our shack, the place was a terrible mess. The floor was littered with T-shirts, underwear, empty

Coke cans and bottles; the wastepaper basket was overflowing. On the desk I saw a plate of leftover food, empty blister packs, an open notebook.

The rest of the room was taken up with canvases, paintpots, brushes, tubes, and easels. There was a smell of fresh paint. Pictures leaned against the walls, desk, and bookcases. Some looked half-finished or only recently begun—or perhaps it just seemed that way to me.

The walk from the cellar had been quite a strain. I collapsed in a heap on the floor, more exhausted than after a day's gardening

Mary fetched a can of Coke from a small fridge and tossed it to me. While I drank, she took out various pictures and arranged them around the room so that I could see them. It was clearly an effort for her to shift the canvases, and I wanted to help, but she motioned to me to stay put.

When she was finished, a dozen pictures were set out along the walls to my left and right.

"These are all things I've done in the last few weeks," Mary said, sitting down beside me, her face twisted in a grimace of pain.

"What's wrong?"

"Nothing. My hip sometimes hurts when I sit down, that's all. It's better now."

I could see in her eyes that this wasn't the truth.

"Can I help you?"

"No," she snapped. "I told you it's better now. I'd rather hear what you think of my paintings."

The pictures on my right were all of blurred, shadowy faces, wreathed in clouds of mist or steam. The eyes and mouths were wide-open— but was it with joy or fear? They could have been skulls, but equally they could have been children's heads.

The longer I looked at them, the more I thought I could see them coming to life before my eyes. There was something mysterious about them that I couldn't describe. They were like mirrors or windows to another world.

"Well? Do you like them?"

"I'm not sure that *like* is the right word," I said, searching for a better expression.

They speak to me. Not right either.

They have power. Sounded odd.

They're alive. No.

They're beautiful. No, they were certainly not beautiful.

Mary waited patiently.

"They—move me."

"In what way?"

Instead of answering, I felt something loosen inside me and before I knew it, there were tears rolling down my face. I saw Santosh again—his eyes, his hesitant smile. He looked as blurred as the faces on Mary's paintings. The emptiness in me gradually subsided. "I can't—I can't describe it."

Mary moved nearer and took me in her arms. She ran her fingers through my hair and stroked my face; she lay down beside me and pulled me close. At last I could cry. I didn't know when—if ever—I had last felt so safe.

I wanted to hide in her arms forever. Hide from the hunger and the virus. From life in the slum. From people who shot other people in the back for rummaging through garbage. We heard footsteps on the landing. Mary held me tight. "It's my father," she whispered. "He goes to the bathroom every night. You don't need to worry. He never comes in. Ever. Not even during the day."

The footsteps came closer.

"Trust me."

"Mary?" Her father's voice.

I froze.

"Yes?"

"Everything all right?"

"Yes, I'm fine."

"What are you doing?"

"Painting."

There was silence on the other side of the door and the hint of a sigh. "You should get some sleep now."

"Yes, I will. Good night, Dad."

"Good night."

We heard a door close, the faint rush of a flushing toilet, and then footsteps moving away.

When all was quiet again, I explained to Mary why I needed more money.

I told her all about our day at the hospital, my mother's improving health, the visit from the police. I had borrowed a pen and a scrap of paper from Bagura and made a list of all my expenses: taxi, doctor, X-ray, medicine, water, cookies, interest.

Mary glanced at the list. "Why the details? 'My mother's life' would have been enough." She smiled.

"The few thousand leik for you are no trouble," she said. "It's the big sum that worries me—the protection money. If that kind of money goes missing, I'm afraid my father might notice after all." She thought for a moment. "My Aunt Kate lives not far from here. Do you remember Aunt Kate?"

"Yes, she used to visit you sometimes. Isn't she married to King Khao, the soy tycoon?"

"Not anymore; they got divorced. But she ended up with the house, a seaside villa, and a good part of his soy fortune. Now she's always blathering on about how rich she is. It drives my father up the wall, so we don't see much of her these days."

"And you think she'd give us the money?"

"No, but the house is empty; Aunt Kate's gone to stay with her daughters, who are studying in

America. There's only a housekeeper in charge, and she knows me. I'll find some pretext to get her out of the house, and we'll have a look around and see what we can find. What do you reckon?"

I was having trouble keeping up.

"We can meet there tomorrow. I'll tell my parents I'm going to paint her swimming pool—I've done that before. My mother will drop me off. Just come to number nineteen, Loi Lam Tam, at twelve. Can you manage that?"

"Of course."

"Ring the bell, I'll be there to let you in."

Mary got up with another brief grimace of pain. She rummaged in her desk, and a moment later she was handing me a bulging envelope.

"What's that?"

"The money for your friend—with interest."

ELEVEN

Early the next morning I went to Bagura to pay my debts, but he had a visitor and I had to wait outside.

Through the flimsy shanty wall I heard a woman in some agitation. Her husband had disappeared. He hadn't been lying next to her when she woke up, though they'd gone to sleep together the night before. She and the children had looked all over the settlement for him. No, there was no one he might have visited in the middle of the night. What a question! No, she had no relatives in town. No, it had never happened before and it wasn't like him at all—as Bagura very well knew. She couldn't make head or tail of it.

Even if I hadn't recognized the voice, I'd have known who it was, and for a moment I thought of going in and explaining everything. But I didn't have it in me to tell the woman that her husband had been murdered. I was too cowardly.

She was crying. Bagura promised to use his contacts with the police. When she came out of the shack, I closed my eyes and pretended I was dozing in the shade.

Bagura eyed me thoughtfully when I went in. "You were out again last night, weren't you?"

I nodded.

"Didn't happen to see Lanky, did you?"

I hesitated. "Hmm."

"What does that mean. Yes or no?"

"No, why do you ask?" I felt wretched.

"He's disappeared. Are you sure you didn't see him?"

I stared at the ground and shook my head.

Before he could ask any more questions, I put the envelope from Mary on the table. "That's the money we owe you. I'll have the protection money this afternoon."

Bagura barely glanced at the envelope. He was staring absentmindedly at the photograph of the little girl on the table beside his bed. I stood there awkwardly. There was another favor that I was embarrassed to ask. "Could you lend me a longyi and a clean white shirt?" I said eventually.

"In your size?" He smiled again. "Not likely."

"The size doesn't matter. As long as they're clean."

"Have a look over there." He gestured toward a pile of clean clothes on a shelf. I pulled out a white T-shirt and a green-and-black longyi and tried them on. They were both far too big. Bagura laughed when he saw me. "You look like a clown."

Maybe I did. But a clean, sweet-smelling clown— and that, I thought to myself, was what mattered.

Before I could set off for Mary's aunt's, there was something I had to do in the settlement. Thida's friend Nai Nai had died in the night, and my mother had asked me to take Thida to the funeral. Since moving to Beautiful Tuscany, I had attended a lot of funerals—sometimes to dig graves, sometimes to see off a dead neighbor, sometimes simply to pass the time. On the whole, the dead had been old, the ceremonies short, and the mourners few. Nai Nai's funeral was different. Crowds of people thronged around the little grave, and there was bitter weeping. Thida wept too, and for a long time she resisted my attempts to take her in my arms and comfort her. I think, secretly, she was still convinced I could have saved Nai Nai.

It was quite a relief to get home and hand her over to my mother.

The property at number nineteen, Loi Lam Tam, took up half a block and was surrounded by a wall higher than the Benzes' villa. I realized that Mary's aunt must be even richer than her parents. Next to the big black metal gate, I spotted surveillance cameras in the bushes, and hoped Mary knew how to switch them off. To be on the safe side, I pulled up the face mask that Bagura had lent me to just under my eyes.

There was also a door next to the gate and an intercom system equipped with another camera.

I rang the bell and shifted nervously from one leg to the other. I had bathed in the canal, cleaned my teeth, and washed my hair, but I was already drenched in sweat again.

Nothing happened.

I was about to ring the bell a second time when I heard a crackling sound followed by Mary's voice. "Niri?"

"Yes." There was a buzz, and the door opened as if by magic. I stepped inside.

Aunt Kate's house resembled two white shoeboxes, one on top of the other, with a great deal of doors and windows. The garden path was edged with palms and the most magnificent hibiscus and oleander. Only the lawn looked as if it could have done with a trim.

Mary was waiting at the door for me. She smiled when she saw me in Bagura's clothes. "Baggy style. Very cool."

We walked through an entrance hall and came to a large room that was entirely glazed on one side. Outside was a roofed terrace with sofas and armchairs and a barbecue; small palms and flowers grew in pots.

The dark-blue tiles of a swimming pool gleamed in the sun. A dozen lounge chairs stood around the pool, a rolled-up towel on each one.

"How many people live here?"

"Just my aunt."

"No one else?"

"No. Except my cousins, of course, when they're over from America. And the staff, who live back there in the garden house—but they're taking care of the seaside villa right now. The only one who's around is Lulu, the housekeeper."

"She's here now?"

"No, she was nice enough to go into town to get me paints and brushes. She'll be gone at least two hours, so we have the place to ourselves for a bit. Are you thirsty?"

"Yes."

"Then come with me."

We passed through a room with a long dining table laid for ten, as if guests were expected at any moment. Powerful wooden fans hung from the ceiling; an AC unit hummed in the background.

Two huge fridges stood in the kitchen. One, with a glass door, was lit from the inside and filled with bottles of wine.

Mary opened the other and handed me a tumbler. "Lime soda? With ice?" She held the glass under an opening and ice cubes tumbled out. Some fell on the floor. I picked them up and didn't know where to put them. Mary pointed at the sink.

"You want me to throw them away?"

"What else? They've been on the floor. They're dirty."

I'd never seen such a clean, shiny floor. Reluctantly, I put the ice cubes in the sink.

I was starting to feel uncomfortable. I'd been longing to see Mary again, but now that I was here with her I felt none of the joy I had anticipated. It was almost as if my joy had refused to follow me into the villa. Something about the place wasn't right. My mother would have said there were no good spirits here—or that they had taken umbrage at the lack of respect and humility shown them. She was convinced that all things and places—trees, shrubs, houses, gardens—were inhabited by spirits. These could be good or bad, friendly or hostile, but they all had great power and were all to be treated with humility and respect. I didn't believe any of that, but even so I had the feeling something was wrong. It was like being in a house with crooked walls, where the furniture shifted when you weren't looking and the pictures spoke in whispering voices, all talking at once. I felt hemmed in, despite all the space.

"What's wrong?"

"What if the housekeeper comes back early?"

"She won't. We're good for two hours."

"Did you switch off the surveillance cameras?"

"I don't know where the switches are. They may not even be on. I can't imagine Lulu watches the videos."

Mary saw me hesitate. "Would you rather leave?"

I didn't have to think for long. "No. I need the money."

"I've already had a look around. There's a safe in the dressing room on the first floor. I think I know how to crack it."

We went back to the entrance hall, where a flight of stairs led to the upper stories. The steps were steeper and more slippery than at the Benzes, and I saw what a struggle it was for Mary to climb them.

"Would you like me to carry you?"

She wheeled around. "Aren't I fast enough for you?"

"It's not that," I said, horrified, "really..."

"You can tell me."

"I only wanted to help."

"Do I look as if I need help?"

She was hauling herself up by the banister, hand over hand, and stopped just before the first landing. "Sorry. But there's nothing I hate more than being dependent on people, or being a burden to them."

I turned and leaned over, offering her my back. "Climb on."

She hesitated.

"What's wrong? Come on up."

"I'm scared of horses . . ."

I waited. "Come on."

She climbed onto my back and wrapped her legs around my hips. She was lighter than I'd expected.

On the first floor I carried her down a long corridor with several doors, stopping now and then to spin her around.

"What are you doing?"

I could tell from her voice that she wasn't afraid.

At the end of the corridor we came to a room with pink painted walls. In the middle was an enormous heart-shaped bed. A picture window stretched from one end of the room to the other.

"Throw me onto the bed," Mary cried.

I spun her around one last time and she clung to me with both hands. I tried to throw her down on the pillows, but she wouldn't let go and we ended up falling onto the bed together. At the last moment, I rolled to one side so as not to land on top of her.

Shoulders touching, we lay there, breathing quickly and staring at the ceiling—a deep-blue sky bright with stars. Then we turned to face each other. Mary beamed at me with her big, beautiful eyes, as if I were very special.

"I hope I didn't hurt you," I said.

"You did, but it was worth it."

"I'm sorry."

She didn't reply, but took my hand, pulled up her dress a little, and laid my fingers on her bare knee.

My heart began to pound with excitement. Mary pushed my hand up her thigh. She was guiding me; I had only to follow. Her skin grew gradually softer until I felt a ridge running across her leg, then another, and another. Her thigh was scarred all over. It felt like the bark of an old palm tree.

Her lips were trembling and she closed her eyes, but not because my caresses gave her pleasure.

The thrill died in me. Instinctively, I made to withdraw my hand, but she held it tight. "No."

"I'm afraid of hurting you."

"You are hurting me. But it's worth it," she said again, looking into my eyes.

"But—but—I don't want that."

"Then you'll have to go." She released my hand.

"Why do you say that?"

"Isn't that how it works? People who get close end up hurting each other."

"No," I said, without giving much thought to her words.

"Oh yes, I'm afraid they do."

"I don't think so."

"Then I'm a sad exception. Even worse."

"I didn't mean it like that."

"So how did you mean it?"

"I'll be gentle. I'll take care. I'll " Mary's eyes told me that this wasn't what she wanted to hear. Tenderly she stroked my face.

"I don't want you to treat me differently."

"But when you're in pain?"

"Then I'm in pain. I can bear it." Mary pushed me gently back onto the pillow and leaned in on me. I closed my eyes and felt her coming closer, until there was only an inch or so between us. I felt her lips touch mine, gentle as a butterfly's wings. Her kiss went right through my body. My hands began to tingle, my heart raced. But I wasn't frightened. I let myself go, unafraid. Unafraid of doing the wrong thing, unafraid of hurting Mary, unafraid of being discovered.

———

Sometime later, Mary started up and looked at her watch. "Oh God, Lulu will be here any minute, we must get a move on."

She led me to the next room, which was all closets and mirrors, and motioned to me to open a door. Inside there was nothing but shoes—there must have been a hundred pairs, in all shapes and colors.

"Wrong closet," she said. "Try the next one."

An entire closet full of dresses. Red ones and blue ones, white ones and black ones, yellow ones and green ones. Shocking pink and old rose. Stripes, checks, polka dots. Short sleeves, long sleeves.

Behind the dresses was a safe that was almost as tall as me and a good arm's length broad and deep. There was a keypad on the door.

"Ouf! How do we get in there?"

"I think I know. But we have two tries, max, before the alarm goes off. If I'm wrong, you must get out of here fast, okay?"

I nodded.

"Here goes, then. 0 4 0 4 2 0 1 0."

"Your aunt tells you her secret codes?" I asked in surprise.

"No, but it's the date of her divorce. She's always telling us how it was the best day of her life and how lucky the numbers are. We've got a shot."

Concentrating hard, I entered the first seven digits. Before the last digit, I hesitated and looked at Mary. She nodded. I entered the final zero.

The door opened with a rasping sound.

When I saw inside the safe, I felt dizzy. Wads of crisp new bills were stacked on the shelves like the books in the monastery library—not just the red-and-blue bills familiar to me, but green bills too, in quantities I'd never dreamed of. Farther down were various drawers that opened to reveal diamonds, chains, rings, and coins—and right at the bottom was a shelf of gold bars.

What does *one* person do with so much money? For a ten-leik bill I could buy a meal for my parents, my sister, and me in a cookshop. Or a new longyi. Or a small bag of rice. Ten leik meant something to me. But in quantities like these, money was no more than a pile of printed paper.

I thought of Santosh, and again that mixture of anger and disgust rose in me.

"Wow," Mary said. "I didn't know there was this much. My father says people don't like keeping their money in the banks anymore, because they're afraid they'll go bankrupt. Looks as if he's right."

"How much is it?"

"No idea. I'm bad at guessing numbers."

"How much do you think I should take?"

"Maybe two gold bars and as many bills as you can fit in your backpack?"

It seemed too much.

"Come on. What's wrong? Do you want me to help you?"

"Yes, please."

Mary kneeled down and took two gold bars from the safe. Then we began to stuff wads of bills into the backpack. "Just leik, or dollars too?"

"Just leik," I replied in a kind of daze.

"Or do you want to take it all? I'm sure we could find another bag somewhere."

"No, it's too much at once."

"Just an idea. It'll be months before my aunt gets back from America and notices."

"No," I said again, pensively. "Not now. Maybe later."

"It's up to you."

A moment later, Mary saw me to the gate. Almost two hours had passed, and now she too was getting nervous. Lulu might come back at any moment.

We stood facing each other awkwardly. "You must go," she said.

"I know," I said, but made no move to leave.

"Do you still have my number?"

"No."

She gave it to me.

"Call me."

I nodded and took her hand.

I didn't want to leave her. Everything in me was resisting.

TWELVE

When I got back to the settlement, I went straight to Bagura. He was sitting on his bed, his eyes only half-open, a battery-powered fan on a stool in front of him and the photograph of the solemn little girl at his side. For a moment I thought he was meditating and that I would have to wait, but then he looked at me. A mournful smile flitted across his face.

"Lanky's dead," he said, adding, before I had time to act surprised, "but you already knew that. Sit down."

I hunkered down on a second stool next to the bed.

"What do you want?"

"I need your help."

"Again?" He sounded as if he was getting better.

I opened the backpack and took out an envelope with money for the mayor and the police. Then I pulled the zipper a little farther to give Bagura a glimpse of the rest of my loot.

"How much?" he asked in a whisper, pushing the envelope under his pillow.

I shrugged. "A lot. Probably a few million. And a couple of gold bars."

I thought he'd be pleased, but he stared at me in horror. "Have you killed someone?"

"No, who do you think I am?"

"So where did you get all this money?" The suspicion in his voice rattled me.

"My source knows the code to a safe."

Bagura shook his head in disbelief. "Who is this source of yours? Is he involved in drugs?"

"What makes you think that?"

"It's always drugs with this kind of money."

"Not in this case."

"So where's it from? Why is your source helping you? What does he get in return?"

"Nothing."

"Come on, you know that's bullshit."

"It's true."

"You don't get something for nothing, Niri," Bagura said angrily. He pulled a large handkerchief from his longyi and blew his nose.

"But it's true," I said again, although deep down in a remote corner of my heart I suspected he might be right.

"Don't do anything stupid."

"What do you mean?"

"You know what I mean. Don't go handing it out this time."

"But what else am I supposed to do with it?"

"Keep it safe and get out of the country as quick as you can."

I'd expected a different answer. "That wasn't the idea."

"Niri," he said, looking at me so intently that I lowered my eyes, "don't you understand what a fortune you're sitting on? If you handle it wisely, you have enough money there to keep you for the rest of your days. You'd never have to work again. Your parents would never have to work again. No more washing and cooking and cleaning for other people. No more mowing other people's lawns. Instead you'd have your own little house with air-conditioning, a TV, a fridge. You could go to a doctor when you needed one."

He paused, waiting for a reply. When I said nothing, he continued. "Think of your little sister. Think of the life you could offer her."

Bagura was right—that was something I'd never thought of. The possibilities he described were alluring, and yet at the same time so alien as to be unreal. It was like hearing about a film he'd seen, thrilling and beguiling, but remote from my life—present and future.

"My father would never agree to that."

Bagura groaned.

"It's not what I want either," I added, to clear up any uncertainty.

"Why not?"

Bad karma, my father would have said.

Bad karma, the abbot would have said.

It was a bit more complicated than that. If I kept the money for myself, I'd be no more than a common, greedy criminal. That wasn't what I wanted. I had taken from someone who had too much to give to people who had nothing. That wasn't theft. It was redistribution. I'd once seen a YouTube video about loading ships. If the load shifts too far to one side, the ship begins to list and will eventually capsize. To prevent that, the cargo has to be redistributed as quickly as possible. That's what I was doing.

"I'm not a thief."

"Then you're crazy." Bagura stared at the wall in silence, his face dark. He was beginning to creep me out.

"Can you help me?"

"What with?"

"Selling the gold bars. Distributing the money."

"No."

"Why not?"

"Because it's too dangerous."

"You'd get your fifteen percent interest, and that would be—"

"Big cash," he said tersely. "I know. I can do the sums too. But that's not the point. Anyone I try to sell those gold bars to will want to know where they come from. They'll ask questions. They'll suspect there's more to be had and they'll sniff it out. People like that have their methods, and they don't hold back. I'm way out of my depth here. I don't want anything to do with this. I'm a small-time crook, not a millionaire thief."

"Please."

He shook his head.

"What else can I do?"

"Bugger off. Today, if you've any sense. Now. This minute. Pack your things and clear out before someone notices they're missing several million leik and two gold bars."

"The owner's in the States. It'll be a while before she notices anything."

"But she will eventually. If you're not a thief, take all this back."

"Are you crazy? You're telling me to put millions of leik and two gold bars back in a safe when we need it so badly?"

"Yes." Bagura waved a hand, as if to end the discussion.

"You talk like my father."

I made no move to get up. Not because I thought I could convince him, but because I didn't know what to do.

"Are you deaf? Get out of here."

I didn't budge. "You're just as much a coward as all the others," I found myself saying.

Bagura looked at me in astonishment.

"You don't even have to get your fingers dirty. You can put all the blame on me. I stole the money. All you have to do is help me share it out. How dangerous can that be? But you'd rather stand by and watch children starve to death after milking their parents for their last cent."

"That's enough," he roared. "I said get out of here. Beat it."

I was quivering with indignation and still made no move to get up. Bagura yelled for Yuri. When he appeared in the door, I rose to my feet.

"Niri wants to leave. Take him home."

"I can see myself out, thanks," I said angrily, pushing my way past a bewildered-looking Yuri.

If Bagura wouldn't help, I'd just have to distribute the money on my own.

THIRTEEN

I felt deep, searing anger. At Bagura, at my father, at the soldiers who had shot Santosh, and at
the virus that had changed our lives almost overnight, while Mary's family was able to stay in their
villa, sitting on their hoard of rice and oil and Scot-
tish shortbread. I was outraged that my mother had
almost died, while stacks of money were languish-
ing in a safe.

Bagura's suggestion that I return the gold and
cash made me furious. I swore to myself that it was
the last thing I would do, though it was true I had no
idea how I was going to distribute my small fortune
fairly and safely without his help. I could hardly
wander around the settlement leaving thousand-
leik bills on people's doorsteps. I didn't even have a
safe place where I could hide my stash for a day or

two. There was no one I could talk to, no one I could turn to for advice.

But if the loot wasn't safe with me, I would have to get rid of it as fast as possible. Not here in Beautiful Tuscany, but in the other slum Bagura had mentioned, behind the General Hospital, on old railway land. The cash, anyway. I'd figure out what to do with the gold at a later date.

It was dusk, the sky was darkening, clouds were gathering. In a few minutes a heavy monsoon would descend on the city. The other settlement may have been smaller than ours, but it was, as Bagura had said, even more of a "shithole." A vile stench wafted toward me long before I reached the metal fence. Young men about my age were loitering at the open gate; not far from them, two black birds perched on a dog's carcass.

The men eyed me suspiciously; they saw at a glance that I didn't belong. My expensive backpack, freshly washed T-shirt, and relatively clean longyi were a giveaway.

I gave them what I hoped was a casual nod and dived between the shanties. After a few feet I stopped and pretended to look for someone. The last days' rain had soaked the ground; I kept sinking into mud up to my ankles. The place was littered with plastic bags and bottles. Most of the people here lived under makeshift tarpaulin roofs. They were dressed in rags, and a lot of the children were running around naked. I wondered why these people were even worse off than us. Bagura was probably right: If they knew what was in my backpack, I'd be dead meat.

I began to have my doubts about distributing the money without help, and was contemplating turning back, when a young woman approached me. There was a baby asleep on her back, and she was so thin that I was amazed she had the strength to carry it. She stretched out a hand to me—she must have seen at once that I was a stranger to the settlement—and started to plead with me in an impenetrable dialect. Then she grabbed my arm and pulled me down a narrow alleyway to a shelter of plastic sheeting. Under it lay a naked boy, perhaps a little younger than my sister, and squatting beside him was a man who was even thinner than the woman, his cheeks hollow, his eyes bloodshot. I guessed that he was the woman's husband. Unlike her, he managed to make himself more or less understood to me. He told me the boy was sick and had been getting steadily worse for days. He needed a doctor and something to eat.

His wife started to say something, but he interrupted her.

It started to rain. Fat drops pelted onto the plastic. Water ran in through holes overhead and gushed down into the shelter from the alley.

I rummaged awkwardly through my backpack, pretending to look for something. A few seconds later, I pulled out a wad of bills.

The man's eyes widened. He was so startled that he didn't immediately take the money. His wife didn't wait to be asked. I put a finger to my lips, hoping they would understand that they mustn't tell anyone what had happened. They nodded.

Then I heard the smacking sound of footsteps in the mud and a moment later two men were standing in front of us. They must have followed me from the gate.

Without a glance in my direction, they began to speak loudly and roughly to the couple, and tried to tear the money from the woman's hands. She clung to it, kicking and screaming. One of the men lashed out at her and caught her face; her husband flung himself between them.

I clutched my backpack and was about to head out of the shelter when one of the men grabbed my arm and tried to hold me back. I twisted myself free, but managed to bring down the plastic sheeting in the process, so that we ended up buried underneath. I was the first to crawl out. As I got to my feet, I saw that we were surrounded by a crowd of onlookers. "Stop that boy!" a voice yelled behind me, and I plunged through the crowd and ran for it.

The settlement was a labyrinth of narrow passages, dead ends, and alleyways. I headed left, knocked over two small children, took a right, had to vault a pile of firewood, almost slipped in the mud, got my balance again, turned into another passage. I was lucky—this one led straight to the gate, and I dashed out onto the street, gasping for breath. The sound of voices behind me told me that I was still being chased, and although I had a head start, I was afraid I wouldn't be able to keep going for long. Stamina wasn't my strong point. I needed somewhere to hide.

The rain lashed my face. I ran past a construction site, saw a gap in the fence, and pushed my way in. On the other side was the shell of a multistory building. Not a safe hiding place—they'd search every floor for me.

In the far corner of the site I spotted a wooden toilet block and dived in without stopping to think. Soon afterward, I heard the voices of my pursuers. As I had thought, they presumed I was in the house and were scouring it from basement to roof.

Through a gap in the wood, I saw two of the men heading for the toilets.

My only chance of escape was the cesspool underneath. I slid into the gooey swill; it came up to my chest and the stink was vile. When I heard someone open the door, I clutched the backpack to me, took a deep breath, held my nose, pressed my lips together, and dived under. Fighting fear and anxiety, I started to count in my head. At twenty, I had the impression there was something splashing about in the cesspool above me. At sixty, my heart started to race; at a hundred, I was having trouble holding my breath; at a hundred and twenty, I thought my lungs would burst; at a hundred and sixty, I had to surface to stop myself from passing out.

Above me, all was quiet.

I waited, suppressing the urge to cough. I listened. It was still raining, but less hard than before. I heard voices moving away, but didn't dare leave the shit until long after they'd gone.

Eventually I pulled myself back up to the toilets and stepped out of the door into the rain. I closed my eyes and felt the water wash the filth out of my hair and face. After a few steps, I heard a sound behind me. Before I could turn around, two hands had grabbed me by the arms and snatched my backpack from me, gripping me so hard that it hurt.

"Stinking idiot," someone said behind me. The voice was familiar. "Yuri? Taro?"

"Shut up."

I wasn't mistaken.

They led me from the building site like a couple of cops leading a criminal, and we headed down the deserted street toward the settlement. There was thunder, and a moment later another even heavier downpour was unleashed. I raised my face gratefully to the sky.

When we passed a torrent of rain cascading off a bridge, they pushed me underneath as if it were a shower. A murky puddle formed at my feet and ran in a rivulet to the gutter.

Bagura was still sitting on his bed, a dish of sunflower seeds in front of him. Yuri and Taro sent me stumbling into the shack with a shove, and blocked the door with their bulky bodies.

Bagura wrinkled his nose at me in disgust. "What have you done now? Been playing the philanthropist again?"

I told him.

"You idiot," he said. "How can anyone be so stupid? Running around doling out alms. Don't you think at all?"

I took no notice of his ranting. "Give me my backpack."

"It's safer with us."

"You lied to me. You told me you're a small-time crook, not a millionaire thief, and now you've stolen my gold. Give it back, or I'll ..."

"Or you'll what?"

"Or I'll fetch it." I made a lunge for one of the stools and brandished it in the air. Even then I was no match for Yuri and Taro, but my resolve made them back off a bit. At least I'd be able to inflict considerable pain on one of them before they got the better of me. "Give me my backpack," I said again.

They threw questioning glances at their father, who shook his head. Then they took a few steps toward me. I hurled myself at them, the stool raised to attack, but this time Yuri was quicker. He grabbed my arm before I could land a blow, and twisted it behind my back. I let out a scream of pain and dropped the stool.

"Let go, you moron," I snarled.

He twisted a little harder.

"Ow! Are you crazy? You'll break it."

"Leave him," Taro said.

Yuri didn't react.

"Leave him," Bagura repeated. Yuri pushed me sprawling onto the floor.

I lay in the dirt, fists clenched, tears of anger and frustration in my eyes. It was all I could do to stop myself from screaming. There was no point, no point at all, in making a second attempt to retrieve my backpack, but I was determined to try all the same. I just had to muster some energy and wait for the right moment.

"You don't give up easily," Bagura said with a sigh, beckoning to me. "And you've got guts too. Come over here."

I got to my feet. "Only if I can have my backpack."

He considered for a moment, then gave Yuri a nod. Reluctantly, Yuri handed me the backpack. Bagura's eyes flitted from me to his sons and back again.

Then he flapped a hand at Yuri and Taro, evidently signaling to them to leave him alone with me. They left the shack, cursing.

"Sit down."

I perched distrustfully on the edge of his bed.

"I warned you, and now we have a problem. Come tomorrow, everyone will know that you're wandering around with a backpack full of money. That kind of thing gets about."

"So? There was a sick child. I thought a doctor and some pills might help."

Bagura shook his head slowly. "Maybe they will, maybe they won't. But you still haven't got it, have you? There are millions of sick children out there, and we'll never have enough doctors and pills to cure them all. That's the way of the world. Didn't your father teach you that?"

"What's my father got to do with it?"

"He's a Buddhist. They think they know a bit about life. You must have been a novice once."

I nodded.

"This wretched life is our karma—don't you believe that?"

"Yes," I said, without thinking. "No. Or, at least—oh, I don't know what I believe anymore."

"I've seen a lot of the world," Bagura said. "I told you I ran away from the whole damn caste system and left India to go to sea. I saw Vancouver and Los Angeles, Singapore and Hamburg, Tokyo and Manila. In those seven years, I learned that there are castes everywhere; they just have different names in different countries. There are rich and there are poor. Some live in villas, others live in filth. Some have access to doctors and medicine; others don't even have a Band-Aid. People starve because they have nothing to eat; others binge themselves to death. That's how it is. It's how it always was and always will be. There are people who live so far removed from reality that they don't know that, or don't want to know, or have forgotten that they ever did. One thing's for sure, though, you can't do anything about it—not if you dole out billions."

"But I'm not talking about Hamburg or Vancouver. I'm here. And every time I give someone money, something changes," I said, surprised at my firmness. "It's the only thing I can do, so I do it."

"If you have a heart, it will end up killing you. Take it from me. Some go sooner than others, that's all."

"And if you don't have a heart, you might as well not be alive."

Bagura shook his head. "Tell me, kid, where did you spend the first eighteen years of your life?"

"At the Benzes."

"What's that? A cult? A monastery? A remote island in the Bay of Bengal?"

"No. A family. Why?"

"Because I have the feeling"—he broke off, searching for the right words—"that you've had quite a protected childhood for an illegal."

I told Bagura briefly of my parents' work, the monastery school, and our years at the Benzes. As I spoke, I realized that he was right. Behind the high wall with the barbed wire and the cameras, we had lived in another world. That wall had protected not only the Benzes, but me and my family. We had been dependent and yet privileged. I'd never had to run away from the police. Until the outbreak of the virus, I'd never been hungry or had to watch anyone else go hungry. I hadn't slept under bridges. I hadn't stood on stinking, toxic garbage dumps, up to my hips in filth, hunting for usable trash. And if I was honest, I had to admit that I'd never given any thought to people who lived like that.

My day-to-day concerns had been brown palm leaves thirty feet up. Long grass. Withered flowers. Weeds.

My ambition, if you can speak of ambition, had been to be a good gardener.

A good son.

A good brother.

"Did you like school?"

"Yes."

"Were you a good student?"

"Yes."

"Weren't you disappointed that you couldn't go to high school because you were an illegal?"

"Of course. But what could I do?"

Bagura mopped his neck and brow with a dirty handkerchief. "That's what I mean, Niri. You can't change things. You can't help everyone."

"I'm not interested in *everyone*. I'm interested in the ones I can help."

He looked at me thoughtfully.

"Imagine you're a father with a sick child," I went on. "Standing in front of you is this guy who could help you, but won't, because he says there are millions of other sick kids and he doesn't have enough money for them all. How would that make you feel? Would it make sense to you? Would it seem logical? We—you and I—are that guy."

Bagura's face twitched. He snorted, his nostrils flared, he looked as if he were about to start yelling at me. My words had touched something in him, but I wasn't sure if he was thinking about what I'd said or preparing to throw me out.

"Do you really think I should take the gold back?"

Bagura still didn't speak. Then, into the silence, he said, "Do you know what one of those bars is worth?"

"No."

"About sixty thousand dollars. That's about six hundred thousand leik. How many do you have?"

"Two. But I can get more."

I could tell from his eyes that he was still thinking. Minutes passed. They seemed to go on forever. I cleared my throat, cracked my knuckles. Bagura didn't react. Hoping to bring him around, I said, "It would be good for your karma."

"I don't give a shit about my karma," he said curtly. "My wife is religious, so are the boys. But not me. Do you hear? I'm not religious. All this hocus-pocus"—he gestured at the poster of Ganesh and the other Hindu gods—"is for them. I'm not Hindu. And I'm not Buddhist or Taoist or Christian or

Muslim or Jewish. I don't believe in heaven and hell or reincarnation or eternal suffering. There was a time when I believed in Marx and Mao, but that's years ago. All I am these days is a zealous adherent of pragmatism.

"And if I help you, we have a very pragmatic problem. I can't sell the gold bars for you; we need a second middleman. He'll want another fifteen percent, at least. In the present climate we can't hope for more than fifty thousand dollars—that's about half a million leik. Minus thirty percent, would leave you with thirty-five thousand."

"That's a lot."

"Not when it should be sixty."

"Doesn't matter. Thirty's thirty."

He shook his head pensively. "You may be good at math, but it doesn't make you a good businessman. Listen, kid, if you want me to help you, you have to trust me, do you understand?"

I nodded.

"That's not easy, I know."

"Why do you say that?"

"Because I don't really trust myself."

"How am I supposed to trust you if you don't trust yourself?"

"It's called friendship. Other laws apply."

He ran both hands through his oily hair. "How much gold is in the safe?"

"Maybe a dozen bars."

"And how much cash?"

"No idea. I didn't count. Millions."

"Only leik?"

"Dollars too."

"American?"

"Are there others?"

He rolled his eyes.

"The bills were green and said *In God We Trust*."

"And if you wanted, you could go back and . . ." He scratched himself thoughtfully between the legs. "I would suggest we start by distributing the contents of your backpack. If all goes well, you can go back and fetch the rest. Agreed?"

"Agreed."

He looked at me searchingly. "There's one thing you must be clear about, kid. If we go ahead with this, nothing will ever be the same again."

I nodded, though I thought he was exaggerating. I needed his help, and if nodding was the price for his support, I would have nodded at anything just then.

"When it's over, we'll go our separate ways—for good. You can give away as much as you like. I'll keep my share and clear out."

"Where will you go? You're not even allowed to leave the city."

He smiled. "It's all a question of money. With enough money, you can get anywhere—out of town, out of the country. I'll buy a small hut for my family somewhere by the sea and watch the fishermen going about their work. I'm not like you."

He reached out an arm. "All right, and now give me that revolting backpack."

He saw my hesitation. "Goodness, kid. I can read your face like a book. You don't know if you can trust me. You're afraid I'll bugger off with the backpack and you'll never see me again. You're right. It's a possibility. But be honest—do you have a better idea?"

I didn't.

Bagura reached into the backpack, took out a wad of damp bills and made a face. "Don't let anyone tell you money doesn't stink."

"Are they still usable?"

"Sure. Just need cleaning and drying." He stowed the backpack under the bed.

I thought of the house on Loi Lam Tam, of the garden, the safe. All that money. The gold bars glinting in the light. But most of all, I thought of Mary. Her body. Her palm-bark skin. Our conversation on the bed. My mind was whirling.

"You all right?" Bagura looked at me in concern, his head cocked to one side.

"Yes. Why?"

"Don't know. You look like someone who's lost his way."

I scanned the room, thinking hard. "Can I ask you something?"

"Anything."

"Do you think that people who get close end up hurting each other?"

"What kind of a question is that?" He raised his bushy eyebrows and leaned over to me. "It's a long time since I was close enough to anyone to ask myself that question. And you? What do you think?"

"I don't think so," I said firmly, although I didn't know what made me so sure.

He smiled. "Of course you don't. I wouldn't have expected anything else of you."

FOURTEEN

Two days later, at the crack of dawn, Bagura came to our shack to fetch me. I could tell from his satisfied grin that the first part of our plan had come off.

My father was far from happy to see him. He didn't even offer him a cup of the tea we had just brewed. Before the two of them could get talking, I jumped up and hurried Bagura out of the shack, mumbling something to my father about having to lend a hand.

A white Toyota minivan was parked at the fence; it looked as if it belonged to the Red Cross. Yuri was sitting at the wheel; Taro stood on the street, holding the door open for me. They both wore face masks and white, freshly pressed uniforms with a red cross on the chest and sleeve. Another uniform and mask were waiting on my seat.

"They're for you," Bagura said. "Put them on."

I climbed into the car. Bagura squeezed himself onto the seat beside me and gestured toward the stacks of gray cardboard boxes on the back seat. "You were lucky. The gold price is soaring. I got over six hundred thousand leik per bar and managed to push down the premium. Together with the cash you pilfered we've got almost two million leik—I've already deducted the money for the car and our camouflage. And I've put aside a thousand leik for every family in this shithole. What we do now is drive to another slum and give every family there a thousand leik. If that goes smoothly, we'll do the same somewhere else tomorrow. If anything goes wrong, we pack up as soon as I give the sign and clear out. Understand?"

"Yes."

"We'll make a note of the names of all the recipients on a list, tick them off when we pay them, and stamp their hands, so they don't go straight to the end of the queue and come back for more. Everything must look as official as possible."

I put on the uniform. It was two sizes too big. In the breast pocket was an ID card with a number and someone else's name. It identified the holder as an employee of the International Red

Cross, Department of Emergency Aid and Crisis Management.

"No long conversations, no photos, no selfies with kids, or whatever else the idiots ask for. If the police show up, just keep calm and get on with your work. Let me do the talking. Got that?"

"I'm not stupid."

"We can't afford to make mistakes. If we're busted, we're in for it. All four of us, but you in particular. Don't think we can protect you. They'll want to know where you got the money, and they'll stop at nothing to get you to talk. You know what happened to Lanky. I tell you, if they arrest us, you'll never see your parents or sister again."

He blew his nose, stuffed the handkerchief back into his longyi, and looked out the window. I was a lot more nervous than I was prepared to admit to myself or the others. Bagura may not have believed it of me, but I knew very well what was at stake.

A few minutes later, we crossed a river, then turned off the road and drove slowly along a bumpy dirt track. There was a settlement on the river-bank, like ours but bigger. Three or four hundred shacks and plastic shelters were crammed into a small space between the bridge and a warehouse.

Yuri parked the minivan on an empty lot covered in puddles. He and Taro got out, fetched three folding tables and chairs from the trunk, and put them up next to the car. On each table they put a bottle of water and a small box with paper, pens, an ink pad, and a rubber stamp. Behind the tables, next to the chairs, they put the boxes of money. Curious children came running up immediately, followed by distrustful-looking men and women.

Bagura settled himself on one of the chairs; it wobbled alarmingly beneath his weight. In his deep, carrying voice he explained that we had been sent by the Red Cross. Thanks to generous donations, we were able to offer every family in the settlement emergency aid of a thousand—"I repeat, one thousand"—leik in cash.

A murmur went through the gathering crowd.

Bagura invited them to queue up at the three tables. One person per family. No cash for unaccompanied minors. There was no need to push and shove—everyone would get the aid they were entitled to. Discipline was crucial. Any fighting or rioting, and the campaign would be broken off immediately, without warning. All attempts at fraud would be penalized with suspension from the aid campaign. Videoing or photographing on mobile phones was strictly prohibited.

Long queues formed at the tables within seconds. I looked nervously at the crowd, embarrassed by all the hungry, expectant faces. Who did I think I was, doling out alms to grown adults? Yuri and

Taro got down to work, as if they'd been doing it all their lives. I didn't move. The air was humid and oppressive, and the sun beat down on us—my eyes ached in the glare.

"Sit down and get a move on," Bagura said.

I sat down and awkwardly took pens, paper, and the rubber stamp from the box.

Across the table from me was a little boy of about Thida's age. He looked at me mutely with big, dark eyes. I picked up a pen. "Where are your parents?"

Silence.

"I'm sorry, but unaccompanied children aren't allowed to queue up."

He didn't move. I was beginning to feel more and more uncomfortable. "Okay, then, what's your name?"

The boy didn't reply, but continued to look imploringly at me.

"Go and get your parents. No children in the queue," Bagura barked at him.

The child flinched.

"Hey, half-pint, didn't you hear what I said? Clear off."

He still didn't budge.

"Are you deaf? Move it."

Bagura turned to the woman who was second in line.

"Your name, please?"

She pushed the boy out of the way. He didn't leave, but stood in silence a little farther around the table. The woman was holding a baby in her arms. I asked her name again, but didn't catch what she said. Behind her, people were jostling and grumbling; someone pushed the woman into the table.

"Stop pushing or we'll leave," Bagura called out sternly. It was instantly quieter.

I slid pen and paper across the table to the woman, so that she could write her own name, but she shook her head.

"If it goes on like this, we'll be here all night," Bagura said. He scribbled a name on the notepad, checked it off, and pressed the rubber stamp—a flying dove—onto her left hand. I counted off five two-hundred-leik bills and gave them to her.

The boy was still standing at the side of the table, his hand outstretched; he had watched everything in silence. I wished I could at least slip him a hundred, but Bagura was keeping an eye on me.

Next in line was an old man; I didn't understand his name either. But I was learning. I wrote down some approximation of what I'd heard, checked it off, and stamped his hand.

After him came a woman who was missing an eye. She spoke loud and clear and held out her hand even before I'd finished writing her name.

Name. Check. Stamp. Cash.
Name. Check. Stamp. Cash.
Name. Check. Stamp. Cash.

I was getting into a rhythm and could feel myself speeding up. But the next man in line didn't take the money I held out to him; he stood stockstill, his eyes fixed on something behind me. Everything went very quiet. I turned around. Two patrol cars were speeding down the dirt track toward us. Bagura let off a loud fart. His sons threw nervous glances at him. The cars stopped and several uniformed men got out.

"Put on your face masks, keep calm, keep working," Bagura said, pulling his mask over his mouth and nose, and ambling over to the policemen.

My hands trembled when I tried to take down the next name. Sweat dripped off my face onto the paper. I tried to concentrate, but couldn't write more than the first letters. From the corner of my eye, I watched Bagura, who was about fifty foot away. He greeted the men politely and talked to them calmly. Pointed to our car. Showed them some papers or other. Then he began to gesticulate. His voice grew louder and agitated; it echoed across the lot, though I couldn't hear what he was saying. I tried to read the policemen's expressions and thought I saw suspicion rather than anything else. The next thing I knew, Bagura was striding toward us. He whipped the fake ID cards from our breast pockets and held them out to the policemen.

"Here you are. This is the name of the aid organization, this is the department, the name, ID number—all present and correct, all official. I don't understand what all the fuss is about."

One of the men took the papers. He clearly had no idea what to make of them and examined them skeptically from both sides.

"We can't help it if you're not informed, can we?" Bagura said, shaking his head in disbelief. "I guess that's bureaucracy for you. But we can call off the campaign, if that's what you want. No trouble at all. The Red Cross will be surprised, of course"—Bagura paused for effect and took a deep breath, as if gathering strength—"but first let me ask you something. Do you have any idea how difficult it is collecting donations these days? Do you know how much time and effort it costs? Do you think the money for campaigns like this is just lying around on the street, waiting to be picked up?"

The policemen looked nonplussed. Bagura went on. "It's scandalous enough that there are slums in this country. A total failure on the part of the government, virus or no virus. The authorities should be glad that *someone is* taking care of things here before there's a revolt."

Bagura had worked himself into a frenzy. All eyes were turned on him.

"The Red Cross has gone to immense lengths to raise millions in countries that, God knows, have problems of their own—they've raised all this money to help the poorest of the poor, and what do the authorities do here? They prevent it!"

Bagura flung his arms in the air dramatically. "They prevent it! They have nothing better to do than harass aid workers. Great. Wonderful."

He held out his wrists to the policemen, as if challenging them to handcuff him. "Come on. Go ahead. I can see the headline now: *Red Cross Worker Arrested at Aid Campaign*. To be honest with you, I can't imagine better publicity for this country's image. And I'm sure your superiors can't either, officers! They'll be thrilled by your good work."

His performance seemed to make an impression—and not just on me. A murmur filled the air and swelled to a rumble. The policemen looked uneasily at their boss. He didn't hesitate long, but returned our ID cards. Bagura gave us firm instructions to get back to work—we'd wasted enough time as it was and didn't want to spend all day in this place. He saw the men back to their cars with an air of control. They seemed to stand to attention before getting in and driving off.

"That was a close call," he whispered to me, as the patrol cars turned onto the main road and vanished. He reached in exhaustion for a bottle of water, drained it in two gulps, and sat down in the shade of the minivan with his eyes closed. Moments later, he was asleep, a line of drool trickling from his half-open mouth.

I can't explain why—it was probably the relief, or perhaps the joy in people's faces when I handed them the money, or the thought of Mary, or something quite different, or everything at once—but soon after the police had left, I felt a rare sense of happiness flooding my body. I felt light and floaty, despite the heat. I could have hugged all these people, instead of taking their names. I, who was usually so awkward about these things, wanted to embrace everyone.

Bagura's sons must have felt something similar; there were smiles lurking on their aloof faces, and Taro even shot me a complicit grin from time to time.

A little old woman stood in front of me. She must have been ancient; her body was bent double and her face covered in deep wrinkles. She wore a small cross around her neck. Instead of telling me her name, she made her way slowly and laboriously around the table to me and clasped my hands in hers. They were as warm and soft as Thida's.

"Thank you," she said, so quietly that I had to lean forward to hear her. "Say thank you to all the donors. For their generosity and kindness. They've saved our lives."

After the police, people were more disciplined. They queued up in an orderly fashion; no one jostled, no one grumbled, even when things didn't move as fast as they could have. Not once did anyone attempt to cheat us.

One man came and stood next to me with his little girl, both of them smiling shyly and gratefully. When his wife took a photo of us with her phone, I didn't have the heart to say no. Bagura couldn't protest; he was still asleep in the shade of the minivan.

Next in line was a young man with a big grin on his face who put an arm around my shoulder and made a victory sign while his father took a photo. After that, I found myself with twin girls on either side of me. They sang a song to say thank you, and their mom videoed it.

Yuri and Taro, too, had forgotten Bagura's warnings and were posing for selfies. I was amazed how many people had phones. They clearly hung on to them for as long as they could.

When the very last family had received their thousand leik, we packed up and got in the car. Yuri maneuvered us slowly through the crowd of smiling, waving people, who formed a kind of honor guard reaching almost to the main road.

Bagura, revived by his nap, laughed about the police, chuckling and chortling in a way that was new to me. Yuri and Taro praised his acting talent. All three of them seemed to think that the campaign could hardly have gone better. I looked out the window at the grateful faces and thought of Mary. I would have liked to have her there with me to share my joy.

Then suddenly Bagura said: "We need another photo of you, Niri. Yuri will take one when we get back."

"What for?"

"Oh, you know."

"Do I?"

"For our next campaign."

I didn't ask any more questions, but I was sure he was hiding something from me.

FIFTEEN

When I was little, my parents had told me that among their people in the Koo tribe, it had once been the tradition for children to *give* presents on their birthday rather than to receive them, because there was more joy in giving. I used to think that weird. Now I understood the logic of it.

I couldn't stop thinking about the grateful faces of the people we'd helped, and I longed to tell my parents about it. Having missed being there when the money was handed out, they should at least get the pleasure of hearing what had happened. But I was afraid my father would be disappointed or angry. I hoped to find an ally in my mother.

The next morning, when my father was out fetching water with Thida, I seized my chance. My mother was resting on her mat, and I went and lay down beside her. Although she still tired more easily than before the pneumonia, she was getting better. She laughed again, got mad at us like in the old days, and had put on some weight. I enjoyed the little time I spent with her. Back at the Benzes, I had sometimes helped out in the kitchen, peeling potatoes, washing rice, scrubbing vegetables, and she had passed the time by making up stories. Today it was my turn to tell her a story.

I told her how nice I had looked in my Red Cross uniform. I described our arrival in the slum, the long lines of people, their grateful faces when I gave them the money.

She listened wide-eyed, letting out an *ah* or an *oh* now and then, just as I used to when she told me stories. When I came to the boxes of almost two million leik, she put her hand to her mouth in astonishment. She felt for the little boy who had stood next to my table begging, and she giggled at Bagura, impressed by the courage and cunning he had demonstrated in tricking the police. I reveled in her attention and admiration, and had the impression that she was very proud of me.

As I came to the end of my story, I embellished and embroidered it as best I could, trying to spin it out for as long as possible. But I kept quiet about where the money came from and how Mary had helped me.

When I had finished, my mother stroked my hair, leaned over me, and gave me a kiss on the forehead. "I didn't know you could tell such good stories. Has your father heard it yet?"

I shook my head.

"That's for the best. He'd probably think you were insane—or that you really did such crazy things. You know what he's like."

I looked at her. "Mom?"

"Yes."

"It really happened. I didn't make it up."

"Oh, Niri..." She propped herself up on one elbow and shook her head very slowly, looking at me as if I were slightly out of my mind.

"I swear to you."

"That's enough now." She sounded stern. I was testing her patience.

We looked at each other, and I knew it would only annoy her if I insisted.

I realized that it wasn't even possible for her to believe me. I could protest all I liked—what I had experienced was quite simply unimaginable for her. I might as well have told her that I'd flown to the moon with Bagura and his sons, and met the Buddha on the way. My pride and happiness melted away, leaving me with a sad, empty feeling.

My mother and I were still lying side by side, only inches from each other, but all at once I felt that we were worlds apart. Something had slipped between us, silently, insidiously.

I gulped and she reached for my hand. "Niri, are you crying?"

"No, I'm okay."

I stood up and reached for the little backpack where I kept Mary's phone.

"Where are you going?"

"See what Thida's up to."

Outside, the sun was dazzling. I paced up and down the fence. Beautiful Tuscany suddenly seemed smaller, more oppressive.

Thida came skipping up, wanting to play. I told her to run off and leave me in peace. I felt hemmed in and wanted to see Mary, but I couldn't go to the house as long as it was light.

After a while, it was all too much for me—too many people, not enough space. I squeezed through the gap in the fence, put on my mask, and set off.

I passed the canal where children were paddling in the water. I crossed wide streets almost empty of cars and pedestrians. It did me good to walk.

Soon the sky began to darken; deep black clouds settled over the city like a blanket. There was going to be a monsoon, but I kept walking all the same. I could have walked forever, out of town and into the country, with no aim and no idea where I was heading. The thunder grew closer; the wind got up.

It swept through the streets, as if someone had switched on a huge fan. It blew leaves and plastic bags along the roads; it shook billboards, power lines, and trees.

My thoughts were with Mary. I'd been wanting to speak to her ever since saying goodbye to her at her aunt's, but I didn't like talking on the phone. It hurt me almost physically to hear the voice of someone I wanted to see and couldn't. Maybe I just wasn't used to it—but even apart from that, I didn't want anyone in the settlement to know I had a phone.

I wondered how she was, whether she'd got home all right. Had the housekeeper noticed anything? Was Mary thinking of me? We hadn't seen each other for three days, and so much had happened in that time. I hadn't realized you could miss someone so much. Instead of calling, I texted her.

Hi Mary, everything ok?

No. Her answer came so quickly, it was as if she'd been waiting to hear from me.

What's wrong?

I miss you.

I miss you too, I wrote, but didn't send the text.

Where are you? she asked.

Out and about.

In this weather?

Yup.

Where are you heading?

Nowhere. Where are you?

In my room, of course. Dumb question.

Sorry.

That's ok.

It started to rain. I fished a plastic bag out of the gutter and wrapped my phone in it. Lukewarm water poured down on me; I was drenched within seconds. My clothes clung to me like a second skin. Lightning lit up the night-black sky; the rain pelted down so hard that it stung my face. All around me, houses, trees, and bushes vanished behind a gray wall of water. After a while I climbed down a bank and took shelter under a bridge. There was no one about—only a few crows overhead, cawing on a steel girder, eyed me with curiosity. Too late I realized that I was standing in a kind of dip, with water gushing at me from all sides.

It was rising fast.

The phone buzzed again. *Can I see you?*

Yes, I replied.

When?

Tomorrow?

At my aunt's?

There was nothing I wanted more than to see her, but I was afraid she might think I was only interested in the contents of her aunt's safe.

Sure?

It'll just be us. Lulu's away.

When?

3. Bring a bag or backpack.

By now the rain had become a torrent; if it kept on like this, the water would soon be up to my waist. I couldn't swim. Plastic bottles drifted past. Pieces of wood. Flip-flops. Dried palm leaves. An old bike tire. I grabbed hold of a plank so that I'd have something to keep me afloat when I was out of my depth. People drowned in floods every year. A novice from the monastery had been swept down the street during a monsoon and never seen again.

The water level was still rising, but I kept calm. The plank was too flimsy to bear my weight for long—I must get to higher ground as fast I could. Just across from where I was standing was the bank I'd climbed down; I could see the bushes sticking up out of the water. If I read the current right, it would carry me straight there. If not—or if I missed the bushes—I was in for a long journey.

I jammed the phone between my teeth and took a few steps. The current caught me, lifted me, and carried me straight to the bushes. I hadn't misjudged it. I let go of the plank, grabbed a fistful of twigs and then another, and pulled myself hand over hand out of the water and up the embankment.

SIXTEEN

It took Bagura almost a week to sell the ten gold bars that Mary and I filched from her Aunt Kate's safe on our second visit. The price of gold had gone up again. Together with the converted US dollars and the cash, there was now approximately fifteen million leik in two sealed metal boxes under his bed.

Fifteen million leik. It was unbelievable. We'd started off with a few bags of rice, and now we were sitting on a fortune.

Bagura amused himself by figuring out how long I would have to work as a gardener at the Benzes before earning that much money. He did the sums three times, because he couldn't believe the result. Almost one thousand one hundred years, including potential pay raises.

He then worked out that the money would allow us to give almost ten thousand families one thousand five hundred leik each, but suggested that it might be better to pay out three thousand leik to five thousand families instead, giving them enough to live off for about six months. Another possibility was to give each family one thousand five hundred in cash and spend the rest on sewing machines, tools, and motorcycles—this would permit them to set up small businesses and workshops to help them through the pandemic. I liked this idea, but in the end we abandoned it as too complicated and risky. We didn't want the authorities asking us questions.

And so it was decided: five thousand families would receive three thousand leik each. If we started at dawn and worked for twelve hours, we should be finished in two days.

This time, too, a Toyota minivan was parked at the fence, but instead of a red cross, it was emblazoned with the words AMITA FOUNDATION.

"Different charity today," Bagura said. He was in a good mood, but his sons, especially Yuri, seemed rather tense. They were wearing blue caps, white uniforms, and vests saying AMITA in big letters. The clothes were too small for them; they looked like sausages that were about to burst their skins, which can hardly have helped their mood. But although unflattering, the uniforms were even more official-looking than the last lot.

The same outfit was waiting for me in the back of the van. There was also a megaphone and several cardboard boxes full of T-shirts and baseball caps emblazoned with AMITA.

"What's *Amita*?" I asked.

"A charity that helps starving children," Bagura replied briefly. "My own invention."

"What's with the T-shirts and caps?"

"We'll give them away. Adds a professional touch."

At the first stop, the routine was the same as before. Bagura explained the rules through the megaphone, and we unloaded the chairs and tables, and set to work. This time, though, I had an uneasy feeling as I took the first thousand- and hundred-leik bills from the box. Everyone waiting could see how big the boxes were and work out how much was inside. We were unarmed. It would have been a cinch to pull a knife and make off with the cash. But this time, too, people were calm and disciplined. No one jostled or cursed when things were slow; no one tried to queue up a second time.

Yuri, Taro, and I worked quickly and intently, without stopping for a break. After six hours, my arm was stiff from all the stamping and writing, and my back ached. Bagura worked us hard and made sure we didn't slack. That evening I returned to the settlement exhausted but relieved. The first day had gone off without a hitch.

The following morning Bagura was sick. He'd been up all night with cramps and diarrhea and looked wretched. Yuri and Taro said that under the circumstances it would be better to call off the campaign, but Bagura wouldn't hear of it. Everything was ready, he said, and we'd shown the day before what an excellent team we were; we could manage perfectly without him.

Reluctantly, they agreed.

Word of our charity work had spread all over the city's slums. Whenever we stopped, we were met by dozens and sometimes hundreds of people. As soon as Yuri cut the engine, they surrounded the car, pressed their faces against the windows, and stared in at us. As in our settlement, nobody wore a face mask.

Yuri and Taro refused to make the announcements. I had no choice but to grab the megaphone and climb onto the roof of the minivan. More than a hundred people stared up at me expectantly. When I raised my voice, it started to crack. I paused and started again, and after a few sentences my voice steadied. In fact, I was surprised at how firm and purposeful it sounded, boosted by the megaphone. Like Bagura, I said a bit about who we were and what our aim was, and explained the rules, cautioning everyone to stick to them and not to take photos or make videos.

Yuri wasn't at all happy about the buzz we were creating. At every stop, his mood grew darker. "We're not a traveling circus," he said. "Too much attention is a bad thing."

In the last place we stopped, I noticed a man of Bagura's age standing a little way off, taking notes. He wore shoes instead of flip-flops and a white shirt damp with sweat; a face mask was slung casually below his nose. Occasionally he would stop someone who had just received money from us and write down what they said; at other times he gave orders to a younger man with cameras around his neck, sending him here and there to take photos.

The pair of them made me feel uneasy; Yuri and Taro were also throwing them worried glances.

"Fuck!" I heard Yuri say. "I think the press is here."

If it had been up to him, we'd have broken off then and there. But the queues were still long, and we couldn't risk any kind of commotion. People might not have let us go; we might have had the police after us again.

While I was wondering what to do, the man made a beeline for me.

"Excuse me, I'm Marc Fowler, an AP reporter."

I rose from my seat and looked blankly at him.

"Associated Press."

I didn't have a clue what he was talking about, but tried not to let it show.

"May I ask you a few questions?"

I nodded warily, rigid with fear.

"What's your name?"

"Niri."

"How old are you?"

I cleared my throat. "Eighteen."

"Where do you come from?"

"From here." I tried to sound polite, but I didn't see what he wanted with all these silly questions.

He noted everything down with an air of importance, as if I'd revealed critical information to him.

I didn't find him unsympathetic; I liked his calm voice and his habit of cocking his head to one side. He waved his pen at my T-shirt. "And you work for this Amita Foundation?"

"That's right."

"What kind of a charity is it? I've never heard of it."

I didn't know what to say.

He waited patiently.

Bagura's words came to my rescue. "It's an organization that helps the poorest of the poor. The corrupt government does nothing to help them, so we have to step in instead."

Marc Fowler nodded, looking at all the people thronged about us, eagerly following our conversation.

"There are so many places like this in our city. It's"—I searched for the word—"it's unjust that people should have to live like this. No one should have to live in such conditions."

Yuri was frantically signaling to me to stop. The reporter continued to take notes. He listened so earnestly and attentively, and the people around us nodded so emphatically, that I felt encouraged to go on.

"All people are equal before the virus, but only the rich have access to doctors and medicine. People are going hungry because they have nothing to eat, while others eat themselves to death." I paused to draw breath. "When those who have fail to help those who have not, it's a—it's a crime. And that has to change. We have to do something about it. Of course we can't help everyone at once. But that's no excuse for doing nothing."

The journalist was still writing, and with every sentence I spoke, I felt more confident—more important.

"What does *Amita* mean?"

I thought for a moment and then, taking a cue from Bagura, I improvised an answer. "The word comes from the Koo language," I said. "It has two meanings. First, *don't give up*. And secondly, something like *make a start*."

"Do you know how the charity is funded?"

"Through donations from home and abroad."

"A more personal question now. You're very young. What do your parents think about your charitable work?"

"They're very proud of me. They support me wherever they can."

"I'm glad to hear it. Aren't you afraid of catching the virus? No one here is wearing a mask."

"No. You can't expect people to buy masks when they can't afford to feed themselves. They're more worried about starvation."

I thought of the night Santosh died, and once again the anger rose in me. "People who resist get killed," I said without thinking.

The reporter looked up from his notepad. "What do you mean by that?"

"I saw a man shot by soldiers for dumpster diving. From behind."

"Where was this?"

"In a supermarket parking lot."

"When?"

"Couple of days ago. The government doesn't help hungry people. It has them shot."

Deep furrows appeared on the man's forehead. "You're a courageous young man. Will you give me your number so I can call you if I have any more questions? I need to look into this."

"I—um—it's not allowed. Data protection. The company's quite strict."

"I see." Frowning, he scribbled something onto a piece of paper and handed it to me. "Here's my number then. You can think about it."

When at last we were finished, Yuri and Taro scrambled to pack up. They couldn't get away quickly enough and kept shouting at me to hurry. After the chairs, tables, ladder, and empty boxes had been stowed in the car, I fell into my seat. But I was too excited to stay still and began to rock back and forth like Thida.

The moment we drove off, Yuri turned and yelled at me. "You pompous bastard. Didn't you have anything better to do than give that idiot an interview?"

"I just answered his questions," I said. "Anything else would have been impolite and might have attracted suspicion."

"This isn't about being polite."

"What did you expect him to do?" said Taro, attempting to keep the peace. "The man spoke to him."

"Don't you start too, you fuckwit," Yuri snarled. "Niri should have fobbed him off with a couple of sentences. Instead he held a fucking speech and was even stupid enough to tell him about Santosh. Are you out of your mind?"

"Santosh was murdered," I insisted.

"What crap is that?" Yuri shouted. "There's a curfew. Santosh was careless. It was his own fault. And now, in a couple of days, the whole world will know about him—and us. The police will read about our campaign in the papers and wonder what the fuck's going on. There are photos. It's only a matter of time till they find us."

"But there's no law against donating money."

This made Yuri even more furious. "Tell me, are you deliberately acting dumb?" he said, slamming his fist down on the steering wheel. "Or do you really think you can come up with a plausible story to explain to the police why a boy like you suddenly has fifteen million leik in his possession?"

He snorted with disgust, his double chin wobbling like mango pudding. "The police will suspect drugs and smell a business deal. The mayor will think the whole campaign's a political conspiracy, or else an early election gift from the opposition. Do you understand?"

"No." The more worked up he became, the calmer I felt. "Even if the reporter does write something, I can't believe anyone will read it. Since when have people in this city cared about what goes on in the slums?"

Yuri stared out of the window with a black look on his face. Taro shot me a furtive glance.

SEVENTEEN

The next day Bagura was better, and it looked as if I might be right. The police left us in peace, and thanks to our donations, there was a mood of near exuberance in the settlement. Kids ran around in Amita Foundation T-shirts, men schlepped bags of rice through the alleys, and the comforting sound of rattling dishes came from the shacks and shanties as meals were prepared.

That afternoon I was playing marbles with Thida and a couple of her friends when a little boy came running up out of breath. Bagura wanted to see me. Right away.

Yuri was stuffing bulging envelopes into a bag when I entered. Bagura was sitting at the table;

behind him, his wife was resting on the bed, breathing heavily. All the shelves in the shack were empty; the posters had gone from the walls; four tightly packed plastic bags stood at the front door. Something awful must have happened, and judging from the look on Yuri's face, I was to blame.

"What's going on here?"

"You're wanted," Bagura said. "The police think you're behind the Noro Hill burglaries."

"Me? Why do they think that?"

Bagura pushed his phone across the table to me; the *Daily Post* website glowed on the screen. "There's an article about you."

BECAUSE THE CORRUPT GOVERNMENT DOES NOTHING! said the headline in big letters. MYSTERY CHARITY DISTRIBUTES MILLIONS IN CASH.

I skimmed the story. The reporter described our campaign in detail, quoting big chunks of the interview with me before going on to speculate about the Amita Foundation. As the whole thing was clearly a fiction, he suggested various theories about who was behind it and where the money came from. One hypothesis was that it was part of the loot from the recent burglaries in the wealthy area of Noro Hill and that we had donated it either to assuage our consciences and improve our karma, or because we saw ourselves as pandemic-age Robin Hoods. Another theory was that the whole thing was a political conspiracy. Wasn't the campaign an indictment of the city council and its grasping mayor? Wasn't it, in fact, a lesson to the ruling class as a whole?

"Now you know," Bagura said darkly. "There's even a bounty on you. A hundred thousand leik."

I collapsed onto a stool. "What do I do now?"

"Idiot," Yuri snarled. "Pompous bastard."

Bagura silenced him with an impatient gesture. "My wife and the boys are clearing out. They'll be picked up in half an hour. You can go with them if you like."

"No," I said, without hesitation.

Bagura nodded, as if it was the answer he'd expected.

"Aren't you going?" I asked.

"I'm staying on a bit. Got a few things to sort out." He waved a hand, as if his plans were hardly relevant. "I'll follow in a couple of days. But you need somewhere to hide."

I was too confused to think straight. I couldn't stay in the settlement. That much was clear. But before I went anywhere, I had to see Mary. She was the only person I wanted to talk to just now. I got up so abruptly that Bagura almost fell off his stool. "I have to go."

"Wait," he called after me. "I have something for you," But my thoughts were already somewhere else.

———

It was dusk when I reached the Benzes' house. I would have to wait a few hours before I could see Mary, but it felt good just to be near her. I found a parked car whose grimy windshield told me that it hadn't been used for a long time, and crawled underneath to wait for nightfall.

Under the car it smelled of oil and moldy leaves. A millipede ran across my arm. Now and then a pair of flip-flops walked past. The longer I lay there, the clearer my mind became. Like noodle soup when the herbs and spices settle at the bottom.

My parents couldn't help me.

I doubted that Bagura could do anything for me.

Mary might be able to hide me in the cellar for a few days, but that wasn't a solution.

I was on my own. For the first time in my life, I was on my own.

I had taken ten thousand leik from our stash, for use in an emergency. It wouldn't last forever, but it would keep me going for a bit.

In the Benzes' garage was the motorcycle that my mother and I used to ride to market. I knew where to find the key.

———

When night had settled on the city, I crawled out from beneath the car, crept around the garden wall, and wriggled under to the other side.

Mary was sitting at the window as if she were expecting me.

We didn't talk much in the cellar. Mary wanted me to go up to her room so she could show me something.

"I didn't know you were famous," she said with a grin, as she closed the door behind us. "There's a big feature on your campaign in the papers. There are even photos!"

"I'm not famous, I'm infamous. The police are looking for me."

Either Mary didn't hear what I said, or she didn't understand the implications. She scrolled through her phone for a moment and showed me the website with the article I had seen at Bagura's. A photo showed Yuri, Taro, and me sitting at our tables, as long lines of people queued up for money. Another picture showed me staring earnestly into the camera.

"'All people are equal before this virus,'" Mary read, "'but only the rich have access to doctors and medicine. People are going hungry because they have nothing to eat, while others eat themselves to death. When those who have fail to help those who have not, it's a crime.' Did you really say that?"

"I think so."

"Wow. Now everyone's talking about you. Really, everyone."

"Talking about me?"

"Yes. On Facebook, YouTube, Instagram—all over the internet."

She sat down on the bed and flipped open her laptop. I sat down beside her. Seconds later I saw the first video of our campaign. It was blurred, but Yuri, Taro, and I were clearly recognizable, pressing bills into people's hands as laughing men and women thronged around us. A second video showed a man in an Amita T-shirt standing next to the minivan, kissing a handful of bills.

Only a few clicks and I saw myself with Yuri and Taro in our Red Cross uniforms. "Look," Mary said, "there you are again. Tell me all about it."

And so I told her about Bagura's idea for the Amita Foundation—how we'd prepared for the campaign, how it had worked, and how Bagura had tricked the police. I told her how happy people had been and how I had stood on the roof of the minivan with a megaphone. The more Mary heard, the more enthusiastic she became.

When I'd finished, she read out the comments people had posted.

Great campaign. More please!

Niri for president.

Cool guy. That's what heroes look like.

Fuck the mayor.

3K leik!!!! When's Niri coming to our slum?

Instead of feeling happy, I buried my face in my hands and lay back on the bed, staring at the ceiling.

"What's wrong? Aren't you pleased?"

"You don't get it. I'm wanted. I may be a hero for some, but there's a price on my head. A hundred thousand leik! I have to run away. And I don't know where. I don't know when I can see you again. What is there to be pleased about?"

"If you run away, I'm coming too," she said.

"You're coming too?"

She leaned over me and her features stiffened. "Why not? Because I can't walk properly?"

"But I don't even know—"

She interrupted me. "Do you think I'll be a burden? Is that it?"

I sat up angrily. "Stop this. What are you talking about?"

"I'm not afraid."

"Mary, this isn't some adventure game."

"Do you think I don't know that?" she said indignantly. "Do you think I've been helping you for the sake of adventure?"

"No, of course not. But once you've run away with me, there's no turning back."

"I realize that."

"You might never be able to come back."

"I don't want to anyway."

"You'd leave your family?"

She nodded.

"Your parents?"

She nodded again.

"Why?"

"Because."

"Because?"

"*Because* is reason enough." She thought for a second. "How are we going to get away?"

"On your motorcycle."

She nodded. "And where are we going?"

"First we'll head south to the coast," I said without a moment's hesitation. "To the beach. Some island. Somewhere where no one will find us. Are you quite sure?" I asked again, and this time I was afraid she might have changed her mind.

By way of an answer, Mary hobbled to the closet and took out a duffel bag. She pulled open drawers, took out clothes, a phone charger, and a few packets of pills, and tossed everything into the bag. "We need money too, don't we?" she said. "Wait here."

I sat on the bed, no longer nervous and agitated, but calm. I had been wrong: I wasn't on my own.

———

Soon afterward, Mary returned with a cloth tote and a paper packet, which she added to the things in the duffel bag. I heard something jangle in the tote. She switched off her phone, tore a sheet from a notepad, scribbled a few lines, and left the note on her bed. "All done. We can go."

I shouldered the duffel bag, and we crept through the house into the garden and then down to the garage, staying in the lee of the bushes. The motorcycle was parked where it always was, with two helmets on the saddle, and the key hung, as usual, in the little box next to the door. I wheeled the motorcycle out into the drive; Mary opened the gate to the street. We hadn't exchanged a word since leaving her room, communicating only with looks.

It was a little after six and already getting light. I strapped Mary's duffel bag onto the luggage rack and swung myself onto the saddle. It was harder for Mary. I heard her curse and give a brief groan of pain.

"You all right?" I asked when she was finally on.

"Yes. Where are we going?"

"First to the settlement. I have to say goodbye."

I parked the motorcycle at the fence and told Mary to wait.

Then I hurried through the alleyways. Early risers were lugging buckets of water; a few sleepy-looking children were sitting on doorsteps. Everyone greeted me cheerfully.

My mother and Thida were still asleep; my father wasn't around. I hoped he wasn't looking for me. There was no paper or pen to write a note, and I hesitated, wondering whether I shouldn't wake Mom and Thida after all. Then I decided against it. What would I have said? I kneeled down between their mats and kissed them both gently on the forehead.

I was on my way to Bagura's when I ran into my father.

"There you are," he cried with relief. "I've been looking for you everywhere. Where have you been?"

"I can't stop now, Dad," I said. "I'll tell you everything later."

"Mom and I have been so worried."

"I'm sorry. But I've no time. I really have to go."

"No time?" I saw the concern on his face morph into anger. "You come with me, please."

"No, I have to go."

"Niri," he said sternly. "What a way to talk to your father."

I wasn't going to hang around and be told off. Not after what I'd been through. "Aren't you ever going to get it?" I asked.

"Get what?" My father stared at me aghast, as if he were looking at a stranger.

"That I can't stand and look on as everyone starves to death. That no one gets a full belly from meditating. That we can't change things by putting bananas on an altar and lighting candles."

"The Buddha says—" my father began.

"The Buddha says, the Buddha says . . . The Buddha doesn't say the world has to stay the way it is. He says we must each bear the responsibility for our actions. But we're also responsible for the things we don't do. Holding our peace, looking away, doing nothing—all that has consequences too. If Mom had died because I hadn't taken her to the doctor, I'd have been to blame. If Thida had starved because I hadn't got food for her, I'd have been to blame."

"No, you wouldn't," my father shouted. "It was right to help, but not the way you did."

"How else?" I yelled. "You went to Mr. Benz to ask for help. What good did that do? Huh?"

My father ground his jaws, but said nothing.

"He wouldn't even speak to you." My voice was close to cracking. "I went to Mr. Benz too. I took what we needed without asking. It was the only way."

"No, Niri, you're wrong there."

"I am not. Would you rather I'd done nothing—just sat around waiting for alms until Mom and Thida were both dead?"

"How can you say such a thing? You stole and you'll end up being punished for it ... One way or another ... It wasn't right."

"I don't care about my karma."

We were speaking in such loud voices that doors began to open in the surrounding shanties and inquisitive heads peered at us in surprise. I didn't care about them either.

"I'm sorry, Dad. But I really have to go now."

He raised his arms and took a step toward me. For a moment I thought he was going to physically restrain me. I backed away and his body went limp.

"Sometime I'll explain everything." We looked at each other. I held his gaze, gave him a nod, and then hurried on past him and down the narrow alley to Bagura's house.

I turned around only once. He was still standing there, motionless between the shacks, watching me go. A small knot of kids had gathered about him.

When I think back to that day now, I feel like crying. Those were the last words we spoke to each other, the last looks we exchanged. No one should ever part from a loved one midquarrel. It would mean so much to me to know that my father understood why I did what I did.

Bagura was sitting outside his shanty in the early light, as if he were expecting me. He was wearing an Amita Foundation baseball cap on his head and an Amita Foundation T-shirt stretched across his big belly.

"Where were you?" he asked dully. "I have something for you." He rose ponderously and signaled to me to follow him into the shack. It looked sad and deserted, with its empty shelves and walls. Only the black-and-white photo of the little girl with big eyes was still there, lying on his bed.

He took two envelopes from his shoulder bag. From one he pulled a red passport and a wad of papers.

"What's that?"

"Have a look."

The passport bore the name of a stranger of my age. He had been born in a different place and on a different day from me, but he had *my* photo. I looked questioningly at Bagura.

"That's your passport. You can leave the country with it. It's been made by pros, so you needn't worry about being caught. The other papers are to confirm that you'll sign on to the MSC *Hong Kong* as a kitchen boy in four weeks' time. The *Hong Kong*'s a container ship—travels mainly between Asia and Europe."

A smile spread across Bagura's face; you could tell he was proud of his coup.

I stood there speechless, holding the passport and papers in my hand.

"I think it would be best if you left the country for a while. It's too dangerous for you here. And you've always wanted to go to sea, haven't you?"

I still couldn't speak.

"Thank you," I stammered eventually, "but I can't accept these." I tried to push the papers back into his hands.

Bagura made one of his dismissive gestures. "You *must* accept them," he said. "Apart from anything else, they were paid for with your money. I was owed a few favors. It was nothing."

"No, really . . ."

"Think of them as an insurance policy. Put them away and take good care of them. You won't get any more."

Then he gave me a second envelope, neatly folded and sealed shut.

"In here are the address and phone number of a friend who might be able to help you until the ship sails. And an old phone with ten SIM cards. You mustn't use any of the cards more than once and you must throw each one away as soon as you've used it. It's possible that someone's monitoring my phone to see if you get in touch. It isn't hard to trace calls. Best not to get in touch until you're about to leave a place. And keep things brief. The shorter the call, the safer it is for you. For me too. Here's my wife's number, in case you can't get hold of me."

I put everything in my backpack. "Thank you," I said again, feeling tears prick my eyes. "Why haven't you left yet?"

"Where would I go?"

"To that hut on the beach. You wanted to watch the fishermen going about their work."

"All in good time."

"What does that mean?"

"You ask too many questions."

"You didn't take any money, did you? That's why there was so much left over after the sale of the gold—because you went without your share."

"You're wrong there. How did you think I paid for my wife and the boys to leave? I'm no Good Samaritan—far from it. Also, Yuri would never have allowed it. Taro maybe, but not Yuri. Never."

"Since when do you let Yuri boss you around?" I asked.

"Don't you worry about me, kid. I can take care of myself. What we need to do now is find you somewhere to hide for the next few weeks. I bet the police will be here looking for you before the day is out."

"I have a motorcycle."

I liked the look of surprise on his face.

"Stolen?"

"Something like that."

"Where's it parked?"

"On the street, by the fence."

"Do you know where you're going?"

"South, to the coast."

"Maybe I've underestimated you," he said approvingly and pushed me roughly out of the shack. "You must go now. Have you seen your parents?"

"Yes, my mom and Thida were still asleep and my dad was out." I didn't want to tell Bagura about the fight. "Will you do me a favor?"

"Another?" he said, with an exaggerated sigh.

"Will you go to them, please, and tell them that I—I—" I couldn't find the right words.

"That you had to leave suddenly, that you're thinking of them, that they mustn't worry about you, that you love them, and that you'll be back soon?"

I nodded, relieved. "Exactly. And that I'm sorry about all the grief I've caused them. Is there any money left over?"

"Not a lot. Why?"

"I'd like you to give them twenty thousand leik. Do you have that much?"

"Yes, but your father will never accept it."

"My mom might though. Will you give it to her, please?"

He nodded. "I will. And now," he said sadly, "I'll see you to the street."

Bagura stopped short when he saw Mary and the motorcycle in the yellow glow of the streetlamps. She hobbled a few steps toward us and then stopped too.

"Who's that?"

"Mary."

"Who's Mary?"

"My source."

He sized her up speechlessly. Mary stared back. She shifted from one leg to the other, but came no closer.

"Is she a cripple?"

"No, she just has trouble walking."

"Then she's a cripple," he said. "And you're planning to take her with you?"

"Of course. We belong together."

His gaze flitted back and forth a few times between Mary and me. "You're crazy. You won't get far with a cripple." He sighed. "I warned you, kid, you don't get something for nothing in this life."

We looked at each other one last time in silence. He bit his lower lip, made a fist, and cuffed me clumsily on the arm. Then he turned and left, walking fast and shaking his head. He vanished through the gap in the fence without looking back.

I gave a few dry sobs.

"Who was that?"

"Bagura."

I climbed onto the motorcycle and Mary got on behind me. With a firm kick, I started the engine.

"Where do we go now?" Mary asked, clasping me tight.

"To the sea."

EIGHTEEN

I opened the throttle as far as it would go. Our bodies quivered from the vibrations of the engine, and the hot wind whipped my chest. We drove onto the freeway; the route to the coast was well sign-posted. Behind me Mary fidgeted restlessly; after about an hour she signaled to me to stop. I pulled over onto the hard shoulder, stopped in the shade of a big billboard, and took off my helmet. Then I waited for Mary to get off, but she didn't.

"What's up?" I asked, turning around to her.

She'd been crying. I got down and helped her off the bike. She stood there in silence, watching the cars drive past and disappear.

"What did your friend say?"

"He wished us all the best."

"You're lying."

"I'm not."

"Tell me the truth."

I turned away from her.

"Tell me the truth," she repeated sharply.

"He said it would be harder with two of us."

"Because I'm a cripple."

"You're not a cripple."

"What am I, then?" she snapped. "Don't act dumb."

"Mary, stop this. I can't argue now."

"And I can't even manage an hour on a goddamn motorcycle." Tears were running down her cheeks again. "It hurts so fucking much." She turned away. I heard her sobbing and tried to take her in my arms, but she shook me off.

"Let's carry on."

A car braked sharply and reversed. The driver let down the window. "Need any help? Gas?"

"No," I said, startled. "We're just having a break."

"Bad place for a break. Don't get caught." He closed the window and went on his way.

Mary watched the car recede into the distance. "I want to go home."

"Now? You're not serious?"

"Yes, I am. Take me back."

For a moment I just stood there, too surprised to say anything. Then anger rose in me. I felt like screaming. I felt like taking a stick and battering the crash barrier or the motorcycle. Why was she doing this to me?

"Get on then."

She opened her mouth to speak, but said nothing—just put on her helmet and heaved herself onto the saddle.

I kicked the engine into life. The rear tire screeched on the hot asphalt, and Mary had to hold tight to stop herself from falling off backward. A sign announced that the next exit was in six miles. I could turn back there. I put my foot down and drove much faster than the limit. At that moment I didn't care about anything. Let the police stop us. Let them arrest us. But the feeling didn't last.

Only three miles to the exit. I was damned if I was going to take Mary home. I'd already spent four years without her, my longing buried between the palms and hibiscus. I wasn't putting myself through that again.

Just two more miles.

Just one more mile. My anger had vanished.

Half a mile.

Instead of slowing, I accelerated. What else could I have done?

"Where are you going?" Mary shouted.

"To the sea."

After another two hours and a brief stop to fill the tank, we left the freeway and were soon rolling downhill on narrow country roads, following handwritten signs saying BEACH. Our journey ended at a small sandy lot where two cars and a few mopeds were parked. I stopped in the shade of three palms, cut the engine, and waited for Mary to get off. But again, she made no sign of moving. My ears were roaring from the wind and the noise of the engine.

I hung my helmet over the handlebars and stretched. "Want some help?"

"If I need help, I'll ask for it." She tried to climb down, but struggled to lift her legs; she tried first one and then the other, groaning with pain. It was hard to sit there doing nothing, so I turned to look at the sea. An almost-deserted beach of fine sand lay before us, and beyond it the water stretched to the horizon, turquoise and then deep blue. Here and there people were lying under parasols, and two children were playing ball in the waves.

The roaring in my ears began to subside, and I realized how quiet it was. There was no sound but the gentle lapping of the surf, the buzz of cicadas, the twittering of birds.

A few moments later, Mary was standing next to the motorcycle on wobbly legs. I got off, put down the side stand, and took her arm.

"Thank you."

Small step by small step, we walked toward an avenue of conifers; wooden huts with roofed terraces stood beneath the trees. Mary moved gingerly, awkwardly, like a child learning to walk.

The huts belonged to restaurants, all of which were closed except one, called Ocean View Grill. We sat down on the first bench we came to.

I was thirsty and fetched Cokes for us. Mary dug a packet of pills out of her bag and took two.

We sat in silence, staring out at the sea.

I was embarrassed, uncomfortable. I had gone against Mary's wishes by bringing her here instead of taking her home, and I wasn't sure how she felt about that. For days I had longed to be with her, but now that we were alone together at last, we didn't seem to know what to say to each other. Here on the beach, after our argument, Mary was more of a stranger to me than back in her cellar or in Aunt Kate's house.

"Are you mad at me for not taking you home?"

"Forget what I said."

"You make it sound so easy."

"I'm sorry, but sometimes the pain's more than I can bear. You don't know what it's like. It hurts so much I could scream, and then I come out with things I don't mean."

I moved nearer to her and took her in my arms. Neither of us spoke, and I had the feeling that with every word we didn't say, we were coming closer again.

"Shall we go in the sea?" Mary asked after a while.

"Can you swim?"

"Of course. Can't you?"

"No."

"Then I'll teach you. We needn't go deep."

She heaved herself up. I offered to carry her to the water, but she took my arm and insisted on walking. The hot sand burned the soles of our feet.

When the water was washing around our ankles, Mary closed her eyes and smiled. "I love the sea."

She let go of me and hobbled in until she was up to her waist, then flopped down into the water, dived under, bobbed up again.

"Come on in."

The sea freaked me out. I took a few steps and then stopped. Mary swam toward me and held out a hand. "Be brave."

"I don't know . . ."

"Come on, you can do it."

For her sake, I went in farther than I was comfortable with—a lot farther. The water was over my belly button. I looked about me nervously, as if afraid a fish or jellyfish might attack at any moment.

A small wave lifted me up and I let out a cry, but a second later I felt the sand beneath my feet again.

"If you take a deep breath and hold it in, you'll float on the water like a piece of wood," Mary said. "You won't sink, promise. Try."

I was tense with fear—unlike Mary, who moved with such ease in the water. "Lie down," she said, holding out her arms.

I did as she said. She eased her hands under my back and I felt myself beginning to swim.

"Trust me."

I started to relax, and an agreeable sense of weightlessness slowly spread through my body.

"You see," Mary cried, at least as pleased as I was. "Hold tight." She waded a few steps farther out. I wrapped my arms around her neck.

Seen from the water, the bay formed a broad U almost a mile across and protected on either side by steep cliffs. The beach was edged with palms— beyond it, inland, a lush hill rose sharply like a green wall. There was a village at one end of the bay, with huts on stilts in the sea and boats bobbing up and down in front of them.

We let the waves carry us back to the beach and sat down in the shade of a palm. The wind and our wet clothes were pleasantly cooling.

"Now I'm hungry," she said. "Do you think there's fresh fish?"

"I'll go and find out."

"The money's in the duffel bag."

The boy at the counter in the small beach bar was a little younger than us. He'd been watching us curiously; now he was engrossed in his phone.

There turned out to be a surprisingly large selection of food: barbecued fish with rice, barbecued chicken, papaya salad, glass-noodle salad, green curry, mango with sweet rice. I ordered two helpings of fish, one helping of mango for dessert, and two bottles of water.

The boy put everything on a tray and totted it all up. "With the two Cokes you had earlier that comes to forty-five leik."

I handed him a crisp new thousand-leik bill. He looked at me as if I were out of my mind.

"Sorry, I don't have any smaller bills."

"I can't change that."

He clearly saw this as my problem, not his.

"Can you put it on our tab?"

He shook his head, confused by my question.

"We're staying a few days."

"Still. My parents won't accept that."

"Then take the money as credit and make a note of what we eat and drink."

His surprise changed to suspicion, but he took the money and fetched pen and paper from a drawer. "What's your name?"

"Niri," I said, without thinking.

He made a note of it and underneath he wrote 45. "How long are you staying?"

"Don't know. Is it possible to rent a hut here?"

"No, but you can sleep on the beach—or on the terrace, if it rains. It's quiet just now, because of the virus. I won't be here tomorrow, but my parents will be around. I'll let them know."

"Thanks." I took the tray and went back to Mary.

We spent most of the afternoon in the sea; Mary said her legs hurt less in the water. She was determined to teach me to swim, and proved a patient teacher. She showed me how to move my arms and legs, put her hands under my belly to hold me up, and praised me even when I thrashed and flailed or splashed about like a puppy dog. Gradually, I started to figure out what she wanted of me and could manage at least a few strokes before sinking.

Afterward I paddled back to the beach in exhaustion, while she swam out so far that I began to worry about her. Her head disappeared between the waves, and I suffered agonies at the thought that it would be impossible for me to rescue her if she got into trouble.

Eventually she came back, worn-out but beaming all over her face.

"God, that was lovely," she said, flopping down beside me on the sand. She breathed deeply and contentedly. "I'd like to die that way. Just swim out to sea, on and on, and never come back."

"I can't imagine much worse."

"Maybe it's different if it's what you want."

I looked at her in astonishment.

"What are you looking at me like that for? Have you never thought of killing yourself?"

"No."

"Really?"

"No," I said again. "Have you?"

"Often." She paused for a moment. "I even tried once."

"When?"

She took a long time to answer. "The riding accident wasn't an accident."

"You mean you deliberately . . ."

She nodded. "My parents had decided to send me to a boarding school in England. I didn't want to leave you."

It was a few seconds before this sunk in. "You tried to kill yourself because of me?"

"No, of course not. It was dumb and childish. Who dies falling off a horse? But I've often thought about trying again since."

"Why?" I said.

"You don't get it, do you?"

"No."

"You think I have everything I need."

"Yes. Maybe not everything, but—"

"Why do you think that?" she said, interrupting me. "Because I live in a big villa? Because I have my own horse and have been to Paris and Rome and New York? Because I don't have to cook for myself or do my own laundry and shopping? Is that everything a person needs?"

"It's everything a person needs to survive."

"I'm not talking about survival. I'm talking about the will to live."

"Why don't you want to live anymore?"

"I do, or we wouldn't be sitting here. But it's tough."

"Why?"

"Because there are so few days when I don't feel sad. Because I'm in constant pain and always will be. Because I feel uncomfortable in my own skin. Lonely. Isn't it the same with you?"

I shook my head.

Mary looked at me thoughtfully. "Sometimes I think I'm not my parents' daughter or my brother's sister, I'm so different from them. Don't you know that feeling?"

"No. Why should I think I'm not my parents' son?"

"Because they're not interested in you. Because they never ask you how you are, and if you tell them, they don't listen. Because on the rare occasions they do listen, they don't have a clue what you're talking about. Because everything they say sounds like something from another world. No one in my family has ever looked at my paintings the way you have. None of them has ever commented on them. I could give you a thousand reasons."

It had never occurred to me to wonder whether my parents were interested in me. Why would they ask me how I was when they saw me every day? We didn't talk much in my family, but it had never bothered me. Okay, so I'd been sad when my mother thought I'd made up the story of our campaign, but that didn't make me think I wasn't her son. My parents were there. They loved me. That was enough for me.

Mary looked at me as if waiting for me to say something.

"Is that why you spent so much time with us when you were little?"

"Yes. And because of you. Even when I was a little girl, I felt more at ease with you than with anyone else. I don't know why."

She laid her head on my chest. I stroked her, and my hand slid up her legs to the scars. The palm-tree skin.

"Does it repulse you?"

"Nothing about you repulses me."

"Swear?"

"I swear. What makes you ask?"

"Because no one in my family has ever touched my scars. Only my mother maybe, once or twice. Do you know who used to rub ointment on them for me when they hurt? *Your* mother."

Before Ocean View Grill closed, I fetched us a candle, two helpings of green curry with rice, and more water. We pitched our camp on the sand under the palms. There was no wind; we ate the curry by candlelight and I thought about our conversation. I couldn't get Mary's words out of my head.

"Is that why you helped me—because you wanted to get even with your parents?"

"No. I helped you because I like you. A lot. And because I don't like myself."

"What's that got to do with it?"

"Maybe I hoped that you'd like me more if I helped you."

"I liked you anyway," I said. "I like you more than anyone else in the world."

"That's not much use to me."

"Doesn't it mean anything to you?"

"Of course it does. I just find it hard to believe. Maybe I thought I'd feel better about myself if I took the money and let you give it to people who really needed it—if I did something useful at last instead of sitting in my room painting pictures that no one ever looks at. And do you know what? When I saw the videos of you distributing the money to those poor people, I felt better than I'd felt for a long time. Alive and full of energy, as if I were there myself."

She moved closer to me. We lay with the tips of our noses almost touching. Tenderly she stroked my head and neck, and closed her eyes.

A few minutes later she had fallen asleep, but I lay awake for a long time. Dark clouds hung over the sea; lightning flickered on the horizon. Later, the clouds dispersed, and white moonlight shimmered on the black water. The steady rush of the surf comforted me, though I couldn't help being afraid that a big wave might come and sweep us away as we slept.

I hadn't understood everything Mary had said, but maybe it didn't matter. She was the woman I loved, not a problem to be solved.

I wanted to be there for her. I wanted to protect her. I wanted to relieve her of her sorrow and pain, even if something told me it was impossible.

———

Just before I fell asleep, I thought of the boy in the restaurant. He must have guessed that that wasn't the only thousand-leik bill in Mary's duffel bag. There had been something in the way he looked at us. I thought it unlikely that he followed the news on the internet and would recognize me, but I felt uneasy all the same. Twice I was jolted awake, thinking I'd heard footsteps and voices. Strange how things turned out, I thought, as I made sure the bag was still there at our heads. Here I was, a poor boy from a shantytown, afraid of being mugged.

NINETEEN

We spent the following days either in the water or in the restaurant or in the shade of our palm tree. Mary said my swimming was coming on nicely, and it's true, I was gradually becoming less afraid of the water, breathing more steadily, improving my strokes. Soon I was confident enough to stay afloat for longer than a few seconds. I swam ten yards, then twenty, then thirty.

The owners of the restaurant had got used to us. They asked no questions, pleased to have customers at last; most days, we were the only ones. They even offered to let us park our motorcycle in a shed behind their kitchen. Just to be on the safe side.

On our second night there, we made love for the first time. If I said it was the most beautiful experience of my life, I would be lying. Neither of us knew what we were doing. We were two nonswimmers on the open sea.

Her body and mine. There was nothing more thrilling, nothing more alien.

We were excited and frightened.

We were full of desire and passion, but had neither skill nor stamina. We sensed vaguely what we wanted, but not how to get it. We followed our senses wherever they took us, but it wasn't the place we'd been longing for.

It was over more quickly than we anticipated.

Mary said it hadn't hurt, but that might have had something to do with the additional painkillers she took just before.

The following night we were more patient with one another. Our desire was greater, but our expectations were more modest. It was a good combination. We began to explore each other's bodies, taking our time.

By the fifth night, we could hardly wait for darkness to fall so that we'd have the beach to ourselves.

After that, I knew that I didn't want to spend another day of my life away from Mary.

We spent the days lying nestled in each other's arms on the sand or going for short walks on the beach. I had the impression that Mary was walking better every day.

Once an ant ran over her hand. She raised her arm to look at it, staring at it in astonishment, as if she'd never seen an ant before.

"What are you looking at it like that for?" I asked.

"I'm marveling at its six little legs and how fast it can go without stumbling."

She lowered her arm onto the sand again, and the ant disappeared under a withered leaf.

Mary let her eyes wander up and down the beach. "No one will ever find us here," she said. "Why don't we stay forever? Maybe we could find a house to rent in the village. Or we could build one. We're not short of money."

I liked the idea. "I could help the fishermen."

"You wouldn't have to. We have enough money to keep us going for a long time. If we were careful, we wouldn't have to work."

I thought of the suspicious look in the boy's eyes when I'd tried to pay with a thousand-leik bill. "I don't think the locals would like that."

Mary laughed. "You're right. I'm talking like a spoiled rich girl. You'd better stick to fishing, and maybe I could mend your nets for you."

She lay with her hands behind her head, staring up at the cloudless sky. I could tell she was pondering something.

"I've discovered the secret of happiness," she said eventually. "I'm going to write a book called *The Happiness Formula*. It'll be a huge bestseller."

I laughed. "I'm glad to hear it. Especially coming from you."

She twisted her face into a smile. "I mean it! Don't you believe me?"

"Of course I do. Will you let me in on the secret?"

"Don't think about tomorrow. And don't think about yesterday."

"That's too easy."

"It isn't easy at all. That's exactly my point. Try it. Come and sit next to me."

I pulled myself up.

"Close your eyes and think of nothing."

I closed my eyes, and my mind was immediately full of images: me floating in the water in Mary's arms; my father's sad, helpless face when we parted midquarrel; me pushing my mother along the hospital corridors; Mary appearing in front of me in the cellar; the two of us making love on the beach.

It felt like my attempts to meditate with my father, or with the monks at school.

"You see," Mary said, as if she could read my mind. "It's not so easy."

"Maybe it's not what I want. I like thinking of yesterday, when you taught me to swim. And I look forward to waking up next to you tomorrow."

"That's the difference between us. If I think of the past, I get sad, and if I think of the future, I get scared."

For precisely one week we managed to stick to Mary's happiness formula. We forgot about the rest of the world. There were just the two of us, the sea and the beach, and occasional visitors or locals, none of whom was interested in us. There was only Mary's soft skin, her gentle fingers, her quivering, trembling body when she let me touch her. There was only her voice, her whisper, her laugh. Nothing happening elsewhere in the country existed for us. The police, the virus, the slums, Bagura—even Mary's family, my parents, and Thida were only a distant memory. Mary didn't once touch her phone to check for messages on Facebook or WhatsApp.

We were sufficient unto ourselves.

Then I saw an elderly man chewing betel nuts. He had a big belly, a white beard, and long hair, and I was reminded of Bagura. I wondered how he was. Had he left to join his family or was he still in the settlement? Was he safe? I thought of calling him, but feared bad news and put it off for another day.

Once it lodged in my mind, though, the thought was hard to shake. I felt my curiosity growing, and while Mary was off swimming I opened the envelope containing Bagura's old phone, the SIM cards, and the list of numbers. I inserted one of the cards in the phone and dialed Bagura's number. It rang until it went to voicemail.

I tried his wife. She picked up on the second ring. "Hello?"

"Hi, it's Niri. May I speak with Bagura?"

"You son of a bitch," she roared. "You revolting mud urchin. You ugly wart on my fat uncle's ass . . ."

"Sorry, I only wanted . . ,"

"Bagura's been arrested," she yelled. "Yuri and Taro have been arrested. I don't know where they are!" She broke into angry sobs. "It's all your fault, you wretched bastard. Where are you hiding? Come back and tell the police that my husband and sons are innocent. Do you hear? It was your money. They didn't—"

I hung up and decided to act as if the conversation had never happened. I ripped out the SIM card and stuffed the phone and list of numbers back in the envelope. As I did so, I noticed a second piece of paper, folded several times. A message to me from Bagura.

Hey kid,
By the time you read this, I hope you're on the Hong Kong, *out on deck or tucked up in your*

berth, bound for Rotterdam, Singapore, or Los Angeles. Anywhere, just as long as you're safe. If you call me before that and don't get hold of me because I've been arrested, for goodness' sake don't do anything. Nothing, do you understand? NOTHING! I know you, it won't be easy for you. But you can't help me, you'd only put yourself at risk. Don't worry about me, okay? I can take care of myself.

You're a good boy. I know that, because I was once one myself. Somehow life got in the way. You'll do better. I'm grateful for being able to help you.

By the way, I've been thinking about the question you once asked me—whether people who get close to each other end up getting hurt. My answer is yes, that's how it is, how it has to be. You can't cook without making a fire, and you can't make a fire without getting burned at some point.

That's life. It needs to be lived. Make something of yours.

Bagura

PS. By the way, "Amita" is a girl's name and means "the boundless one." Boundless, like happiness, love, sorrow.

I read the letter twice.

Mary came back from her swim. She saw at once that something had happened.

"Bagura's been arrested," I said, and told her of my brief phone call with his wife.

Mary took her phone from her bag, signed onto the restaurant Wi-Fi, and handed it to me. "Maybe there's something on the news."

The *Daily Post* website popped up on the screen a few seconds later. The first items were about the virus, the financial crisis, tensions between China and the US. I scrolled down to the national news; the second headline was NO TRACE OF MILLIONAIRE'S DAUGHTER. There was a photograph of Mary. She saw the look of horror on my face and grabbed the phone from me.

"They're looking for me all over the country," she said when she'd read the article. "My parents think I've been kidnapped." Furiously, she threw the phone into my lap. "I left them a message, saying that I was going of my own free will and they weren't to look for me. Why couldn't they just believe me?"

She took the phone back, stood up, and walked a few steps toward the sea. Then she stood with the water behind her, tied her hair into a ponytail, and smiled into the camera.

"What are you doing?"

"Making a video. I'll put it on my Facebook page. Then everyone can see I'm all right." She began to record herself.

"*Hi, Mary here.* This is a message for my family and friends and for the police. I haven't been kidnapped. Anyone who says I have is lying. I left home of my own free will. And I'm very well. See for yourselves." She panned slowly across the bay and back again. "Please stop looking for me. I'm eighteen. I'm an adult. I can do or not do whatever I want, and I've decided to live a different kind of life." She paused and took a deep breath. "Mom and Dad—I didn't want to worry you. I know I'm a disappointment to you, but I can't help it. I think it's best if we don't see each other anymore."

She lowered her arm. "Okay? Convincing?"

"Very," I said.

She came back to me, thumbed her phone frantically, waited, thumbed again. After a few minutes, her voice and the roar of the sea came from her phone and she smiled, satisfied. "It worked," she said with relief, and switched the phone off again. "Now everyone will see I'm all right. Let's hope they leave us in peace now."

Mary and I were in the water when I saw the police car drive onto the parking lot. Two uniformed policemen got out, looked our way, and then went into the restaurant to talk to the owners' son. A moment later they were joined by the owners themselves. All five of them kept turning to look at us.

I was holding Mary in my arms and slowly walked a little farther out to sea. By now I was a strong enough swimmer to venture out of my depth, but there was nowhere for us to hide at sea, however far we went. If they wanted to talk to us, they had only to wait. Sooner or later we'd have to come out of the water.

"What's wrong?" Mary asked, feeling me tense up. But she didn't raise her head from my shoulder.

"Nothing."

"That's good," she said, and began to hum softly to herself.

Soon afterward I saw the police snooping around the closed restaurants and inspecting the beach. Then they went back to their car and drove away.

Mary and I stayed in the water a little longer. After a while she was thirsty, so we went back to the beach to get something to drink.

The boy was sitting behind the counter, and I could see that he was desperate to tell me what had happened. He handed me two Cokes and added a ten to our growing tab. "The police were here," he said.

"I saw," I said, as casually as possible.

"They're looking for a young couple." He flashed a conspiratorial smile at me. "Apparently the man's broken into villas in the capital and may be the woman's kidnapper. She's the daughter of a rich family. He's asking for a ten-million-leik ransom."

I felt nauseous.

"They asked all about you." He paused to give the words their full effect. "Wanted to know who you are, what you're called, where you're from."

"What did you say?"

"That you call her Sara and she calls you Chaka and you're from around here." He grinned.

I made no attempt to conceal my relief. "Thank you. Do you think they'll come again?"

"Probably. They're looking for you everywhere. I even saw it on TV."

"Fuck," I said.

His parents came out of the kitchen. They looked at me. I couldn't tell what was in their eyes, but suspected a mixture of curiosity and distrust.

"You're Niri, aren't you?" the boy asked.

"Who?"

"The guy who handed out money in the slums with a bunch of friends."

"Why do you think that?"

Mary was getting impatient. "What's taking you so long?" she called out. "You'd better bring two for me. I'm parched."

"Coming," I called back.

"The videos went viral. You're a hero, man." He scrolled through his phone, and a Facebook page popped up under the name of "Niri." "You've got fifteen million followers. Crazy. Yesterday it was only thirteen. Look—the latest video has eighteen million likes."

"That—" I stammered, "that's not me, that's not my—"

He didn't let me finish, but clicked on one of the latest videos. It showed me without a mask, talking earnestly to the AP reporter. "All people are equal before this virus," I heard myself say, "but only the rich have access to doctors and medicine. People are going hungry because they have nothing to eat, while others eat themselves to death." One of the bystanders had videoed my interview with Marc Fowler and uploaded it to Facebook.

I stared. First at the phone, then at the boy, then at his parents. They laughed. All three of them looked as happy as if I'd just handed them ten thousand leik each. The mother stuck up her thumbs, the father made a fist and gave me a look of encouragement. "Mega," the boy said, and there was awe in his voice.

Then he started scrolling through his phone again and showed me the police Facebook page. The bounty for any information leading to my arrest had been raised from a hundred thousand leik to a million. I felt suddenly suspicious. Why hadn't they betrayed me?

Mary sipped her second Coke thoughtfully as I told her what had happened.

"We're not safe here anymore, are we?"

"I don't know. If the family were interested in the bounty, they'd have betrayed us by now. The police were here half an hour ago."

"But they might change their minds anytime."

"What shall we do? Find another bay to hide out in?"

"Tricky." She thought for a moment. "We have to get right away from here. They'll search every beach in the area."

Fear gripped me. For the first time, perhaps, I realized that somewhere, someday, our getaway would end. I took Bagura's friend's address from my backpack and handed it to her. "Any idea where that is?"

She gave a surprised smile. "On Shark Island."

"Shark Island?"

"It's in the shape of a shark's fin. I went there on vacation a few times. A friend of mine had a house there. It would be a good place to hide. Do you know your friend's friend?"

"Not yet."

On the second ring, a deep male voice replied. He knew who I was almost before I told him.

"You can come, but not after eight," he said, and hung up.

I looked at Mary doubtingly.

"Can we trust him?" she asked

"Do we have a choice?"

We logged into the restaurant Wi-Fi and looked up the island on Google Maps. Two hours south of us was a harbor from which three ferries left daily. We decided to set off early the following morning.

Neither of us could sleep that night. We went for a swim, and afterward made love as fiercely as if it were the last time.

TWENTY

In the morning the boy and his parents saw us off as if we were family. They had made us a picnic of ice-cold Coke, spring rolls, and barbecued drumsticks—if we'd had more room on the motorcycle, I think they'd have given us a whole week's supplies. We managed to persuade them to keep the change from the thousand-leik bill.

On their advice we took a narrow, single-track road along the coast, through small villages, and past paddy fields and water buffalo pastures. Children playing by the roadside waved as we passed. We drove up hills that offered sweeping views of the sea: The wind dotted the water with white horses, and fishing boats followed their lonely paths. Mary held me tight with both arms and stroked my belly under my T-shirt. It was a comfort to feel her hands on me. Leaving our bay had been more of a wrench to me than to her. I sensed dimly that we would never again be as alone and undisturbed.

The light was dazzling, and the sun beat down on my arms. An insect flew into my mouth soon after we set off, and for some miles I had the nasty feeling that it was buzzing in my stomach.

An hour into the journey, I noticed that there was something wrong with the engine. It was running fitfully, sputtering whenever I stepped on the gas. We slowed to a halt, and I pulled over to the side of the road.

"What's the matter?" Mary asked.

"I don't know. Something's not right."

Mary got off. I opened the gas cap and moved the motorcycle back and forth a bit, so that I could hear the gas sloshing around in the tank. It was still a quarter full.

"Do you know anything about engines?"

"Not a lot." My father had always taken care of the motorcycle; I had just handed him the tools he needed. He would invariably explain what he was taking apart or putting together, what might be causing the problem and how it might be resolved, but I only ever half listened. To his great regret, I was that rare thing, a boy who isn't interested in engines.

"Maybe it just overheated?"

"Don't think so." Not knowing what else to do, I checked the spark plug connector and made sure the throttle cable wasn't too tight.

It took me five goes to coax the engine back to life; we weren't going to get far. The bike sputtered its way up the next rise at a crawl—fortunately, by the time it conked out at the top of the hill, we were already approaching a big, sprawling village. We freewheeled down to the valley and I got off and pushed it for the last few hundred yards.

A busy two-lane road ran through the middle of the village. We passed a teahouse, a bakery, a supermarket, and several stores selling fruit and rice, then came to a small gas station with a workshop. A mother and her daughter were sitting under a sunshade decanting gas into plastic bottles to sell. They knew even less about broken engines than me. Inside the workshop, five young men with oily hands were sitting around a partly dismantled Royal Enfield, talking animatedly.

I explained the problem, but they didn't seem particularly interested. There'd be a wait, the oldest said without looking up, and went back to fiddling around with the Enfield.

Mary sat down on a stack of old car tires, and I stood in the shed, feeling slightly lost and wondering what I could say to hurry them up a bit.

They took little notice of us until one of the young men got up to fetch something. Our eyes met, I smiled, and he did a double take, stared at me, checked something on his phone, and showed it to one of the other mechanics. This guy whispered something to a third, and soon all three of them were staring at us.

"You're Niri," one of them said.

I pretended I didn't know what he was talking about.

"Of course you are," another said.

I shook my head defensively. The three young men came over and showed me a video where I was clearly recognizable. It would have been ludicrous to claim I was anyone else.

"You're right, it's Niri," Mary called out.

For a moment there was surprised silence. Then everyone spoke at once. The men laughed delightedly and gave us a thumbs-up. The oldest wiped his greasy fingers on a cloth, joined his hands in front of his chest, and intimated a bow.

"Thank you," he said. "Thank you. At last someone is helping us poor people."

He promised to repair the motorcycle right away. Judging from my description, it was just a dirty carburetor—it would only take them an hour, two hours max, to take it out and clean it and put it back again. They pushed the motorcycle into the garage and set to work. I offered to help, but they only laughed.

News of our arrival spread fast; a few minutes later, a small crowd of people had gathered in front of the workshop. They called out my name, and when Mary and I stepped outside, they clapped and cheered as if we were Bollywood stars. The crowd grew. I remembered with alarm what Yuri had said: *Too much attention is a bad thing.* I may have been a hero to some, but I was also a wanted man with a large bounty on his head. Mary was smiling; she looked incredulous but happy. The crowd led us across the road to a teahouse. Mary refused my arm. We took small steps and she walked with a limp, but I hadn't seen her walk so well unaided since her accident. A man pushed his way through the throng to us and told us to sit down—it was, he said, an honor to serve us in his teahouse. A moment later, we were sitting in front of a pot of tea and a huge plate of cakes.

"I can't believe this is happening," Mary whispered. People thrust phones in our faces, photographed us, videoed us—some even handed us pen and paper and asked for autographs. They all thanked us. I'd never heard *thank you* so often.

One woman came forward with outstretched hand, mumbling something about a sick daughter and asking for money. The people around her turned on her before I could reply. What was she thinking of, pestering us like that? She wasn't the only one who needed help—couldn't she see that we weren't there to hand out money? We'd be doing that again soon enough, but not now, not today, not to her. Annoyed and disappointed, she retreated into the crowd and vanished.

Then the talking and shouting sank to a murmur that slowly subsided until an eerie silence filled the air. A corridor formed in front of us, and two burly men in uniform appeared, heading our way. My stomach turned.

The police gawped at us; they probably couldn't believe that Mary and I had managed to draw such a crowd.

"What's going on here?" the older of them asked. No one spoke.

He looked at us sternly. "Who are you?"

We, too, remained silent.

"Stand up and answer me when I talk to you." He grabbed me by the arm and pulled me roughly from my stool. A murmur went through the crowd. "What's your name?"

"Let go of me, please," I said, calmly and firmly.

The policeman was a whole head taller than me, and twice as broad. He looked at me in astonishment and strengthened his grasp.

"I'm the one giving orders here," he shouted fiercely. "What's your name?"

"Niri," a woman called out and was immediately silenced by a barrage of loud, angry voices.

"Niri?" It took the policeman a second or two to grasp the significance of what he had just heard. Then: "Niri," he said again—gleefully this time.

Mary and I sat frozen in the back of the police car. We had refused to answer any questions. The police had dragged us to the car, but the crowd had been uncooperative, and despite much bullying and cursing, it had taken them several minutes to get us the few yards from the teahouse to the road.

Mary edged a hand across the seat to me and I squeezed it, feeling her tension. Our getaway would end here. There was no way we could escape from the car. No one had called the police; they had happened to be passing. Now they were taking us to the police station in the next town "to clarify the situation." I had no doubts about what would happen next: Mary and I would be put in separate cells and we'd never see each other again.

There wasn't a lot to clarify. They knew who we were; they knew we were wanted. The police car was surrounded by people who showed no sign of getting out of the way. The whole village seemed to be out in force. Old and young, men and women, they peered through the car windows, their faces curious but also angry. A loud chant rose and swelled, ringing through the streets. "Set them free. Set them free."

The younger policeman sat at the wheel, fat beads of sweat on his forehead. He had locked the doors and now sounded the horn several times and revved the engine, but the villagers remained unfazed. The car couldn't go backward or forward; any attempt to get through the living wall would have meant knocking down several men, women, and children. I doubted that he could get anywhere at all with the crowd as dense as it was.

The older policeman slammed his fist down on the dashboard, spitting curses. Then he wound down the window and turned on the crowd, calling them lazy bastards, idiots, morons, and yelling at them to get out of the way. Instead of complying, people began to press down on the trunk and hood, setting the car rocking like a small boat.

"Stop that," he shouted.

When the car began to sway more violently, he pulled his pistol, stretched his arm out the window, and shot into the air.

I don't know what provoked what happened next. Was it the shot? Was it a particular insult or the cumulative weight of events? Or was it years of pent-up anger suddenly let loose? Several hands darted out of the crowd, grabbed the arm holding the pistol, and brought it down against the roof of the car with such force that the policeman cried out in pain and dropped the gun.

Seconds later it was pointing at him.

"Cut the engine," someone said.

The other policeman cut the engine.

"Get out," said the man holding the gun.

Mary and I didn't dare move. For a few seemingly endless seconds, neither of the policemen moved either. Then the older one gave his colleague a nod. Very slowly and cautiously, they opened the doors and got out with their hands up. The second gun was also seized.

The crowd had gone quiet. Perhaps people were shocked by their own courage and power—or perhaps they no longer needed the reassurance of noise. It was impossible to tell.

"Take off your uniforms."

Reluctantly, the men began to unbutton their uniforms and strip to their underpants. Nimble fingers whipped the clothes away and spirited them into the crowd.

Mary opened the door and was helped out of the car by friendly hands. I got out after her. There was a loud hiss as someone slashed one of the rear tires with a knife, followed, seconds later, by another hiss. When all the tires were flat, an uneasy silence descended on the crowd again. People looked at me as if waiting to be told what to do next.

"Thank you," I cried. "Thank you for helping us!"

"You should clear out now," said the man holding the first gun. "Before it's too late." Just then, one of the young men from the workshop appeared, pushing a motorcycle through the crowd. It wasn't ours; it was a 250-cc Honda, but my backpack was hanging over the handlebars and Mary's duffel bag was strapped to the luggage rack.

"This is for you," said the young man, handing me the key. "Yours won't be ready in time."

On the last leg of the journey, Mary clung to me tighter than ever, her exhausted head resting on my back. I concentrated on the driving; I'd never ridden such a fast motorcycle. Afraid of missing the ferry, I took the highway and drove all the way without stopping.

The boat to Shark Island was still in dock when we reached the harbor. There was already quite a crowd of passengers on deck, some of them with chickens, pigs, or baskets of fruit and vegetables. Was this a good idea? I wasn't happy at the thought of spending three hours on a boat with so many strangers. The shock of our brief arrest was too recent, and I was terrified of being recognized again.

Only a hundred yards away, long-tail boats bobbed up and down at a pier. A faded sign promised unforgettable tours to remote, unspoiled beaches.

In one of the boats, two men lay dozing in the shade. They seemed surprised that we didn't want to take the ferry, but obligingly rustled up two planks, wheeled the motorcycle on board, and lashed it fast. Then they asked us to wait a moment while they went to fetch gas. We climbed into the rocking boat and sat close together in the bows.

"I was so scared earlier," Mary said quietly.

"Me too."

"Who'd have thought we'd get away?" She didn't wait for a reply, but went on as if she were talking to herself. "It was . . . To think they did that for us . . . They don't even know us . . . Not personally, I mean . . . The risk . . . Giving us the motorcycle like that, without asking for money . . . What was in it for them?"

Her voice died away and she stared down at the water, lost in thought.

"What do you think they'll do to the policemen?" she asked at length.

"No idea."

"Do you think they'll kill them?"

"No. Helping us to escape was one thing. Murder's in a different league."

"Are you as tired as I am?"

"I'm all right," I said, though I was having trouble keeping my eyes open.

Mary laid her head on my shoulder. I stroked her neck.

"You're still trembling."

She took my hand and pressed it to her face.

I kept an eye on the pier. Part of me just wanted to sleep; the other part was hyperalert. Secretly I was afraid that the men might have recognized us— that they'd gone for the police, not gas.

Minutes passed.

The ferry was untied. It hooted three times and I thought I heard sirens in the distance.

Would I be able to unmoor the boat and steer it if the police turned up? We wouldn't get far. But just as I was about to go ashore and look for the boatmen, I saw them hurrying along the quay with a heavy canister. They apologized for keeping us waiting, hefted the tank on board, and asked politely for the crossing charge of eight hundred leik.

Mary reached into her bag and rifled through her clothes—once, twice.

"The money's gone," she whispered to me.

"Are you sure?"

"The envelope with the gold coins is still there, but not the other, with the cash."

Someone in the workshop must have gone through her things and been unable to resist temptation.

"What a low trick," Mary said, disappointed rather than angry. "Pretending to help us . . ."

"They did help us," I pointed out. "How much money was it?"

"Fifty thousand? Maybe a bit more."

I rummaged in my backpack, which seemed not to have been meddled with—at any rate, the thousand-leik bills were still there. I gave one to the boatman, and a moment later he was skillfully maneuvering the boat out of the narrow harbor and heading for the open sea.

The sea was choppier than it had looked from the shore. The boat pitched and tossed, and waves crashed against the wooden sides, making it shudder. We stowed our things under a tarpaulin. Spray swept over us, leaving us drenched within minutes. I licked the drops from my lips; the salt water was pleasantly cooling.

When the island appeared before us, I asked Mary to give me the envelope from my backpack so that I could find the address.

"What's this?" she asked, holding up the passport and documents that Bagura had organized for me.

Startled, I made a grab for them. "That's the wrong envelope," I said. "Give that to me."

Mary pulled back her hand. "But what is it?" she asked, looking curiously at the red passport. "Is this yours?"

"Yes," I said, embarrassed. "Bagura got it for me."

She turned the pages as if she hadn't heard, read out the name, peered at the photo. "It's you, all right. But the name's fake." She set the passport aside and skimmed the documents that identified me as a future kitchen boy on the MSC *Hong Kong*. The ship was due to sail in a little under three weeks.

Eventually she dropped her arms. There were tears in her eyes. She looked at me with disappointment and, worse still, with suspicion.

"Mary, it's not the way you think."

"What way do I think?"

"That—that I'm going to leave you in three weeks to work on a ship."

"That's what it says here."

"It's wrong."

"It's what it says here," she repeated, almost tonelessly. "Why didn't you tell me?"

"Because I'd forgotten all about the papers. Because they weren't important to me." I could see her restraining herself from interrupting me.

"Have you ever," she asked, forcing herself to speak calmly, "had a real passport?"

"No, of course not."

She took a deep breath. "So you have a passport that would see you to safety, and papers for a job you've always wanted to do, and you're trying to tell me you'd forgotten them both?"

"Yes." I could hear how unlikely it sounded. But it was the truth.

"I don't believe you."

"But it's true," I insisted.

"I still don't believe you." Her voice trembled.

"Why not?"

"Because it doesn't make sense."

"How do you know what makes sense to me?"

She shook her head, as if my question weren't worth answering.

"It was Bagura's idea. He organized everything and gave me the envelope when I went to say good-bye to him. He didn't know we'd run away together. He wanted to make sure I was safe. Bagura meant well; he didn't know about you, I swear."

Mary turned away and stared out to sea in silence.

I couldn't tell what she was thinking. If only she'd scream, I thought. Curse me, spit at me, hit me. Her silence was harder to bear than any fit of rage.

"I'll never leave you. Ever."

"If you don't need the papers, why don't you just throw them away?"

What could I say? They meant nothing to me. I hadn't thought of them all week. So why had I hung on to them? Out of thoughtlessness? Negligence? Because it did no harm to keep them, just in case—as a kind of insurance policy, should Mary change her mind and want to go home after all? Any attempt to explain what even I didn't understand could only make matters worse.

"I don't know."

She didn't move.

"Mary, are you listening?"

She looked at me gravely, her eyes flashing with rage. "Without me, you couldn't have helped your family, right?"

I nodded.

"Without me, your sister would have stayed hungry, your mom would have gone untreated, there'd have been no money for you to give people. Without me, your friend Bagura wouldn't have got his commission, right?"

I nodded again.

"If that's all that mattered to you and you want to go on your way alone, then tell me right now and I'll get these men to take me back to the mainland."

I didn't want to dodge her gaze, but I could hardly hold it. I gulped. Had I hung on to the papers because, unconsciously, I wanted to leave myself the possibility of breaking with Mary? If I had, there wasn't the slightest doubt in my mind now. I loved her, I needed her. Maybe even more than she loved and needed me.

How hard it is to find the right words, I thought. Simple words that lay no blame. That make neither reproaches nor excuses. Words that make no false claims and do not seek to accuse or exonerate. Words that say things the way they are, that forgive and understand.

Mary was still looking at me, waiting.

"No, never," I said. "I don't want to be without you. I love you."

"So what are these for?" She held up the papers.

I took them out of her hand, passport and all, and threw them in a high arc into the water.

TWENTY-ONE

Baguma's friend lived on a shady avenue lined with small, brightly painted wooden houses—there was even the occasional stone building. It was a spruce-looking neighborhood; the houses had metal roofs and proper doors and windows, and there were motorcycles and in some cases cars parked in the drives.

We stopped outside number twenty. A sign hung above the door, its paint peeling like eucalyptus bark. If I guessed the missing letters right, it said HANCOCK'S REPAIR SHOP. The front garden was strewn with metal and plastic piping, cable drums, rusty tools, and a motley assortment of old appliances. A beat-up Toyota pickup truck stood in the middle.

Mary followed me onto the veranda. The curtains were drawn at the big front window, but the door was open a crack. I knocked.

"Who is it?"

"Us," I said.

"Who's 'us'?"

"Bagura's friends."

"Come in."

We stepped into a room that was kitchen, living room, and bedroom all in one. Beyond, through a half-open curtain, I could dimly make out a workshop and storeroom. There was a smell of stale smoke, burned food, and alcohol.

A man perhaps a few years older than Bagura stood leaning against a sink. He was gaunt and tall—at least a head taller than me—and wore his white hair neatly parted. Deep furrows marked his cheeks and forehead; his small eyes were set far back in their sockets; his unusually long nose gave his narrow face a strange, flinty look.

He greeted us with a friendly smile that was at odds with his stern features.

"Bagura called a week ago and told me all about you," he said. "Take a seat."

The only free seat was a wooden chair. Since Mary was clearly in pain after the hours on the motorcycle and in the boat, I left this to her and sat down on the floor at her feet. Old newspapers, dirty dishes, and empty cans and bottles littered the bed and armchairs, and a pan of leftover rice thick with flies stood on the table, surrounded by eggshells and shriveled bits of cut-up vegetables. Bagura's friend lit a cigarette and scrutinized us; a look of concern crossed his face.

"You look exhausted. Especially you," he said to Mary. "Would you like something to eat?"

She shook her head.

"A drink?"

"Water would be good."

He fetched a bottle from the fridge and gave it to her. Mary produced two pills and took them with the water.

"Call me Hancock—everyone does."

He took a drag on his cigarette but said nothing more.

"Did Bagura tell you we need somewhere to hide?" I asked.

He nodded. "For how long?"

Mary and I exchanged glances. "We don't know yet."

"That's all right," he said. "You can stay as long as you like. No one'll find you if we're careful. Probably best if you put your motorcycle in the garage behind the house. And I wouldn't go out during the day if I were you—neighbors are always nosy. You can go to the beach after dark—it's just around the corner—but be careful about swimming; there's a strong current in the monsoon season."

He thought for a moment. "And another thing: The house is yours all day, but at night, I'd like you to leave me in peace. I don't want to be disturbed after eight, all right? Got that?"

Mary and I nodded.

"Why don't you have a rest now?" Hancock dug two moth-eaten blankets out of a chest and showed us to the workshop.

"What's up with you?" he asked Mary, when he noticed the awkward way she was moving. "Why do you walk in that funny way?"

"I have a gimpy leg."

"Motorcycling accident?"

"No. I fell off a horse."

Hancock looked at her in surprise. "You ride?"

"Not anymore."

"Do you want crutches? I think I've got a pair somewhere."

"I'm all right, thanks."

Shaking his head, Hancock showed us to the far end of the storeroom. The place was piled high with old radios, toasters, television sets, and food processors. Two motorcycles were propped against a row of fridges that stood along one wall. There was a smell of oil and old grease.

Along another wall were two cabinets filled with boxes of screws, washers, and coils of wire; I helped Hancock pull these out to make a space where Mary and I could camp. We needn't worry about being discovered, Hancock said—he was the only person who ever came to this part of the house. We could stay here a hundred years and still feel safe.

We made up beds for ourselves, and Mary lay down so quickly that I thought for a moment she had fainted. I stretched out beside her, suddenly aware of what a long day we'd had and how draining it had been.

Mary stared at the ceiling. We weren't touching despite the cramped space. Since I'd jettisoned the passport and papers, we'd hardly spoken.

"Mary?" I whispered.

Silence.

"Is it soft enough for you?"

"Yes."

I could tell this wasn't the truth, so I folded my blanket and pushed it under hers. I was used to sleeping on a hard surface and had no objection to lying on floorboards. It wasn't as if I could sleep anyway.

Mary's eyes fell shut, her body twitched a couple of times, and soon she was breathing steadily.

Whenever I closed my eyes, I saw the policemen standing in front of us. Their grins when they recognized us. Mary and me in the car.

Sleep was out of the question.

After a while I was thirsty and got up to have a drink. It was quiet in the house. Light from the front room fell through the curtain into the workshop. I peered out through a narrow gap. Hancock was sitting in one of the armchairs with his back to me, staring out the window and smoking. Beside him stood a glass and a bottle of SomSom rum. The front door was open.

"What is it?" he asked, as if he had eyes in the back of his head. He spoke slowly and his voice was thicker and deeper than earlier. "Can't you sleep?"

"I'm sorry, I didn't want to disturb you."

"Well, you have. But I'll let it pass, just this once." His tongue was sluggish; it was hard to make out what he was saying.

"I'm thirsty."

"Then come here."

I walked around and perched on the edge of the couch. In the cold glow of the fluorescent light, his gaunt body looked even gaunter and his white hair even whiter. He poured himself half a glass of rum, knocked back a hefty slug, and put the glass down. "Want some? The glasses are over there."

"No, thanks. I don't drink."

His eyes left me and went back to staring out the window; I wasn't sure if he'd heard me. After a while, he picked up his glass again, drained it, and refilled it, holding the bottle upside down to get the last drops. He seemed so far away that I didn't dare ask for water.

Through the open door came the rasp of cicadas and the noise of croaking frogs.

"Bagura's friends," Hancock said under his breath, as if he were talking to himself. It didn't sound as if he expected an answer, but I said "Yes," just in case.

"He doesn't have many friends." Hancock spoke with surprise, rather than suspicion. "Never did."

I sat there in silence, watching him drink. He took small sips at intervals, belching loudly after each one, his movements growing slower and more ponderous. Soon after the last sip, his body went limp. His shoulders slumped, his arms slipped from the armrests, his head tipped back. He began to snore softly, his mouth slightly open. I waited a while, so as not to wake him. Then I got up and fetched myself a bottle of water, closed the front door, turned out the light, and went back to Mary.

Soon afterward I, too, was asleep.

———

The next morning I was woken by short, sharp hammer blows. Hancock was busy in the workshop. He sawed something, put in screws, resumed hammering. Mary woke up and looked at me sleepily. I reached out to take her hand, but she pulled it away.

A short while later we heard a door open and close, and a truck drive off.

I helped Mary up. Two homemade crutches were propped against the cabinets outside our hiding place. I offered them to Mary, but she shook her head firmly.

Hancock had tidied up. The empty bottles and cans had vanished; the dishes and frying pan had been washed up, the newspapers stuffed into a paper bag, and the table wiped clean. On the kitchen counter was a bowl of bananas, mangos, and papayas.

Behind the fridge was a door I hadn't noticed the day before. It led to a small bathroom with a washbasin and a flush toilet. A showerhead was attached to the wall above the toilet; Hancock could shower while he was taking a shit.

Mary hobbled to the fridge. It was filled with bottles of beer and a few jars of sauce; in the vegetable drawer was a bunch of limp spring onions and half a dozen eggs.

In a cupboard we found a carton of cigarettes and three boxes of ramen noodles. I took out two pots and put water on to boil.

We spooned out our soup in silence; we hadn't spoken all morning. Mary looked out the window. She was still mad at me, I could tell.

"I think we're safe here for the moment, don't you?" I said, hoping to draw her out.

She went on eating as if she hadn't heard me.

If she really believed I had deliberately kept quiet about the passport and papers, she must think me a vile, ungrateful little traitor. It was a wonder she could bear to sit in the same room as me.

When I could stand the silence no longer, I said: "Do you want to go home?"

She gave a start, then turned to me. "Niri," she yelled, so loudly that I was afraid the neighbors would hear. "You still haven't got it, have you? My home is with you. I don't have another—not anymore." Then she began to cry as I have never seen anyone cry before—not even my parents when Mayari died. She shook all over, her body wracked with sobs, as if her grief were a big wave that might sweep her away at any moment.

I got up and took her in my arms, but that only made her cry more.

"Mary," I said. "I'm here. I'm not going to leave you."

She pushed me away roughly, but pulled me close again a moment later.

After a few minutes, the sobs began to subside.

"I'm sorry," I said softly. "Please don't doubt me. All the time we were on the beach, I didn't—"

Instead of listening, Mary took my head in her hands and kissed me—not tenderly, but with fierce desire, as if her life depended on it. "Love me," she whispered. "Love me."

I carried her back to our hideout and undressed; she slipped off her blouse and trousers, and we began to make love. It was different from on the beach. Instead of stroking me, Mary hit and clawed at me until my skin ached and bled. I couldn't figure out if it was lust, anger, or desperation—or perhaps a combination of all three. Afterward we clung to each other, drenched in sweat, her body clamped to mine.

Hancock didn't return until dusk. He had been shopping and came in laden with rice, oil, vegetables, canned tuna, eggs, and cookies.

He seemed glad when I offered to cook, and asked if I could make fried rice. While Mary helped me to chop the vegetables, he fetched himself a bottle of beer from the fridge, opened a can of tuna, and sat down to join us. He was much chattier than the day before.

"Do you know why I'm called Hancock?" he asked. "No, of course you don't. Why would you? I was named for the superhero."

Mary and I must have gawped at him; at any rate he laughed loudly.

"Don't you know the movie with Will Smith?"

"No."

"Doesn't matter. Hancock's a superhero—one of those invincible guys with superhuman powers. My oldest son gave me the nickname." He took a gulp of beer and looked for a moment as if he might not go on. Then he said: "I fished a friend of his out of the sea. They were playing on the beach and I happened to be passing by. There was a riptide—knocked the boy over and pulled him out. He wasn't a strong swimmer and would have drowned. It was a near thing—I was almost killed myself. Since then, everyone's called me Hancock. Not bad, huh?"

He liked finishing with a rhetorical question.

"You two are in pretty deep shit," he said, putting a forkful of fish in his mouth and washing it down with beer. "Had a look on the internet this morning to get the lowdown. They're scouring the country for you—up and down the coast and all over the islands. I hope your ferrymen keep their mouths shut." He laughed. "You must have a whole bunch of doppelgängers."

"What do you mean?" I asked.

"There are people claiming to have seen you everywhere—north, south, east, west. You've been spotted on almost every island too. Either they've all got their eyes on the bounty, or they're trying to confuse the police in order to protect you. I suspect the former."

Remembering how half a village had rescued us from the police, I wasn't so sure.

"The police have had so many tip-offs they've asked people to stop sending them information for the time being. Pretty funny, huh?"

He laughed again—a loud, infectious laugh. This time, Mary and I joined in.

Half an hour later, our supper was on the table. Hancock took only a small helping and even that he didn't finish.

"Don't you like it?" I asked, disappointed.

"Oh yes, I do. You're a good cook. But I'm never very hungry in the evenings—you'll have to get used to that. Do I look like someone who eats a lot?"

After his third beer, Hancock fetched a bottle of rum from a cabinet in the workshop—I glimpsed at least another dozen bottles in there. It took him about half an hour to drink the first glass, and when he'd finished, he was quieter. After the second, he wanted to be alone.

Early the next morning, I heard Hancock in the workshop again. Mary was still fast asleep. I got up and offered to lend him a hand.

He looked pleased to see me. "Know anything about engines?"

I shook my head.

"Electrical appliances?"

"A little," I fibbed. "Though plants are more my thing. I used to be a gardener."

He handed me a water pump. "Take that apart for me."

I took what I thought were the right screwdrivers from the toolbox, but when I tried them, one was too big and the other too small. It was a while before I found what I needed and could set to work. I didn't get far.

"You're all thumbs," Hancock said, taking the pump back. "Like Bagura. Make us a pot of tea instead."

We took the tea out onto the veranda. Hancock said the neighbors wouldn't notice me—they were too busy at this hour of the morning.

He still wasn't hungry, but smoked a cigarette with relish while I ate up the remains of the fried rice. We sipped our tea in silence. Birds twittered, geckos darted across the veranda, rays of sun fell through the dense foliage of a banyan tree. It was warm, but not yet too hot. I could hear the roar of the sea in the distance.

"When does your ship sail?" Hancock asked.

I started.

"Bagura told me your plans. Does your girl-friend know?"

"I'm not getting on that ship," I said curtly, without looking at him.

He nodded, unsurprised. "Bagura thought you'd say that. He asked me to try and talk you around."

"No way. Why is it so important to him?"

"Maybe because he likes you, because he's worried about you." Hancock looked at me sidelong. "You remind me of him."

"Of Bagura?" I laughed, thinking it must be a joke.

"Not the way he is now. The way he was at your age. Bagura was a quiet boy, very serious. No interest in machines, just like you. There's even a physical resemblance. Has he never told you that?"

"No."

"When you look at me with your head on one side, I see Bagura when he was twenty. You could be his little brother. Maybe that's why he's so fond of you."

"Have you known him that long?"

"We grew up in the same village. Our families were neighbors; we used to play together."

"Are you a Dalit too?"

"Yes. Bagura's two years older than me—I know you wouldn't think so to look at us. He was like a big brother to me. When he said he wanted to be a teacher, I said I wanted to be a teacher too, and my parents beat me for my dreams just as his parents beat him. When he moved to Mumbai, I followed him. We slept rough and worked as day laborers. We fell in love with the same girls. First the rag-picker's daughter, then the knife grinder's daughter. Neither was interested in us." Hancock grinned. "Bagura became a cook, I became a handyman. When he went to Communist Party meetings, I went too. We joined the crew of a ship together and traveled the world for seven years, Bagura in the galley, me in the engine room. When Bagura signed off, I stayed on for another three years. Then I fell in love while I was visiting him on leave, and soon after that I got married and settled here with my wife. If you can mend a ship's engine, you'll always have work on an island. Bagura had plans to move here, too, and open a restaurant, but it didn't come to anything. It was a shame. I'm fonder of him than anyone, apart from my wife and sons."

Hancock paused, staring out at the empty street and the old tools and appliances in the front garden. "Why don't you want to work on the ship? It would be an opportunity to escape poverty. And you'd be safe."

"I can't go without Mary."

"You don't stand a chance together."

When I said nothing, he continued: "If you went your separate ways, Mary could go back to her parents—I'm sure they'd forgive her. It wouldn't have to be for long. You'd go to sea for a few years, until all this has blown over, then you'd come back to her."

I shook my head.

He sighed and spat a tea leaf onto the veranda.

"Don't get me wrong—you can stay here as long as you like, I just don't know how long you want to camp out on the floor behind a couple of cabinets. It's no solution. But you won't find anywhere else to hide. You're too famous. And I can't get you fake papers; you have to be in the city for that, and I don't have the kind of contacts Bagura has. Niri," he said urgently, "think it over."

"If you don't want us here, we can leave."

"That's not what I said. But if they arrest you and Mary, you'll never see each other again. You probably won't even survive."

"They won't arrest us."

Hancock and I spun around. Mary was standing in the door. We hadn't heard her coming. The warm glow of the morning sun lit up her face, and she looked lovelier than ever.

"We won't let them arrest us," Mary said slowly, emphasizing every word. She hobbled onto the veranda and came over to me. Hancock contemplated us, smiling. He looked as if he were going to say something, but didn't.

When I think about it now, I believe he must have heard something in Mary's voice that I wasn't aware of at the time: an absolute that brooked no argument, a love that knew no bounds. What she said was beautifully simple: If we can't live together, we will die together. No power in the world can separate us. It's the two of us or nothing.

Hancock leaned back, frowning and rubbing his face. There was a wistfulness in his eyes that I didn't understand at the time. He gave another deep sigh and got up, offering Mary his chair. "Maybe you're right," he said. "Maybe I'd do the same if I were you." He went into the house and reemerged a moment later carrying his tool bag. He waved to us from the pickup before driving off.

Mary sat down and watched him go. Then she turned to me. "They won't arrest us," she said again, but this time there was less conviction in her voice; the words sounded frail and thin. "Will they?"

"No."

She took my hand and kissed it all over. I slid off my chair, kneeled before her, and laid my head on her lap. Tenderly she stroked the back of my neck. We stayed like that for some time, and in that long, drawn out moment, I knew she was right: the police wouldn't arrest us. And so what if they did?

They could do what they liked to us—they would never get at what mattered. There was something between us that was stronger than fear or brute violence.

Mary and I soon learned to fit in around Hancock's rigid routine. Every day, he rose soon after dawn, worked in the workshop until late morning, drove away for a few hours, came home sometime in the afternoon, and returned to the workshop. He wasn't very chatty first thing; if we happened to bump into him, we never got more than a nod and a curt good morning.

At six p.m. on the dot, he put down whatever he was working on, opened a beer, and began to drink. The first beer was followed by a second and often a third; after that he moved on to rum, putting away half a bottle and sometimes a whole one. The alcohol made him garrulous—at least in the early evening, when he liked to have us around, asking him questions. He laughed a lot, making jokes and telling us funny stories about his work in the houses of the local rich. After the first beer, it always felt as if his upbeat younger brother had dropped in on us.

He did the shopping, and Mary and I did the cooking, though we rarely made anything more adventurous than egg-fried rice with canned tuna and sweet corn. Hancock wasn't a discerning eater, and neither Mary nor I were skilled cooks.

At Mary's request, Hancock bought paper and pencils. She started to draw again, and asked me to fetch the little mirror from the bathroom so that she could draw herself. Then it was my turn to sit for her. I sat on the couch, trying not to move and relishing the intentness of her gaze.

I wasn't allowed to see the drawing until it was finished. It was of Mary and me riding a horse bareback. Our hair fluttered in the wind, and we were looking ahead, our gazes intent, but without fear or concern. You couldn't see where the horse was going—only that it was preparing for a big leap. When I looked closer, I spotted tiny trees and houses at the bottom of the picture. It looked as if we were flying or floating through the air. As with all Mary's pictures, I was amazed at how lifelike it was.

One evening when we were having supper, Mary pointed at the appliances in the front garden.

"Why do you keep all that old stuff?" she asked Hancock, who was on his second beer and at the talkative stage.

"For the spare parts," he said. "I repair things. Kitchen appliances, water pumps, cooling units, engines. Luckily for me, the more gadgets people have, the more quickly they break. Do you know why?"

"The law of probability," Mary said.

"Wrong. It's because when people have too many things, they stop looking after them. As soon as they have more of something than they need, they start to waste it. Simple as that. It infuriates me. Because these things"—Hancock pointed at the kettle, his phone, the lamp over the table—"may not have souls, but they do have value. Do you know what I mean? I'm not talking about their financial value in leik or dollars or euros." He picked up his phone and held it out to us. "Take this cellphone. A bunch of smart programmers and engineers have done some pretty hard thinking to make this thing work as well as it does. People have stood in factories from morning till night screwing the parts together. And before that, the raw materials had to be sourced. Copper, aluminum, iron, tin, cobalt. You don't find them lying on the street or growing on trees. Nature doesn't give them to us unasked. We have to go get them—wrest them from the bowels of the earth. That's miserable, dirty work. Little kids risk their lives crawling through cobalt mines so that we can make calls on these things.

"Do people appreciate that? Do they treat their phones with care? No. What do they do when their phones stop working or when the battery stops charging? They chuck them and buy new ones. Same with their toasters, TVs, fridges, radios. They have no respect for their value. I try to restore that value by repairing the things and selling them on. It's the least I can do."

He drained the bottle and wiped his mouth on his sleeve.

"I spend a lot of time in the houses of the rich," he went on. "They trust me, because they've known me a long time—they know I'm just a harmless old boozer. I've lost all desire to be wealthy myself. I don't want to live in a luxury villa or drive an expensive car. I don't want to drink vintage wine or eat rich food. Money means nothing to me, as long as I have enough to buy myself a bottle of rum every day. I don't envy the rich their wealth; it leaves me cold—though I am sometimes repelled by their affluence."

He fetched himself a third beer from the fridge and raised the bottle to us.

Mary and I said nothing. After a while I cleared the table and prepared to wash up.

"Don't bother," Hancock said. "I'll do it in the morning. Tell me instead: Did Bagura ever confess to being a gifted cook? Did you know he even had his own cookshop for a time?"

I nodded.

"And did he tell you that it was twice set on fire by jealous neighbors?"

I nodded again.

"And that he lost his wife in the second fire and almost lost his daughter?"

I stared at Hancock in disbelief. "But—his wife's alive," I stuttered.

"I thought as much," Hancock said. He shook his head and gave a loud sigh, followed by an even louder belch. "That's his second wife. A widow with two sons—what are their names again?"

"Yuri and Taro," I said tonelessly.

"That's right."

"And his daughter?"

"Her name was Amita. She was three at the time."

Amita. I closed my eyes. *By the way, Amita is a girl's name and means "the boundless one."* Why hadn't Bagura told me about her?

"What happened to her?" I asked, though I'd already guessed the answer.

"She died. I thought you knew."

It was so quiet that I could hear the faucet dripping.

"A long time ago?" Mary asked tentatively.

Hancock took a swig from the bottle. "Yes. She died three months after the fire. Bagura always thought she starved to death. His wife was dead, and he couldn't work because of his burns. They slept rough and had very little to eat. Amita fell ill, and Bagura couldn't take her to the doctor—not without money; you know how it is for illegals. No-body helped." He looked piercingly at me. "There was no Niri to help them. Things might have been very different otherwise. One day, Amita didn't wake up. Bagura was a different man after that."

"So Yuri and Taro aren't his?"

"Not his biological sons. He used to not get on with them very well. Maybe that's changed."

All the things I hadn't understood suddenly made sense.

Every afternoon when Hancock came home, Mary took his phone and checked the internet for news of us. Several videos of our arrest and liberation had been posted on YouTube and Facebook. The naked policemen were the laughingstock of the country.

Mary's family continued to claim that she had been kidnapped; the police refused to comment. In the course of their investigations, they had discovered the ransacked safe and figured out that she was my accomplice. Once it became known that more than fifteen million leik had been plundered from "King Khao's ex" and that it was presumably

Mary who had let the thief into the house, the newspapers began to call us "Niri and Mary," "Robin and Maid Marian," and sometimes even "Bonnie and Clyde." As far as the press was concerned, there was no doubt that we were on the run together. Daily bulletins and feature articles reported on the futile search for us and charted our popularity among the country's poor. There was speculation on whether we were still in the country or had managed to flee—on who was helping us, and when we would next strike. A so-called expert wrote articles analyzing our relationship. She believed either that I had seduced Mary and had her at my mercy, or that I was attracted by her wealth and was in thrall to her.

In the Indian state of Kerala, the first copycat crimes were reported. Two men had robbed a bank, sprayed "Niri" on the wall, and thrown part of the haul out of their car window as they drove away. There had been riots on the street as passersby fought over the scattered money. Mary read the story aloud to us, and Hancock laughed so much he almost choked on his beer.

Somewhere in Europe, in a place called Palermo, burglars had cleared out the contents of a supermarket and carried everything to a nearby market square. By the time the police showed up, there was very little left, and no trace of the perpetrators, who had sprayed "Niri" in big letters on the cobblestones.

At a holdup in a jeweler's in Los Angeles, a policeman and one of the three robbers were shot dead. According to the newspaper report, the dead man had had "Niri" tattooed on his arm.

There were "Niri" Facebook pages in countless languages and countries.

"I don't get it," I said one evening, when Mary had read us yet another of these articles. "Why are the police hunting us as if we were terrorists or dangerous criminals? We haven't taken anyone hostage or robbed a bank or killed anyone. All we've done is stolen money from a safe and given it to people who were in dire need of it. Why does that make us celebrities? We visited maybe a dozen slums in one city, and people are acting as if we'd saved the world from starvation."

Hancock smiled. "Do you really not understand?" he said, picking up his bottle of beer and leaning back in his chair.

"No."

He drew pensively on his cigarette and slowly exhaled. "People are celebrating you," he said at last, "because you give them something more valuable than money."

"And what might that be?"

"Hope."

"Of what?"

"That their fate might change. The police are searching for you for the same reason. Hope, inspiration. That's why the bounty on your heads is so high." He laughed at the look of confusion on my face. "You're way more dangerous than your average bank robber or kidnapper, because there's this fear that others will follow your example. It's already starting to happen. Just imagine—instead of one Niri, or ten, or a hundred, you have thousands of Niris. No one knows how much poverty, oppression, and humiliation has to be endured until people revolt. There's no knowing who or what makes them do it. But when it happens, the world is a different place—that's what frightens the powers that be."

I pondered this as I ate the green chicken curry that Hancock had brought home from a cookshop. It was so lip-stingingly hot that I had to take a break after every spoonful. Mary helped herself to seconds, seemingly oblivious to the chili. Hancock had eaten as little as always. Now he lit a cigarette and looked out at the rain; fat drops pelted the window and trickled down the glass. Mary hadn't taken her eyes off him all the time we'd been talking.

He opened his third bottle of beer.

"Why do you drink so much?" she said abruptly.

I gave a start. I'd been wanting to ask the same thing, but hadn't dared.

Hancock didn't respond. He went on staring at the rain, as if he hadn't heard her.

"Why do you want to know?" he asked at length.

"I want to understand why someone would intoxicate themselves every evening."

"Because I like the taste. Because it gives me pleasure. Because it does me good. Is that enough reasons?"

"It does you no good at all," Mary said. "You're slowly but surely killing yourself."

"You're probably right. But that's not my objective—only a regrettable consequence."

"So why don't you stop?"

"Why do you think?"

"Because you're in pain?"

"That's one possible reason. Can you think of another?"

Mary pondered the question. "Loads."

Hancock turned to face us. His features were suddenly softer looking, almost boyish.

"Depression might be a reason, mightn't it? Melancholy, the blues, the black dog. It has many names. Maybe you know what it's like. Maybe you don't. I've suffered from it for as long as I can remember. I must have been born with it, the way other children are born with one leg shorter than the other, or one finger too many. Some people are troubled only fleetingly, sporadically. Not me. My whole life has been overshadowed by depression. Apparently there are drugs that keep it at bay—I find that hard to imagine. There have been times when I've thought I've seen the last of it—when I met my wife, when our children were born, when we found this house on this beautiful island. But each time, it came back. I have no talent for happiness. It runs through my fingers like water; I can't hold on to it. My wife sometimes asked me why I was so depressed—I never knew what to say. I could have given her the easy answer: Because I was born a Dalit; because the other kids saw that as a reason to throw dog shit at me; because I saw my own dad run over by a drunk truck driver and dragged a hundred yards down the road. Because the world is the way it is. Sounds plausible, doesn't it?"

Hancock leaned forward and looked from one to the other of us. "But do you know what? It would be a lie. A despicable form of self-pity. The truth is, I don't know why I get depressed. I don't even know if there's a reason. Other people have been through far worse than me and *they* don't drink. If I were asking the questions, I'd want to know why not. Seems to me that's more of a mystery than my drinking.

"My wife used to hate it when I came home drunk, but I never raised my hand to her or the children. Never even raised my voice. I went to bed and slept. Alcohol doesn't make me aggressive—you know that. It makes me tired. It numbs me. It wraps around me like a big blanket and cushions me from the shocks of life. It helps me to bear my grief.

"My wife didn't want me to drink myself to death. I understood that. She told me I was an egoist—told me to think of her and the kids too. I tried. But it made no difference.

"'If you really loved us, you'd stop,' she said.

"'I do love you,' I told her.

"'Not enough,' she said.

"I explained that I loved them as much as I could. You can't ask more of a person than that, can you?

"But it wasn't enough for her. That, too, I understood. I didn't remonstrate with her. Different people need different things to be happy—and some need more than others.

"One day, we'd said all there was to say. She packed what little she had and took the kids to live with relatives in the north. I drove them to the ferry.

"We talk for an hour or two on the phone every month. She's doing well, and that's good to know. The kids are doing well too. They're grown up now. Both teachers. I'm proud of them. My wife says she'll come back if I stop drinking—says it's up to me. But it's not quite as easy as that."

Hancock's voice had dropped very low. He leaned his head back in exhaustion. "Any more questions?"

Yes, I thought. Loads.

"No," Mary said softly.

He turned to look at her. "You know way too much for your age. It isn't good for you."

TWENTY-TWO

When Mary and I went into the kitchen the next morning, Hancock was on the phone. He greeted us with a brief nod and headed for the veranda. His voice was unusually soft and cheerful for the time of day, and he kept saying to whoever was at the other end of the line how sweet it was of them to remember.

"Is it your birthday?" Mary asked when he came back in.

"Yes. But birthdays aren't a big deal when you're my age."

"Many happy returns!" she said. "Why didn't you tell us?"

"What? So you could organize a surprise party for me?" He laughed. "We'll have a drink this evening. I must get to work now." He put two packs of cigarettes in his tool bag and went on his way.

"We should give him a present," Mary said as the door closed behind him.

"But what?"

She thought for a while. "He ought to have a birthday cake. Everyone likes birthday cake."

"You think?"

She gave me a sidelong glance. "Oh, come on, Niri. You like birthday cake, don't you?"

"I've never had one."

"Never? Don't you celebrate birthdays?"

"Yes. We go to the monastery. One of the monks blesses the family, we give alms, and then we go home again. Do you even know how to bake a cake?"

"No, but what's the internet for? We'll find a recipe we like the look of and watch the tutorial." Mary turned to fetch pen and paper to make a note of the ingredients, then remembered that although Hancock had two gas burners, there was no oven in the kitchen—and no mixer or cake pan either. Disappointed but undeterred, she suggested that I take the motorcycle to the next village to look for a cake and candles. This seemed like a good idea. Apart from anything else, it gave me an excuse to ride the motorcycle.

I fetched the bike from the garage and set off for the island's biggest village. It didn't take me long to find a 7-Eleven with an in-store bakery on the main street. I put on a mask and went in.

I'd never been in such a glamorous 7-Eleven.

And I'd never seen such a vast range of products. The candles alone filled several shelves: altar candles and temple candles in all different sizes; birthday-cake candles in all colors of the rainbow. I chose a pack of red, blue, and green candles for Hancock's cake, and headed for the bakery.

Here, too, the choice was overwhelming: strawberry cream slices; lemon, pineapple, and mango gâteaux with fancy frosting; chocolate-filled buns; rice cookies, and freshly baked sponge cakes. I hesitated between a plain unfrosted pineapple loaf that would have been relatively easy to transport in my backpack, and an iced gâteau with "Happy Birthday" in colored letters. I asked myself what Mary would have taken, and finally settled for the gâteau.

At the checkout, I spotted a display case filled with liquor. Wine from Australia, champagne from France, a variety of whiskies, and a fancy-looking bottle of SomSom rum with a golden label saying "Royal Prestige." It was a "limited edition," the man at the till told me—a special gift for special occasions. It cost a hundred and fifty-five leik—three times as much as a normal bottle—but I took it anyway. It was Hancock's birthday.

When I got back, the kitchen was changed almost beyond recognition.

Mary had made bunting from the peeled-off labels of Hancock's empty bottles and strung it diagonally across the room. Somewhere in the house she had found colored paper and cut out birds, palm trees, candles, hearts, and stars to stick on the walls. She had picked three dark-red hibiscus flowers from the bushes in the garden and put them in a beer bottle.

"Do you like it?" she asked, clearly pleased at my surprise.

"Yes." It really was beautiful, though not what I was used to.

The drive home hadn't done the cake much good. It was rather squashed, and the writing had run in places, but Mary said Hancock wouldn't mind. She restored it to its former shape as best she could, wrapped the bottle of rum in newspaper, and tied a bow around the neck with a length of wire. Then she arranged everything on the table with the flowers.

When Hancock's truck pulled up outside the house, we lit the candles and waited for him to push open the door so that we could sing "Happy Birthday."

He stood there as if rooted to the spot. His eyes flitted about the room, and for a moment I was afraid that Mary had been wrong—that instead of being pleased, he would dismiss everything with a sullen shake of his head or a brusque hand gesture.

But the opposite happened.

His eyes beamed. A big smile spread across his face.

"It's years since I celebrated my birthday," he said. "Or anyone's birthday for that matter. Thank you."

He put down his tool bag and fetched three bottles of beer from the fridge. We drank to him. The beer tasted as vile as the rice wine I had once tried, but at least it didn't burn my gullet. Mary insisted that Hancock blow out the candles and make a wish.

Then he cut the cake, and we talked and laughed a great deal. Hancock told us about his years on board ship with Bagura, their shore leave, their plans to open a combination restaurant-workshop in the States. He took photos to send his wife and sons—of the birthday table, of us, of Mary's decorations.

Later that evening, he produced a box of old family photos. They reminded me of the few pictures of my family: solemn-looking people staring into the camera, their eyes betraying nothing of their feelings for each other.

The best photos were those of Hancock and Bagura. Two good-looking young men in sailors' uniforms, laughing and happy to be alive—only a little older than Mary and I now. They were unrecognizable. One picture showed them outside a red-tiled restaurant front, their arms around each other's shoulders. CUNEO, it said in neon lights over the door.

"That was in Hamburg, Davidstrasse—our favorite restaurant when we were in port there. Amazing place. Great owner. Crazy guy. 'If we can't hold time back, we can at least enjoy it,' he used to say, and he'd serve us pasta at two in the morning— the best pasta *all'arrabbiata* in the world." Hancock grinned. "They had a jukebox. Bagura and I would dance into the small hours—can you imagine? Wild neighborhood. The streets were heaving at night."

"Why the cheeky laugh?" Mary asked.

"Oh, you know."

In another photo they stood arm in arm in a chasm of skyscrapers, as a short-skirted passerby turned to look at them in their uniforms. On the back someone had written *New York, Summer '85*.

"Those were the days," Hancock murmured, chuckling to himself. It was touching to see how happy the memories made him.

Then his phone buzzed. He glanced at the screen, checked the number, and ignored it, but a moment later it started up again. This time he took the call.

There was a man at the other end of the line. I didn't need to hear what he was saying to know that something terrible had happened. Hancock's small eyes widened and then narrowed. He opened his mouth as if to scream, but no sound came out. The call lasted a minute or two and in all that time he said only a couple of soft yeses and noes. When it was over he threw the phone down on the table and stared out the window.

"Bagura is dead."

It took a few seconds to sink in. My eyes filled with tears.

"The police say he died of a heart attack during interrogation." Hancock looked so angry, I was afraid he might get up and trash the house.

"That's—that's not possible," I stammered. "He was in good health. You don't just die being interrogated."

"Depends on the interrogation methods," Hancock said, his voice thick with rage. "They will have tried to make him tell them where you are. He didn't betray us, or we'd have had the police here long ago. The bastards will have tried to beat it out of him. Not everyone's heart can take that."

Hancock stood up. He paced up and down, then stopped and pounded so hard on the bathroom door with his fists that the wood splintered. He went to the sink, fetched three dirty water glasses, slammed them down on the table, opened the bottle of SomSom Royal Prestige, and filled the glasses almost to the brim.

Mary reached for my hand and squeezed it. I sat beside her in a daze, feeling empty and drained. Bagura was dead, murdered. I opened my mouth to say something, but couldn't string two words together.

"Drink," Hancock ordered us.

Mary and I sipped the rum.

"Drink, I said."

I took a big gulp. It tasted revolting and burned my gullet and stomach. I choked and spluttered. Mary hesitated for a second, then emptied her glass in one gulp, as if she were drinking water. I followed suit.

The rum didn't take long to kick in. A deep sense of calm came over me, and I felt my body relax. Nothing seemed to matter anymore. Someone had put life on mute.

Bagura was still dead, but my pain was numbed. I felt a serenity that was at once soothing and unnerving.

Mary and I exchanged glances. Her face and neck were flushed, but she looked relaxed.

Hancock refilled our glasses in silence. Mary downed hers again, and again I did as she did.

Then Hancock stood up and fetched a bottle of regular SomSom from the cupboard.

I could taste no difference, but after the third glass I started to feel dizzy and nauseous. Everything spun around me. I tried to focus on the candles, but it was no good; the room just went on spinning. The paper cutouts on the wall, the Som-Som-and-beer bunting, the remains of the birthday cake. I closed my eyes, but that only made things worse. I clutched the arms of my chair and heaved myself to my feet. The floor gave a lurch. Mary tried to get up to help me, but fell back onto her chair. I made it to the bathroom just in time to vomit. I have no memory of how I got to bed.

In the morning I woke with a piercing headache and a ravening thirst. I was still dizzy and queasy.

Bagura was dead, and life was no longer on mute. For a few hours, alcohol had kept grief at bay, but that was over now. At the thought of all that rum, I felt the nausea rise again, worse than before.

I got up. Every time I moved, it was like banging my head against a wall.

Hancock was still asleep in his armchair. I drank a bottle of water and sat down with another.

"Bagura is dead," I whispered and closed my eyes. "Bagura is dead." For the first time, I grasped the meaning of the words.

Grief and anger swilled around in me. I saw images of Bagura, like a video in my head. That dismissive wave that was so typical of him. The way he used to sit outside his shack, mopping his brow and scratching himself between his legs. The black-and-white photograph of Amita next to his bed. The dramatic flourish with which he had held out his hands to the police, challenging them to handcuff him. The proud twinkle in his eye when he produced the envelope with the faked passport and papers for the MSC *Hong Kong*. Would he be disappointed by what I'd done, or would he understand?

I breathed deeply in and out, the way my father had taught me when we meditated together.

In and out.

In and out.

Sitting next to him, I had never managed to do it right, but now it came quite naturally. I began to relax a little.

I didn't want to let my grief and anger get the upper hand. But at the same time, I thought, I didn't want to get rid of them altogether. I wanted to be free in the midst of my emotions. I wanted to turn the power of those emotions to good use.

Again I saw Bagura: He was coming toward me
down one of the narrowest alleyways in the settlement, an Amita Foundation T-shirt stretched
across his big belly, while behind him Santosh stood
and waved in an Amita Foundation cap. Bagura
looked pleased to see me; he laughed and leaned toward me. I heard him whisper, I heard him speak,
and I could swear that it was he who gave me the
idea of what to do next.

Hancock pulled me back into the house. He
shook me by the shoulder, and I opened my eyes.

"Everything okay?" he asked in concern.

"Yes," I said. "I was just dreaming."

Hancock looked as sad as the evening before.
He stayed and had breakfast with us instead of
rushing off to work. I boiled water for noodle soup
and made strong black coffee that he drank noisily
from a mug.

I'd been busy making plans and was now waiting
for the right moment to tell him and Mary my idea.
When I'd finished eating, I pushed my polystyrene
bowl into the middle of the table and cleared my
throat.

"I've been thinking," I said.

Mary and Hancock looked at me.

"I'd like to work for the foundation again."

"What foundation?" Hancock asked, puzzled.

"The Amita Foundation."

"Why would you do that?" He fixed me over the top of his mug as he slurped his coffee. Mary smiled at me; she knew at once what I meant.

"I'd like us to distribute some more money to the poor on behalf of the foundation."

"Who is this 'us'?"

"Mary and me."

"And where are you going to get hold of this money?" Hancock looked at Mary. "Maybe you have another rich aunt, here on the island?" he said teasingly.

"No, we'll have to do things differently this time."

"But how?"

I took a deep breath. This was, of course, the crucial question, and the answer depended on him. "Didn't you say that you have access to the houses of the local rich? That people trust you?"

He stared at me, and I thought of Bagura telling me he could read my face like a book; it was certainly easy to read the expression on Hancock's face. He took a gulp of coffee as he pondered what I'd said—then took another gulp as he began to see where I was headed.

"You want me to be your accomplice?"

Mary and I nodded, almost in sync.

"And how exactly would that work?"

"It's pretty simple," I said. "You go about your work as usual and I come with you as a kind of assistant. While you're fiddling around with the swimming pool pump or the electric garage door or the air-conditioning, I slip into the house and see what I can find in the way of cash, jewelry, and other valuables." I paused in case he had questions or objections; when he said nothing, I went on. "As soon as we have enough money together, we'll do what Bagura did. We'll have T-shirts and caps printed, we'll have the name of the charity painted on the side of a car, and we'll distribute the leik we've collected in a slum on the mainland."

"You might as well turn yourselves in to the police. Every child in the country knows who's behind the Amita Foundation."

"I don't think anyone will give us away. And if they do, we'll be long gone by the time the police show up."

"You want me to go thieving with you." Hancock shook his head. I wasn't sure if that was a no or merely an expression of disbelief or astonishment. For a long time he said nothing. Then he got up and fetched a glass and a bottle of rum from the cabinet. He set them on the table without opening the bottle and sat down in front of them.

"I have my life here—I'd be putting it on the line. And for what? Where do you get the idea I'd help you?"

"You're already helping us by hiding us," Mary said.

"That's different."

"So why are you hiding us?"

"Because my oldest and best friend asked me to."

"Your oldest friend has been murdered," Mary said. "Another campaign would be a way of showing that he lives on."

"He's dead," Hancock said dully.

"If we kept the Amita Foundation alive, we'd be creating a kind of monument to Bagura."

He buried his face in his hands. "Monuments don't bring people back to life."

"You said we gave people hope and inspiration," I said.

"*You*, not me."

But for the first time, I heard equivocation in his voice. "Don't you want to help us?" I asked.

"No."

"Why not?"

"Because I don't want to end up like Bagura."

"Nor do we," said Mary and I with one voice.

"But you will."

Mary looked at me. We said nothing. Long seconds passed.

Then Hancock shook his head fiercely. "You're asking too much. I can't help you."

"Why not?" I asked again, almost beseechingly.

"Because I've stopped believing that I can change anything or anyone, starting with myself."

"Because you prefer to sit at home getting drunk," I retorted angrily.

For a moment there was silence.

"Who the hell do you think you are?" he said, his voice quivering with rage. "I ought to throw you out of the house. Even if you are Bagura's friends."

My heart pounded in my throat. What had I done? Insulted the only person we could trust, the only person who had offered us protection. I had let slip the words in my excitement, but at the same time I had meant them and had no intention of taking them back.

We were silent.

Hancock turned his head away and finished smoking his cigarette.

"I didn't want to hurt you," I said.

"You were rude and disrespectful."

"I'm—"

He interrupted me. "There may," he said, "be some truth in it, but that's my business. I'm answerable to no one. Least of all to you."

"Yes," I said. "I'm really—"

"Oh, shut up." He opened the bottle, poured himself a glass of rum, and left the room with it. We saw him on the veranda, drinking it in little sips. It was the earliest we'd ever seen him drink.

"That was stupid of me."

"It was spot-on," Mary said. "You spoke the truth. And the idea's good. If he won't help, we'll find some other way to make it work."

We waited. I was so nervous that I slid off the chair and stretched out on the floor. Without Hancock's help, it would be uphill work. Mary began to jiggle her left foot up and down.

"Does your leg hurt?"

She shook her head. "Just a stupid habit."

"Do you think he'll change his mind?"

"Yes."

"Why?"

"For the same reason that Bagura helped you."

"Hancock didn't have a daughter who starved to death."

"No, but his best friend was murdered."

Time passed. I wondered whether there was anything I could say or do to convince Hancock, but I could think of nothing.

Eventually we saw him get up and cross the front garden to the street. Then he turned and looked back at the house, as if afraid he might never see it again.

Finally he strode calmly back to the house and into the kitchen. Mary moved closer to me.

Hancock's eyes scanned the room, taking in the bunting and the paper cutouts and the remains of the cake on the table. His expression had changed. "All right," he said. "I'll help you. But this time the charity will be called the Bagura Foundation. Tomorrow you start work as my assistant."

TWENTY-THREE

Hancock prepared me thoroughly for my part. He
found a pair of blue overalls that more or less fitted
and a big toolbox where I would hide the money. We
agreed that I should stick to taking cash, because
Hancock didn't have the same kind of contacts as
Bagura and wouldn't be able to sell jewelry.

He rubbed my hands with grease and oil until
I looked as if I'd spent all my life taking engines
apart and putting them together again. He also
gave me a cap and a face mask, these too smeared
with black streaks.

Our first job was to unblock a swimming pool
filter. "Good customers," Hancock told me on the
way there. "Three kids and a lot of breakages. Nor-
mally live in the city, but they came to the island to
flee the virus."

He announced himself at the intercom, and a moment later the heavy iron gate slid soundlessly open. The big house—a smaller version of Mary's aunt's shoeboxes—was concealed behind a high wall and surrounded by a large garden, better kept than Aunt Kate's. The curving drive was edged with tidily pruned hibiscus bushes; the lawn was neatly trimmed; the palm trees free of withered leaves. There was clearly a diligent gardener at work here.

Parked outside the garage were two SUVs and a motorcycle. We were greeted warmly by a maid who seemed to know Hancock well, and I pulled my mask up to under my eyes, to be on the safe side. Hancock introduced me as his new assistant, took his bag of tools from the truck, and walked around the house with me to the pool. A man in shorts was sitting on the terrace, staring at a laptop; he paid us no attention. Through an open door came the sound of children's voices.

The pool was at least sixty feet long and lined with dark-blue tiles. Two inflatable donuts floated on the surface; used towels lay on the poolside lounge chairs. Beyond was a small building containing changing rooms, toilets, and a shower—it also housed the filter unit. Hancock had no need of my help; he was familiar with the system and accustomed to working on his own. I squatted down beside him, feeling superfluous. I had assumed that the house would be empty and that I could wander around it as freely as at Aunt Kate's. "How am I going to get in?" I asked.

Judging by his look, Hancock hadn't given the matter much thought either. "I mended a leaking window in the bathroom here a few months ago," he said. "Tell them you need to check the gaskets after the last monsoon." I threw a wrench or two into my toolbox and edged toward the terrace door.

The maid looked surprised to see me in the house, but unsuspectingly offered to show me the way to the bathroom.

It was pleasantly cool inside. We walked through a big living room strewn with toys, and headed up to the first floor. Two children passed us on the stairs without giving me a second glance. The bathroom was light and airy, with two washbasins, two showers, and a bathtub, but no toilet. The counters next to the basins were littered with bottles, jars, and tubes, a jar of toothbrushes, a razor, and a vase of flowers. I thanked the maid, and she went back downstairs. I opened the two big windows, pretending to check the new gaskets, and tightened the already tight screws in the frames.

Children's voices floated up from the terrace, and the voice of another woman, not the maid. In the rooms around me, all was quiet; it looked as if

I was on my own up here. I closed the window and tiptoed out into the passage, which had several doors leading off it. I listened. Nothing. The first door was ajar, and through the crack I could see a child's bedroom. A stuffed panda bigger than Thida sat on the bed; several more stuffed toys were lined up beside it. I'd never seen so many toys in my life. Dolls, a doll stroller, a miniature dressing table, a fully equipped playhouse, a toy kitchen, picture books, a CD player.

Next door was a boy's room. There was a car racetrack on the floor, and on the wall a big Manchester United poster and a signed Manchester United shirt.

I felt more than uncomfortable snooping around up here while the children were playing downstairs. Worse still, I kept hearing my father's voice, his disapproval. Here in this stranger's house, without Mary at my side, I felt for the first time like a real burglar. I wasn't stealing because my little sister was hungry. I wasn't stealing to provide my neighbors or a particular slum with rice or cash. Things had got more complicated.

I crept on. The next door opened onto the parents' bedroom. If I was going to find cash anywhere, it was here.

But before I could go in, I heard a voice.

"What are you doing here?"

I wheeled around and saw a young woman about my age eyeing me suspiciously.

"I'm a workman. I was checking the bathroom windows."

"And what are you doing in my parents' room?"

"Nothing, just looking for a toilet."

"The guest bathroom is downstairs, off the hall," she said tersely.

"Thanks." I walked past her to the stairs as casually as I could.

She stood at the top, watching me closely. "First door on the left," she called out after me.

When I came out of the toilet, she was still there. I glanced up at her and she pointed me to the front door.

Hancock laughed when I told him about it in the truck as we drove away.

"What's so funny?" I asked petulantly.

"World-famous thief chased out of house by eighteen-year-old girl?"

"There's no need to laugh. What else could I have done?"

"Tell her you had to check the windows in her parents' room. Ask her to help you—or at least keep out of your way." He chuckled.

I didn't feel like laughing and stared out at the passing countryside, furious at myself. Hancock opened his window; hot air streamed into the truck. He lit up thoughtfully, took a drag on the cigarette and exhaled slowly through his nose.

"You won't have anything to distribute un less you take something," Hancock said. "Quite straightforward. When Bagura and I were your age, we had this theory that it was the rich who'd started the stealing—that their money wasn't honestly earned."

"And now?"

"Bagura's dead and I'm too old."

"Too old for what?"

"For bold theories. Next time you have qualms about taking things, just tell yourself you're not stealing; you're collecting a kind of tax on luxury."

I liked the idea. Really, I thought, people who paid taxes should be happy; it meant they had something worth being taxed. That wasn't anything the slum dwellers of Beautiful Tuscany could boast of.

On our next job, I didn't even get to see the house. The garden gate was stuck, and Hancock repaired it in twenty minutes while I stood idly looking on.

At the third place I was at least able to make myself useful. A boy had flown his drone into a coconut palm and it had gotten stuck. Hancock watched in astonishment as I climbed the tall trunk to get it down.

Our last stop was at a villa where Hancock had been asked to pick up a broken fridge. The owners and all their staff were away in the city for a few days and had left the fridge in the garage.

A connecting door led from the garage into the house. Using a picklock, Hancock opened the simple lock and sent me in to have a look around. He promised to keep guard and to warn me if anyone showed up.

Having the house to myself made things easier. I worked my way through the rooms as swiftly as I could, trying not to be sidetracked by thoughts of Bagura or my father. On the first floor were two bedrooms and an office. I rummaged through closets and chests of drawers, looked behind books and CDs. In a desk drawer I found a fat envelope stuffed with thousand-leik bills; the next drawer down yielded a black metal box with a lock. I nabbed them both and returned to the garage.

Back at home, it took Hancock less than five minutes to open the cashbox. Inside were ten thousand

US dollars and ten thousand euros in crisp new bills. Hancock handed them to us and opened a bottle of beer, but seemed disinclined to talk.

We had decided that Mary should be responsible for our pickings. She counted the money twice, noted the amount on a piece of paper, and hid the bills in a box in the workshop behind a carton of wires and cables.

Even after his second beer Hancock remained taciturn.

After supper Mary and I washed up and withdrew to our hideout.

Mary was chattier than she'd been for a long time, livened up by our plans for the Bagura Foundation. She wanted to hear all about my day, and suggested places where she thought rich people might hide their money (under the bed, spread between several purses, in books, behind books, in the oven). She thought we should plan our campaign as minutely as possible, leaving nothing to chance, because she was afraid that her slowness would be a hindrance to us.

What we didn't talk about was our plans for after the campaign. We wouldn't be able to stay at Hancock's—he would probably have to lie low himself. But where could we go instead?

I think we both sensed that there wasn't much to discuss—and if you can't talk about something,

you're best keeping quiet about it. It wasn't that
we had a limited number of options: we had none
at all.

We made love that night and all the following
nights—though never until I'd crept through the
workshop to check on Hancock. I would find him
fast asleep on the couch or in his armchair, an
empty bottle of rum within reach on the table.

Mary said there was no better analgesic than
making love. It was only when I touched her and
turned her on that her body stopped feeling the
pain.

When Hancock and I got back from work
the following afternoon, Mary was sitting on the
veranda, drawing. I could tell immediately that she
hadn't had a good day.

Spread out beside her were several pictures,
each bleaker than the one before: a huge skeletal
hand clawing at two children at play; the body of
a cat she had found dead on the road outside the
house; a self-portrait in a mirror with a skull in the
background.

"How can you stand it?" Hancock asked.

"What?"

"Thinking about nothing but death all day."

Mary shrugged, as if she didn't understand the question. "I don't think about death all day."

He gestured toward the pictures. "So what are these about?"

She looked at them. "The end of life."

After supper Mary had a yen for the sea and asked me to drive her to the beach. Hancock had no objections. It was dark and windy; the beach would be deserted. But he was adamant that we shouldn't go swimming—the current in the bay was treach erous at the best of times; in a high wind like this, anything might happen.

The parking lot was deserted. Hancock had been right: there was no one around.

The surf was impressive. Wave after wave rolled to the shore, rising higher and higher until it crashed on the beach and rushed at us, then turned to retreat only inches from our feet, leaving the beach covered in a carpet of white foam. The water was sucked back as if pulled by a magnet, uncovering stones and shells and sand as it prepared for the next attack. We stood in silence, staring at the churning sea as it vanished into the distance. The wind played with Mary's long hair; flecks of white spray danced over the beach. I sat down on the warm sand and Mary sat between my legs. I put my arms around her.

"What's wrong?" I asked.

"What do you mean?"

"You look so sad."

"Have you thought about our chances of escape?"

"No. Have you?"

"All day today. They're not high."

"Didn't you tell me you'd discovered the secret of happiness?" I said, in a pitiable attempt to cheer her up. *Don't think about tomorrow.*

"That was a game," she said grimly. "In real life it's impossible."

Her mood was darkening by the minute. I drew a boat in the sand to distract her, and a heart-shaped sun shining down on it. "What do you think this is?"

She didn't even look at it.

I tried to tickle her, but she wriggled out of my arms. "Stop it."

For a long time she stared into the darkness. Then, all of a sudden, she said, "Shall we go swimming?"

"When?"

"Now, of course."

"No, it's too dangerous."

"Oh, come on. Swimming in surf is fun, believe me."

"No, you heard what Hancock said."

She waved this aside. "He doesn't know what strong swimmers we are. Please come with me."

I shook my head, bewildered by her persistence. "I'm not a strong swimmer."

Mary heaved herself up and hobbled toward the sea.

"Stay here," I called, jumping to my feet, gripped by a sense of foreboding.

The water rushed at Mary, lapping at her knees and legs. She hobbled on and I followed. Now the sea was sucked back again, fifty or sixty feet, and a wall of water reared up, growing taller and more formidable by the second, towering over us, twice our height. The wave swept Mary off her feet before I could reach her, hitting her with the force of a big truck. Then it knocked me down too, spinning me around, pushing me under, dashing me against the sand. By the time I got my head above water, I could see nothing but the white, raging sea.

Suddenly, a few feet away, Mary's body surfaced beside me. I grabbed one of her feet and held it fast. The next wave was already rolling up—it dealt me another hard blow, spinning me through the water again, but I didn't let go of Mary. Grasping her tightly by the leg, I pulled her closer. Her hands sought mine. The sea released us again, retreating as if to return with even greater force and swallow us forever. I took Mary in my arms, and she wrapped her arms and legs around me. The water was only up to my knees now, but the undertow was so strong I could hardly keep on my feet. We won't get out of here alive, I thought. Not a chance. I put all my strength into running and managed a few yards before the next wave broke behind us. It sounded like an explosion. I teetered but didn't fall. Instead of swallowing us, the wave lifted us up and washed us onto the beach.

When the water began to flow back, I braced myself against the undertow and dragged Mary higher up the beach toward the palms, out of reach of the next wave.

"Are you crazy?" I shouted, completely out of breath. "We could have drowned."

Mary lay at my feet on the sand, breathing heavily. I kneeled down to her.

"Why did you do that?" Never in my life had I yelled at anyone so furiously. "Why?"

"Because I don't want them to arrest us." Water spilled out of her mouth.

"They won't arrest us, you said so yourself."

"Of course they will. You shouldn't have pulled me out of the sea." She lashed out at me, but I caught her arms and held them tight.

"Calm down, Mary. We have plans, you and I, have you forgotten?"

"No, I haven't. But I don't know if it's what I want."

"Why not?"

"Because I'm scared of being arrested—why can't you get that into your head? You heard what happened to Bagura. I don't even want to imagine what they might do to a young woman. I don't want to be at their mercy. Is that so hard to understand?" She closed her eyes. I let go of her arms and dropped down beside her. My hair, ears, nose, and teeth were full of sand, and I felt that I might throw up at any moment.

A short while later, all I wanted was to feel Mary's body. I rolled close to her and put my arms around her from behind. *I love you,* I wanted to whisper. *I'll take care of you. We'll find a way.* But I was too exhausted to speak.

"Why didn't you swim out with me?"

"Because I don't want to die, Mary. I want to live. With you. Don't do anything like that again."

She said nothing.

"Never again. Promise me."

"I can't."

"Please."

"Don't force me to lie to you."

When we got back, Hancock was asleep in his armchair, his head slumped to one side, his mouth open, and in front of him two rum bottles, one empty, the other partly drunk. I pushed a cushion under his head and put his legs up on a chair.

Although it was warm in the house, Mary was still shivering. She took off her wet clothes and I wrapped her in one of Hancock's blankets and made her tea.

She retreated to our hideout. I didn't know what to do. Part of me wanted to be with her and hold her in my arms; another part told me it would be best to leave her in peace.

I sat down on the veranda for a while. My confusion had given way to deep sadness.

After a few minutes, I'd had enough of being without her and went back inside.

I lay awake, thinking of the surf and Mary's bleak words. Mary tossed and turned too, but I was used to that; she often took a while to settle into a comfortable position. She reached for my hand and held it tight. Gradually we both grew calmer. "Thank you," she said, turning to me. "I'm sorry."

"Will you promise—"

Mary put a finger to my lips.

"Shh. You mustn't ask people for promises they can't keep."

"You can't leave me on my own. I love you."

She was silent for so long that I thought she'd fallen asleep. Then I heard her whisper something. "All right," she said. "I'll promise, but only if you promise me something too."

"What?"

"That we won't get arrested, no matter what."

"Promise."

The next day I distracted myself by helping Hancock with a few jobs. We spent most of the day setting up a robotic lawn mower. It was quicker, quieter, and more thorough than I had ever been, and I felt like programming it to drive straight into the ornamental pond.

When we got back in the afternoon, Mary was waiting for us on the veranda. I didn't recognize her at first. Her long, wavy black hair was gone. She hadn't cut it to her shoulders, or in a bob or with bangs. She'd shaved it all off so that she looked like a young nun.

"Do you like it?" She pulled a sheepish face, but I sensed that, underneath, she was relieved, as if she'd freed herself not only of her hair, but of a weightier burden.

At first I was too surprised to say anything.

She twisted her head this way and that. Her hair was about a quarter of an inch long, if that, and her head was the perfect shape for a buzz cut.

Hancock was the first to recover his voice. "Suits you," he said approvingly, and went into the house.

I nodded. She looked like Mary, and yet different—older, no longer girlish, her expression clearer and more determined than before, though in no way harsh or masculine. In fact, the short hair brought out the delicacy of her features. She looked so unfamiliar and so beautiful that I found myself groping for words.

"Do you like it too?" she asked when I said nothing.

"Yes."

"Sure?"

"You're even more beautiful than you were."

"Really? I've been wanting to cut it for so long, but never been brave enough. It's the first time I've ever had it short. I saw the electric razor in the workshop and decided the time had come."

"To cut your hair?"

"To be brave."

The next few days were busy. Hancock and I replaced broken security lights and surveillance cameras, changed makeup-mirror bulbs and fish-tank pumps, repaired awnings and sun canopies. We spent an entire day in a villa overlooking the sea, where Hancock had been asked to transform a first-floor room the size of his workshop into a playroom for cats. Downstairs in the same house, a group of workmen were installing a gym—luckily for us, since they kept the maid busy with their questions and would later deflect some of the suspicion. While Hancock assembled scratching posts, ladders, and climbing walls, I had plenty of time to search for cash.

It was my fifth day as Hancock's assistant, and I was no longer troubled by my father's voice. My fear of being caught was gone, as were my qualms about snooping around strangers' houses and taking things that didn't belong to me. All I felt was a determination to raise as much as possible for the Bagura Foundation. I didn't care whether the wealthy villa owners had made their millions honestly or not—what mattered was that they had money to spare. If they weren't going to part with this voluntarily, I would just have to help them along a bit with my tax on luxury.

Still, I was disappointed when the end of the week came and we'd collected only half a million leik. It was clear that we would never amass as much as we'd found at Mary's aunt's—that safe full of gold bars and wads of bills had been a stroke of luck, a one-off. Apart from anything else, it was only a matter of time before we were caught. Someone would catch us in the act—or Hancock's employers would start to notice the thefts—and sooner or later suspicion would fall on us.

"What's wrong?" Hancock asked when he saw my gloomy face.

"We'll never get there at this rate."

"What are you talking about?"

"We'll never get enough money together."

"How much is enough?"

I shrugged.

"Five million? Ten? Twenty?"

"I don't know," I said. I thought of the bulging box of thousand-leik bills that we'd distributed on behalf of the Amita Foundation and felt even more despondent.

"How much did you have for your second campaign with Bagura?"

"Almost fifteen million."

"Wow." Hancock gave an astonished whistle. "Compared with that, of course, half a million's not a lot." He thought for a moment. "How much did you earn as a gardener?"

"A little over a thousand a month."

He calculated. "Then look at it this way: we've collected forty years' wages in the space of a week. Does that sound better?"

"It's not about me," I said. "Once we start dividing up the money, half a million will be gone in no time. If we give every family a thousand leik, we've only just enough for five hundred families."

"Less, if you deduct expenses," he said quietly, "but that doesn't matter."

"Yes, it does."

"No. It makes no difference if they get a thousand, two thousand, or three thousand. This isn't about money anymore."

"What then?"

"It's like I said before when I was explaining why you're so popular. If you and Mary make a comeback, you'll renew people's hope and inspiration. You're putting out a message: Niri is still around. Mary is with him. They're not afraid—and if they are, their courage is greater than their fear and that's better still. What matters isn't the amount you hand out. What matters is the gesture. You rouse people from their apathy, and that apathy is one reason they live in such misery. They've given up the fight, given up trying to change their fate. You show them that it can be done."

TWENTY-FOUR

It took Hancock almost a week to make arrangements for the campaign. Several times he drove to the mainland and didn't return until evening. Most of these trips were connected with finding a white car that could be disposed of without a trace when the campaign was over.

One morning I woke with no one beside me. Where was Mary? I leapt up in alarm, and running through the workshop to the front of the house, I found her on the veranda, deep in conversation with Hancock. They were so engrossed that I didn't want to interrupt, so I watched them from the kitchen. I still hadn't got used to Mary's short hair.

It was hard to say—had they really not noticed me or were they pretending? Hancock's thoughtful gaze was fixed on Mary; occasionally he nodded or shook his head or said something. Whatever Mary was telling him or asking of him was clearly urgent. She leaned close to him, took his hand for a moment. I couldn't hear what they were saying, but I could tell from Mary's tone of voice that it was serious.

When I stepped out onto the veranda, they broke off abruptly.

"Sorry. I didn't want to interrupt."

"You're not interrupting," Hancock said, a touch too loud and fast. "Mary woke up early. We've been having a little chat. Come and join us."

Mary averted her eyes awkwardly. It looked as if she was wiping tears from her face.

I sat down on the steps. None of us said a word. "Is there anything I can do?" I said after a while.

"No, I'm nearly ready. Give me another day or two. I was just saying to Mary, day after tomorrow at the latest we'll be good to go."

Now, he said, it was my turn to hear the plan. I was sure that wasn't what he and Mary had been talking about, but I listened anyway, of course.

"We'll take the first ferry to the mainland at dawn," he said, "and drive to a village a few miles from the coast to switch cars. Then we'll head twelve miles south to a small seaside town where an illegal refugee camp has recently sprung up. A lot of workers live there with their families— people who were more or less guaranteed work in the tourist industry before the pandemic. The beaches were always very popular with sun-starved Europeans and Americans—especially in the winter. Now they're practically deserted. There are about three hundred families in the camp, natives and illegals."

He had prepared enough envelopes for everyone. It was important that we didn't hang around for more than an hour. This time, there was a higher risk of coming to the attention of the police or being betrayed by someone, so the campaign would have to be more low-key than those organized by Bagura. In order to keep down the number of people who were in on it, Hancock had decided that we should paint the T-shirts ourselves. He'd got hold of the necessary materials.

Of course, there was no guarantee that people wouldn't start to riot and tear the envelopes from our hands. They lived in immense poverty. We would just have to trust to their common sense and discipline.

Hancock would instruct everyone to form lines; Mary and I would distribute envelopes of one thousand five hundred leik each. Hancock thought it unlikely that anyone would be wearing a mask, and though we could wear ours if we liked, it was important that people were able to take photos and make videos in which we were easily recognizable. This time the publicity counted for even more than the money. The pictures of us would soon go viral, turning our small gesture into a huge campaign in Bagura's honor.

We would stay at the camp an hour, max, then return to the village, dump the car, and catch the midday ferry. If all went well, we'd be home before the police had noticed anything.

"Any questions?" Hancock asked. "Suggestions, objections?"

For the first time that morning, Mary looked at me. She shook her head. "No," she said. "You, Niri?"

"No."

We spent the rest of the day painting T-shirts. Mary had designed a logo to go above the words *Bagura Foundation*. We only managed a couple of dozen, but Hancock said it was enough for the photos. Mary conscientiously labeled all three hundred envelopes with the charity name and logo. We didn't want anyone to miss Bagura's name.

None of us talked much during the journey. On the ferry, Mary and I pulled our masks up beneath our eyes and pretended to sleep, though we were far too excited to relax. I had cramps and diarrhea when we stopped to switch cars, and Hancock and Mary had to wait while I went in search of a bathroom.

The car was a rickety old Toyota with cable ends sticking out of the dashboard, no speedometer, no ventilation, and broken window cranks. The back seat was so worn you could feel every spring. Mary had taken two extra painkillers as a precaution.

From the outside, however, the car made a good impression. It was sprayed white, with BAGURA FOUNDATION emblazoned in big letters on the hood, roof, and both sides of the body.

Mary took my hand and I shifted closer to her. She put her head on my shoulder. Once we were on the coastal road my stomach began to settle.

As we approached the camp, we changed into the Bagura Foundation T-shirts. Mary looked proud and happy, as if a long-cherished wish were coming true. She had counted out the money before we left and put it in the envelopes, checking several times to make sure that the rubber stamp worked and that her phone was charged so that she, too, could take photos and make videos.

The refugee camp looked as godforsaken as our settlement. Everywhere were makeshift shanties—flimsy shacks of driftwood and plastic sheeting. Stray dogs roamed the alleyways, and there was a familiar smell of cesspit.

On Hancock's orders, people formed long lines and patiently waited their turn. I stamped their hands; Mary distributed the envelopes. At first she was nervous, but with every envelope she handed out, she looked happier and more content.

Despite the desperate poverty, there was only one dispute, when a family tried to line up twice. Fortunately, others in the queue intervened and the matter was soon settled.

The real problem was the excitement caused by our arrival. Almost everyone in the camp had heard of us, and everyone wanted to be photographed or videoed with Mary or me, preferably both. We held babies in our arms, signed T-shirts, hugged children. We were surrounded by families holding their money up to the camera, singing and jumping up and down. People made thumbs-up and victory signs.

Hancock had been right. The amount of money was irrelevant; these people were no less delighted than those who'd received twice as much.

This was about more. Much more.

Because of all the photos and videos, we couldn't get away as soon as we'd hoped, and after an hour

Hancock began to get nervous. One call to the police was all it would take.

But at last we were done. Hancock maneuvered the car through the crowd, hooting loudly and cursing under his breath. People stuck their heads in at the windows and ran alongside us, thanking us over and over. The last thing we heard were shouts of "Niri, Niri!" The last thing we saw were fathers holding their kids in the air to wave to us.

Back in the village, we switched cars again and arrived at the harbor just in time to catch the midday ferry.

When we got to Hancock's in the afternoon, he went straight to the cabinet and poured out three glasses of rum.

"To Bagura," he said.

"To Bagura," we echoed, clinking glasses.

Hancock downed his rum in one gulp, poured himself another glass, and collapsed into an armchair with a loud groan.

It was only now that I saw how exhausted he was.

Mary and I also drained our glasses, and the alcohol soon made itself felt. A pleasant, floaty feeling suffused my body, and Mary kept giggling, like Thida when I tickled her.

I was hungry and made fried noodles with the leftovers in the fridge. The first bottle of rum was quickly emptied.

We could hardly wait to see whether news of the Bagura Foundation had reached the internet. While Hancock proceeded to get drunk, Mary and I stared at his phone, watching his prediction come true. Thanks to Facebook, YouTube, Twitter, and Instagram, our small gesture had swelled to a campaign of unbelievable proportions. We sat up late that night, playing new videos, replaying old videos, and reading the news and comments on the websites of the *Daily Post*, the *Evening News*, and the *International Standard*. It suddenly came home to me how rife the virus was in other countries too. How many people all over the world it had robbed of jobs, homes, and loved ones. How many people it had plunged into famine. Just as I had once failed to look beyond the Benzes' garden wall, I had been blind to what was going on beyond the borders of our country. I'd had no cause to look farther.

At a certain point in the evening, I'd had enough. But Mary couldn't stop. With pride in her voice, she read out quotes to me and translated posts from English.

We were a glimmer of hope in the dark times of the virus.

A bright spot in the fight against global injustice.

A thorn in the rotting flesh of apathy.

An outcry against indifference.

We were skimming off the cream and should keep at it.

We were an example to everyone.

We should watch out—heroes died young.

As I listened, I thought of Thida and how it had all begun.

With her hunger. Her tears.

And for the first time I understood that Thida's hunger and tears were the hunger and tears of the whole world.

TWENTY-FIVE

We were no longer safe on Shark Island. The first rumors of theft had already begun to circulate. It said on the internet that the police were planning to cordon off the island and all those surrounding it, and search every house in every street. Then it said that this was ridiculous because we'd been sighted on the mainland and had almost certainly taken refuge in the caves and woods in the national park. Hancock read the news with growing alarm.

"You'll have to leave," he said eventually. It was the morning after our campaign. "A lot of people are claiming to have seen you on the ferry. The police will soon be scouring the island."

"But where can we go?"

"The only place where they probably won't look for you and certainly won't arrest you is a monastery. The bigger, the better. I'll take you to Holy Lake; it's the most famous monastery here in the south. Used to be part of an old palace—a royal summer residence. The monks will look after you."

"When would we leave?"

"Right now."

Mary and I had hardly slept; we were too tired to think of alternative solutions.

It took us only a few minutes to gather up our belongings. Hancock packed a duffel bag and stowed everything under the passenger seat of his pickup, together with a brown-paper package and two bottles of rum. He washed the dirty dishes, tidied up, and locked the house as if he were setting off on a long journey.

"Are you planning to be away for some time?" I asked.

"I think it's probably best if I clear out for a few weeks. Maybe I'll drive to the mountains and see my wife. Or the boys. It's been a while."

Mary and I climbed into the truck bed, and I spread out blankets for her to lie on. Hancock covered us with a black tarpaulin, weighing down the corners with his toolbox, some lengths of piping, and other spare parts. The journey would take a good five hours, he said, counting the ferry crossing, and it wouldn't be much fun. Hot, uncomfortable, and full of hazards. The police could stop us at any time. They could pull us over because his left brake light wasn't working, or because he had license plates from another province—or simply because they felt like bumping up their salary by fining him for some offense of their invention. If that happened, there would be nothing more he could do for us; our getaway would be over.

Mary took three painkillers and I lay down behind her and pulled her close, cushioning her head on my arm and holding her as tight as I could. Even so, I heard her groan at every pothole, every jolt. I put my other arm around her and stroked her belly.

The journey seemed to go on forever. The ferry was noisy—voices talking only a few feet from the truck, chickens clucking, people laughing. Later we stopped briefly to fill up the tank. Someone asked Hancock for a lift, and he apologized profusely and mumbled an excuse. Then the road worsened; the tools and spare parts rattled at every bump and soon my bones, too, were aching. The heat under the tarp was almost unbearable; our bodies were drenched in sweat, and in all the excitement, we'd forgotten to pack bottles of water. I ought really to have fallen asleep in exhaustion, but thirst and pain kept me awake.

At last, we slowed to a crawl. Hancock braked, cut the engine, and got out. We heard him talking to a man; we heard another man get in the pickup.

Their voices sounded grave. Then someone banged the side of the truck.

"You can come out."

When I pushed the tarpaulin aside, I saw how pale Mary was. She was in such pain she could hardly get up—Hancock and I had to help her out.

Before us stood three young monks. They exchanged embarrassed glances and seemed not to know how to proceed. I had the impression that at least one, if not all of them, had recognized us, despite our masks. Hancock suggested that they take us to the abbot and let him decide what should be done with us.

We walked in silence across a large courtyard. Mary refused to take my arm or let me carry her; she walked slow but straight beside us, her head held high.

Hancock had brought us to the biggest and most beautiful monastery I had ever seen. The grounds were surrounded by a high wall and dotted with pagodas of every shape and size, some painted white, others gleaming gold in the low evening light. Scattered between these were dark-teak houses, dormitories, and prayer halls. Little bells rang in the wind. A long roofed wooden bridge on stilts connected the temple with the former palace. From one building we could hear children's voices chanting a mantra.

The abbot was deep in conversation with an elderly couple, who seemed to be in the process of donating a large sum of money to the monastery. Two monks were unloading bags of rice, packets of cookies, and cans of coconut milk from the trunk of a Mercedes-Benz and carrying them to a storeroom.

We followed our monks onto a veranda outside the prayer hall and sat down on the floor to wait. Now and then a child walked past and stared at us. We kept our masks on, to avoid being recognized. A novice brought us a tray of tea and dry cookies, and a bottle of water each. Mary and I drank the water in one go and were immediately given more.

The abbot saw off the elderly couple and came to join us. He looked younger than Hancock, with a round, friendly face, fleshy fingers, and a hefty paunch straining his robes. One of the young monks spoke to him in a whisper, and he nodded intermittently, casting searching glances in our direction. I could see in his eyes that he knew who we were—and that we weren't welcome.

"How long do you want to stay?" he asked, getting straight to the point.

Mary and I just shrugged. Hancock, too, was silent.

"Two or three days, maybe four," the abbot said. "We can't keep your presence a secret for longer than that. You're too famous. We have a lot of guests and pilgrims in the monastery, even now, and there's a million-leik bounty on your heads. I wouldn't want to lead anyone into temptation." He jerked his head toward a cluster of inquisitive children who were watching us from a respectful distance.

I wondered whose safety the abbot was concerned about—ours or his? But what difference did it make? I glanced at Mary and Hancock. They looked as dejected as I felt.

"Take them to the room behind the storeroom," the abbot said to the novices, rising to his feet. Then he turned and vanished into the semidarkness of the prayer hall.

The young monks led us into another prayer hall and down some steps to a basement room with a screen door. One of them unlocked the lock that was securing the door, and we traipsed past stacks of canisters and bags of rice to a small room in the far corner. Inside were two plank beds; high in the wall, a barred window looked onto the courtyard. I put our bags down on one of the beds.

"Could we have another couple of blankets?" I asked.

"It doesn't get cold at night."

"I know. Still."

One of the novices disappeared and returned a moment later with two blankets.

We stood there, six people crammed into a tiny room, not knowing what we were waiting for. What now? I wanted to ask, but I knew that none of us had an answer.

"I'll be going then," Hancock murmured, chewing his lip, and making no move to go. He clearly didn't like the thought of leaving us there.

Eventually he stirred himself and we headed for the courtyard with him, the novices following close behind.

At the car we stood about awkwardly

"I wish I could take you with me," Hancock said softly. "But it's no solution. Driving around with me is even more dangerous than staying here. Maybe the abbot will change his mind. Or think of somewhere else for you to hide."

He didn't sound convinced.

Then he opened the truck door, took out the brown-paper package, and gave it to Mary.

"Thank you," she said.

He smiled sadly. "I should be the one saying thank you. Good luck to you both. I'll miss you."

I wanted to reply, but my voice failed me.

Hancock gave us a nod, scrabbled into the car, turned on the engine, and vanished in a gray-brown cloud of sand and dust.

I took the package from Mary; it was heavier than I'd imagined. She took my arm and we headed back to our hiding place.

"Anything else you need?" one of the novices asked.

"No, thank you."

"If you think of anything, just let me know. My name's Chai. You can ask for me." He locked the door behind us. Mary hobbled into the room and I stopped and looked back through the screen door. The monks turned around, and Chai smiled at me. The place felt more like a prison than a refuge.

Mary was lying on one of the beds. I pushed the other up against it. "What shall I do with Hancock's package?"

"Hide it under the bed."

"What's inside?"

She thought for a moment. "A surprise."

"May I see?"

"Yes, but not yet."

"When?"

"Soon."

A little later Chai was in the door again, holding out a dark wooden pot with a lid. "It's a special healing cream," he said, "for easing pain. You need to rub it in several times a day."

He'd vanished before we could thank him.

I unscrewed the lid. The cream had a reddish tinge and smelled strongly of chili, cinnamon, and menthol. "What do you reckon?"

"Might as well give it a go. It can't make it any worse."

The gong rang for evening prayers.

Mary took off her skirt and lay down, and I began to massage the cream gently onto her hip, into the welts on her thigh and the rough palm bark of her skin.

Overhead the monks were chanting their mantras. The monotonous singsong was deeply familiar to me, but something in me resisted it. Too many memories. Mary found it soothing.

I dipped my fingers in the cream again and continued to massage Mary's scars until she fell asleep.

The following morning there was a tray outside our door with two bowls of rice, some vegetables, and a pot of tea. When Mary picked up one of the bowls, she found a scrap of paper underneath.

We think you're amazing. Don't give up! it said in spidery writing.

We ate our breakfast in silence. Afterward Mary asked me to massage her again; the ointment had helped.

As I was rubbing cream into her skin we heard someone at the door. A moment later, Chai and a handful of other novices were in our room, staring at us with big, awed eyes. "Hello," I said, covering Mary's bare legs with a blanket.

One of them stuck a thumb in the air and the others laughed. Chai seemed to be the oldest.

"You're heroes," he said bashfully. "Can we help you in any way?"

"Do you have a better hiding place for us?" Mary asked.

They looked gloomily at the floor and shook their heads.

"Then I don't know how you can help us."

They gave us a key. "This is for the lock."

"Thank you," I said.

"Do you need any more blankets?"

"No."

"Anything else to eat?"

"No."

"Does the cream help?"

"Yes, it's great. Thank you."

"Would you like some more?"

Mary made a polite gesture of refusal. "No, thanks, there's still plenty left."

They stood there, not wanting to leave.

"Do you think you could get me a pen and notebook?" I asked. "I'd like to make some notes."

Two of them went out. They returned a moment later with biros, two new exercise books, and a handful of candles and matches.

We thanked them and they withdrew, happy to have helped us.

I picked up a pen and one of the exercise books and began to write this story, haltingly at first, then faster. Soon the memories were coming so thick and fast that my hand could hardly keep pace.

Mary drew as I wrote, or lay and rested with her head in my lap.

That afternoon, the abbot summoned us to his office, a small book-filled room off the prayer hall. He looked at us with cool, dark eyes and asked us to sit down.

"I've been reading some articles about you and watching videos," he began. "What you do is not lawful. Neither under state law nor under Buddhist rules."

"It may not be lawful," I said, "but it's just." I was sick of being preached to. I was sick of people telling me what was right or wrong, good or evil. I was sick of swallowing my anger, with its increasingly nasty, bitter taste. "If the law isn't on our side, then I ask myself what kind of a law it is. Certainly not mine."

"Who decides that?" he asked in a piercing voice. "You?"

I was about to reply, but thought better of it. I could tell from Mary's thin lips that she, too, was angry.

"*My law*. Isn't that rather a presumptuous way of talking for someone as young as you? According to *your law*, if I'm not mistaken, everyone can take what they need—or think they need. Is that any kind of solution—a world where everyone takes what they like?"

I wasn't in the mood to argue with him. I was sure he had nothing to tell us that I hadn't heard before, from my teachers in the monastery or from my father.

"No, but a world where everyone has what they need," Mary said, coming to my rescue. "Then there'd be enough for everyone."

"That's rich coming from a young woman as wealthy as you," he said, smiling sarcastically.

"I know what I'm talking about."

The abbot shook his head. "You two have let your anger get the better of you. When your anger controls you rather than the other way around, you will sooner or later come to grief. Rage is not a good counselor, believe me, and laws are in place to be followed, not broken. They're there to protect us— all of us, including the weak, including you."

Mary averted her gaze and said nothing.

"I'd like you to leave the monastery by dawn to-morrow. You're putting us in danger. If the police track you down, they'll end up arresting us all. And it's only a matter of time till they find you. Have I made myself clear?"

I wondered if it was worth asking for reprieve, worth explaining that we had nowhere to go, and that, given Mary's state of health, it was hard . . . No, she wouldn't want that—and neither did I.

We nodded.

"And now, go."

Neither of us could think of anyone who might help us. Then I remembered the reporter who had interviewed me. Maybe he could do something for us.

I dug his number out of my backpack and called him using the second of Bagura's SIM cards.

He picked up on the third ring. "AP, Fowler."

"Hello, it's Niri."

"Niri? I don't think I know a Niri."

I was about to hang up when he cried, "*The* Niri?"

"Yes, that's right."

"Wow, Niri," he whispered, his voice suddenly excited. "Where are you? Is Mary with you?"

"Yes."

"Can I see you?"

"If you'll help us."

"In what way?"

"We need somewhere to hide."

Silence at the end of the line. "I'm sorry, I can't give you that kind of help."

"Why not?"

"First, because I'd be liable to prosecution. And secondly, because I don't know of anywhere—and even if I did, journalists can't do stuff like that. We're observers, not actors."

"What do you mean?"

"We ask questions and listen and research, and we write down what we find out. But we don't get involved."

"I see," I said, disappointed. Not getting involved is also a form of involvement, I thought, but I wasn't going to argue with him.

"Can I ask you a few questions?"

"Sure."

"I'll have to prepare them. Can you call back in a few minutes?"

"No, you can ask them now."

He gave a kind of grunt. "Okay, hang on a sec, I'll just get something to write with."

I heard rustling paper, then the sound of something falling and shattering. He cursed.

"Okay, I'm ready. How much time do we have?"

"A few minutes."

"You're not in safety, is that right?"

"No—or at least not for much longer."

"Are you scared?"

"Yes." Then I thought for a moment and said, "Actually, no. Not anymore."

"Are you planning more campaigns?"

"Of course. Loads."

"The government thinks you're acting on behalf of the illegal Communist Party. Is that true?"

"No, that's bullshit."

"How about the police's suggestion that you're in the employ of foreign secret services?"

"That's bullshit too. We only act on behalf of the Bagura and Amita Foundations."

"But they don't exist; they're inventions of yours. I've looked into it. No one in the capital has ever heard of them, and there's nothing about them on the internet except in connection with your campaigns."

"Oh, so because there's nothing about them on the internet, they don't exist?" His answer made me furious. "No one in the capital has ever heard of Amita either, and there's nothing about her death on the internet, but she lived and died all the same. There's nothing about Hancock on the internet, but that doesn't mean he doesn't exist."

"Who are Amita and Hancock?"

"It doesn't matter." I was wasting my time.

"Why do you do it?"

"Why do we distribute money to poor people? I don't understand the question."

"Why are you and your girlfriend putting your lives at risk? Things won't end well for you."

"I still don't see what you're getting at."

Now he became impatient. "You know what I mean."

"No, I don't." It was self-evident why we did what we did.

"Okay, forget that. New topic. How did the whole thing start?"

"When did the world start accepting that some people have everything and others nothing? When did people start ignoring everyone but themselves? When did people start being 'legal' or 'illegal'? You tell me."

He let out a loud noise, half groan, half sigh. He didn't seem to like my answers.

"Was it your idea to steal the money and distribute it in the slums, or was it your girlfriend's?"

"Neither nor."

"So whose idea was it?"

"How should I know? The idea is way older than us."

"What do you mean by that?"

"What I say."

A moment's silence at the end of the line. Then: "Do you and Mary know how famous you are?"

"Yes."

"Was that part of your plan?"

"No."

"But you like being famous."

"It's all the same to me." The longer we talked, the less sense his questions seemed to make.

"You have followers—here in this country, but in India too, I believe, and even in Italy and America. That must feel good."

"Yes, but it's not really a big deal to me." Maybe, I thought, I didn't actually want to tell him anything—didn't want to explain or justify myself. Maybe there weren't words for what I did. Maybe I said what I had to say through my actions. People either got it or they didn't.

"You still there, Niri?"

"Yes. But this'll have to be the last question."

He thought for a moment. "Is there anything you'd like to add?"

"Hmm. I'm sorry to have caused my parents such worry. I always wanted to be a good son, and I'm not. I'm sorry that I can't be there for my little sister. I always wanted to be a good big brother to Thida and that's something else I'm not. I'm sorry that—"

"If you're so sorry about all these things," he said, interrupting me, "do you regret your actions?"

I was silent for a moment, pondering this question.

"Was it worth it?"

"That's a question that only an *observer* could ask," I replied, knowing that he wouldn't understand me, no matter how long we talked. I pushed a button on my phone and ended the call.

TWENTY-SIX

The day was dawning. The last candle had almost burned down; I had written all through the night. The twitter of birds was drowned out by the noise of a helicopter. The monks left off chanting their mantras. Hurrying footsteps and shrill, excited voices echoed overhead.

The sky outside our window was ablaze with light.

Searchlights. They'd found us.

It had been only a matter of time.

Mary woke and looked at me. "What's that noise?"

"Helicopters. They've found us."

For once, there was no sign of pain in her eyes. She reached under her bed, pulled out Hancock's package, and ripped off the brown paper, revealing a cardboard box that had once contained a water pump. Carefully she lifted the lid. Inside were two pistols.

"We won't let them arrest us," she said. "You promised."

"What are you thinking of doing? The monastery's probably surrounded by hundreds of police. We won't get anywhere with two pistols."

"Yes, we will." Mary passed me one of the guns. The metal lay cold and heavy in my hand.

"Do you understand?"

"Not yet."

Mary sat up. She was quite calm, as if she knew exactly what she was doing. "We'll get the monks to tell them we surrender. Then we'll go out into the courtyard with the pistols hidden under our Bagura Foundation T-shirts. They won't arrest us as long as we're in the monastery—that's what Hancock said. So we'll walk slowly toward the exit, with me leaning on your arm. And as soon as we're out of the temple grounds, we'll pull the guns . . ."

It didn't take much imagination to guess what would happen if we pointed our guns at the police. I looked at the pistol in my hand. My knees were trembling.

"What's wrong?"

I was crying and hadn't even noticed.

The noise of the helicopter grew louder. Soon it was joined by a second. They flew lower and lower.

I held Mary close. Her heart was pounding as wildly as mine. I thought of Thida. My parents. Bagura. Hancock. And for some reason I couldn't fathom, I was flooded with relief. I felt no fear—only a calm, quiet happiness.

In the course of the past weeks, I had learned that fear can be overcome. And that courage is a force that we have more of than we realize.

No one—really, no one—knows what they're capable of when they are in danger or in need.

The next thing we knew, there was excited whispering and splintering wood as someone kicked in the storeroom door. We heard several men approaching and whipped the guns under our T-shirts before they entered our cell. The men were wearing monks' robes. I recognized Chai and one of the novices who had brought us the exercise books, but I didn't know the others. They were all very agitated.

"Come with us," they whispered. "Quick."

Mary and I hesitated.

"Come on. Hurry."

I noticed that the strangers were not barefoot or in flip-flops like monks, but had black leather police boots on their feet.

"Where?"

"We're going to get you out of here."

"It's a trap," Mary cried. "They want to arrest us without a struggle."

"No," Chai said. "There's an old underground passage leading from the monastery to the palace. We'll get you out of here and take you to safety. Trust me."

I saw fear in Mary's face. "How? I'm too slow."

"We'll carry you."

One of the strangers made to lift her onto his back; I intervened, pointing at his police boots.

"They're on our side," Chai said. "It's all organized."

"Get on with it," the man said.

Did we have a choice?

I took Mary in my arms. Her heart was quivering. "Come on."

This is the end of my story. This is where I stop and close the book. I've written down what happened for anyone who's interested, trying not to gloss over anything or make things sound better than they were.

My father once said, "Most of what we say is unimportant and the most important things cannot be said." He was right, of course, but I've tried anyway.

The young monks have promised to do all they can to deliver this little book into my parents' hands. Into Thida's hands. I want Thida to know why I acted the way I did. I want her to know why she won't grow up with a big brother at her side.

How it all ended.

And how it all began.

With her tears.

EPILOGUE

"NIRI AND MARY" DODGE ARREST
By Marc Fowler (AP)

MURIN PROVINCE—An attempt to arrest the notorious criminal couple known as "Niri and Mary" has failed. Massive security forces surrounded the Holy Lake Monastery compound in Murin Province early this morning after reported sightings of the couple in the monastery buildings.

"Niri and Mary," who have a substantial following, have been on the run for more than three weeks. According to a spokesperson for the Ministry of the Interior, the police used helicopters and search dogs, but were unable to find the couple.

It remains unclear how they were able to escape the closely guarded area. Law enforcement officials suspect that sympathizers from among their own ranks and from the monastery may have helped the criminals. Several young monks and novices have been reported missing.

The monastery's abbot and five senior monks have been taken into police custody for questioning.

"ROBIN HOOD COUPLE" ON THE RUN
By Marc Fowler (AP)

TAMA PROVINCE—Police searched villages in the far north of Tama Province yesterday after witnesses claimed to have seen "Niri and Mary" in the area. The couple were allegedly accompanied by a man known as Hancock.

The operation lasted all day, causing serious unrest. Hundreds of people built roadblocks and attacked security forces with stones, metal pipes, and slingshots. Several injuries were reported, three of them severe. The police made dozens of arrests.

Later in the day, law enforcement officials set up checkpoints throughout the province. All buses and trains entering and leaving the area are currently being searched.

At a hastily arranged press conference a government spokesman expressed his conviction that it is only a matter of days until the couple are caught and brought to justice.

He announced that the million leik ($100,000) reward for information leading to the arrest of "Niri and Mary" has been raised to 10 million leik ($1 million).

MILLIONS TAKEN IN CASINO ROBBERY
By Marc Fowler (AP)

TAMA PROVINCE—Unknown robbers raided the Royal Lucky Star casino late last night. In what may turn out to be one of the biggest heists in recent years, the thieves reportedly made away with more than 100 million leik ($10 million).

The Chinese-owned casino had recently reopened after lockdown and operated in strict compliance with health and safety requirements. It is the country's most popular destination for Chinese tourists.

It is not yet clear how the unarmed perpetrators managed to enter the high-security casino vault. Police suspect that they had accomplices among the security guards. Videos showing the gang in masks and Bagura Foundation T-shirts are currently circulating on social networks.

The thieves left the casino in two vans before the police arrived. The vehicles were found abandoned a few hours later. There has since been no sign of the perpetrators or the casino money.

Police claims that "Mary and Niri" were among the thieves remain unconfirmed by independent sources.

The Chinese government demands an immediate investigation into the case.

COUPLE MOUNT SPECTACULAR GIVEAWAY
By Marc Fowler (AP)

TAMA PROVINCE—In an unprecedentedly bold move the criminal duo "Niri and Mary" gave away more than 50 million leik ($5 million) to the poor yesterday. The couple, who were working on behalf of the little-known Bagura Foundation, were assisted by a dozen accomplices.

The campaign was held simultaneously in several slums in Tama Province, the country's poorest region. Photos and video footage show people in "Niri" and "Mary" masks handing out stacks of 100-leik bills. The campaign went on all day and was received with dancing and celebration in the streets of the slums.

It is not yet clear why the police failed to intervene. According to initial reports, residents built roadblocks to prevent the police from accessing the slums. More recent reports suggest that officers refused to act, and that they did not leave their posts to try to break through the roadblocks. It has yet to be established whether the military took a similar stand against intervention or was simply not notified. There is an ongoing internal investigation. The chief of police of Tama Province has been suspended. The perpetrators remain at large.

NIRI AND MARY SURFACE IN PARIS
By Marc Fowler (AP)

PARIS—"Niri and Mary" are back. The philanthropic gangster duo, who disappeared from public view some weeks ago and were feared dead by their supporters, are alive and kicking. The tired-looking couple posted a video message on Facebook yesterday, with the words "Liberté, Égalité, Fraternité" visible in the background. French police say they have no reason to doubt the video's authenticity and believe that it was filmed yesterday, outside the Palais de Justice, the court-house in the heart of the French capital.

In their message, "Niri and Mary" thanked their millions of followers around the world for their continuing support: "Without all you brave and determined people, we would never have managed to keep dodging the authorities!"

The couple also announced their intention to withdraw from public view for a few weeks for health reasons, but they also said that their fight for justice and a fairer world has only just begun.

According to unconfirmed reports, the French government refuses to consider an extradition request for the couple, who have a huge international following.

ACKNOWLEDGMENTS

My heartfelt thanks go to all the people I met on my many journeys through Asia who provided the inspiration for this story.

I would like to thank my US publisher and editor Judith Gurewich and the whole team at Other Press for their trust, passion, and commitment. I couldn't think of a better home for my books.

Several friends have helped me during my work on this novel. I would like to thank Stephan Abarbanell and Ulrich Genzler in particular for being patient enough to read various drafts.

Special thanks also go to Tilo Eckardt for his suggestions, ideas, and critical questions—in a word, for the passion he brought to the making of this book.

Thanks to my son Jonathan, I didn't listen to Beethoven, Brahms, and Mozart while I wrote this book, but instead to Kygo, Robin Schulz, and Tez Cadey. His "Jonathan's Chill" playlist introduced me to the various forms of house music.

I am as ever grateful to my wife Anna for her encouragement, patience, and trust, and for providing unfailing support when it was most needed.

JAN-PHILIPP SENDKER, born in Hamburg in 1960, was the American correspondent for *Stern* from 1990 to 1995, and its Asian correspondent from 1995 to 1999. In 2000 he published *Cracks in the Wall*, a nonfiction book about China. *The Art of Hearing Heartbeats*, his first novel, became an international best seller, and was followed by two sequels, *A Well-Tempered Heart* and *The Heart Remembers*. He lives in Berlin with his family.

IMOGEN TAYLOR was born in London in 1970 and has lived in Berlin since 2001. She is the translator of Sascha Arango, Dirk Kurbjuweit, and Melanie Raabe, among others. Her translation of Sasha Marianna Salzmann's *Beside Myself* (Other Press, 2020) was short-listed for the 2021 Helen & Kurt Wolff Translator's Prize and the 2020 Schlegel-Tieck Prize.